First edition.

Everlast

THE CHRONICLES OF NERISSETTE

Other books by Andria Buchanan

EVANESCENT

INFINITY

Everlast

THE CHRONICLES OF NERISSETTE

ANDRIA BUCHANAN

Entangled Publishing, LLC
2614 South Timberline Road
Suite 109
Fort Collins, CO 80525
Visit our website at www.entangledpublishing.com.

Edited by Libby Murphy and Danielle Poiesz
Cover design by Libby Murphy

Print ISBN   978-1-62266-006-3
Ebook ISBN   978-1-62266-007-0

Manufactured in the United States of America

First Edition September 2013

To Ainsley
For always being there to remind me how to be brave,
even when I don't want to be

Chapter One

As it always did, my dream started with an inky blackness that I couldn't see through. The world began and ended in a darkness that stood like walls a thousand feet high around me.

"Hello?"

The sound of my voice never went farther than my lips before it stuttered and died, a victim of the monster that haunted the emptiness around me.

"Hello?" I said, louder this time.

Still nothing.

I sank to the floor, slowly, looking around to try to see if there was anything I could recognize—something that would tell me where I was.

Scritch.

I turned my head toward the sound, listening, trying not to breathe. Waiting for the monster to move again.

Click. Scritch. Click-clack. The clipped sounds of something sharp against the solid stones, invisible beneath my feet because of the dark.

I brought my hands up to cover my nose and mouth, desperate to hide from whatever was making the noise, whatever was hunting me.

"You can't escape me, Princess," a slick, serpentine voice said, hissing the last word.

A male dragon stepped out of the darkness, his scales as red as blood and eyes like glowing emeralds. A long, black forked tongue snaked out of his snout, like he was searching for a scent.

"You…" I sidled away from him, my hands out in front of me. "You're not real. This is a dream, and you're not real."

"Am I not?" he asked. "Isn't *this* real?"

He opened his mouth and I pressed farther back, trembling at the sight of rows of razor-sharp teeth. He lifted his head and flames poured from his mouth, setting the air above our heads ablaze. "Are the flames not real, Your Highness? Do they not burn?"

"This is a dream." My eyes darted around the room, trying to find a way to escape.

"Is it?"

"This isn't real. This is a dream, and you're nothing but a dragon from a book of fairy tales my mother used to read to me. You're Kuolema, one of the great dragons of the Bleak. You haunt the world of dreams with your brothers, tormenting those too cowardly to stand and meet their fate."

"Very good." The dragon's tongue flicked out again in front of my nose. "Very clever, Princess. Now continue with the story. Finish it."

"The brothers—Death, Fear, Hatred, and Despair, the last of the great dragon lords—were sentenced to the Bleak at the will of the stars, eating the bones of those who commit unforgivable crimes."

"How well do you know your stories?" he asked. "What types of criminals do we hunt?"

"You hunt those who let others die in their place, who are too scared to go up against a greater evil. Mom pounded that into my brain so I'd never forget it. You're the monsters sent to destroy the selfish. To punish them for their greediness. But you're a *story*. A stupid story from a stupid book that used to give me nightmares. You're not real!"

"Am I not?" The dragon's tongue curled along the length of my neck, flicking once behind my left ear as he kept his eyes fixed on mine.

"You're not real," I whispered. My shoulders began to shake as I tried to keep from cringing away from the beast that still stared deep into my eyes.

"Soon you'll see, little Princess," the dragon said, his voice nothing but a breeze. "Soon you'll see just how real I am. Fate is coming, in her cloak of broken promises, and she will bring destruction in her wake. We will bathe in the blood and the tears that she rains upon your face. We will dance to the music of your screams."

"No." I shook my head. "Fate isn't real, and even if she were, what would she want with me? I'm no one. I'm just a girl."

"Fate is coming for you, Princess." The dragon brought his snout closer.

I could smell the stench of rotting meat on his breath and tried not to gag.

"Fate is coming with her terrible swords and her cloak and her fire, and when you fail her I will burn you alive, and my brothers and I will feast upon your bones."

The dragon lifted his head again and roared, the sound echoing around me as the world burst into a brilliant white. The darkness vanished as the blinding light replaced it, banishing the blackness from every corner.

An instant later it was gone. The light. The black. The world around me was only gray. Stones boxing me in. A prison with no windows or doors. Another picture from the same book. Kiirastuli, the Place of Waiting, where souls whose great deeds had not yet come were trapped.

"This isn't real." I rubbed my hands up and down my arms. "None of this is real."

"It's coming," a sharper, female voice said. It startled me and I jumped, surveying the empty room as terror licked down the length of my spine.

"What's coming?" I asked no one.

"The time has come, and Fate demands her payment. Her debt must be paid."

"Where are you?" I asked. "*Who* are you?"

"I'm so sorry," the voice said again from behind me. I spun around to find myself face-to-face with a hazy, washed-out vision of a large black cat. A large, black, *talking* cat…

"Six thousand days seemed like such a long time when I agreed to it. Such a very, very long time. A lifetime."

"Six thousand days for what?"

"Fate is coming, and with her, the souls of a million realities, the lives of a hundred worlds."

"I don't understand. What do you mean—"

"*Beep.*" The cat crossed her eyes and then shook her head. "*Beep. Beep. Beep. Beep.*"

I jerked upright, my heart pounding, gasping for breath,

and looked around my tiny bedroom. *Beep. Beep.* My alarm.

I slammed my hand down on the black plastic alarm clock and sucked in a lungful of air. I ran a shaky hand through my hair and tried to breathe evenly. The dreams were getting worse. This time I'd actually smelled the dragon's breath and felt the flames. And the cat. Where the heck had she come from? She'd never been in my dreams before.

"Allie?" Gran Mosely called from downstairs, her voice echoing in the narrow stairwell outside my bedroom door. "Allie, are you awake?"

"Yeah," I said, my voice quivering. "I'm awake, Gran."

"Good. Hurry up and come down. Your friends are here, and I'm making breakfast."

I scrambled out of bed, pulling off my oversize nightshirt as I went, and grabbed a pair of black sweatpants. I froze.

Today was Saturday. Time to work on my English Literature group project at the library. With Winston Carruthers—the most gorgeous guy in school—who also happened to be one of my closest friends and usually told people I'm "just like one of the guys."

Even though I'd been completely friend-zoned by him, there was no way I was going to spend the entire day with him in a pair of ratty sweatpants looking like I'd just rolled out of bed.

"Allie?" Gran called up the stairs again.

"Coming!" I looked at the sweatpants in my hand and then at my closet. Did I have time for a shower? I checked the clock: 9:30 a.m. We were supposed to be there at ten. No time.

"It's not a big deal," I said to myself. Nothing to freak out about. Nothing at all. "He probably won't even notice."

"Allie, eggs are done," my best friend, Mercedes, yelled up

the stairs. "Come down now or I'm eating your share."

"Be right there!" I hurried over to the closet and grabbed a pair of jeans and a long, forest-green henley that sort of brought out the red highlights in my mousy brown hair. Or at least that's what Gran had said when we bought it. Even if Winston didn't notice, I'd still look somewhat okay.

I tugged my clothes on and then pulled my hair up into a loose ponytail. Did I have time for makeup? Lip gloss, maybe? 9:33. It was twelve blocks to the library. Definitely no time for lip gloss.

"Your eggs are on my plate," Mercedes voice rang out in the stairwell. "I'm going to munch down their runny, over-easy goodness. Yummy, yummy eggs for me."

I snatched my worn, purple book bag off the back of my desk chair and jerked the door to my bedroom open before pounding down the stairs. I jumped from the third stair into the tiny, yellow-and-white kitchen, and my bare feet slid a little on the worn linoleum.

"Nice," Mercedes said. I glanced up quickly to see her sitting with Winston at the kitchen table, eating my eggs, with an empty plate beside her.

"That was my—" I stopped and stared at her. Thick black glasses, old-school video-gamer T-shirt. Chubby cheeks. Holy smokes. "What did you do to your hair?"

"An unfortunate chemical accident with Clairol." She patted her formerly raven and now mint-green hair and grinned. "I was trying for platinum."

"It didn't work," Winston said. He shoved an entire piece of bacon into his mouth and then winked a twinkling, chocolate-colored eye at me, his coffee-colored skin even darker than normal against Gran Mosely's bright-yellow tablecloth.

My breath caught as I gawked at him, and I tried to remind myself that we were most definitely just friends.

"I, um, I can see that." I snagged a piece of buttered toast off the chipped plate in the center of the table and took a bite, trying to pass off my moment of idiocy by focusing on the food.

"Mom says I have to live with it until I can afford to pay for a pro to color it—or it grows out," Mercedes said.

"And?" I asked through a mouthful of toast.

"I'm thinking I could rock a crew cut."

"No, you couldn't." Winston rubbed his own close-cropped black curls. "The itch of it growing back in would drive you nuts. Besides, you're better as a leprechaun."

"Shut up." She narrowed her eyes at him. "Or I'll tell everyone about how you once told me you wished—"

"So," Gran Mosely said, interrupting their usual bickering. "Mercedes said you're all spending the day at the library. The fairy-tale project. How's that going?"

"Yeah." I took another bite and purposely didn't meet her eyes. "It's going good."

"We're working with Jesse and Heidi, or as I like to call them, the zombie twins, and they're slowing us down." Winston scraped his fork across his plate, scooping up the last bit of egg yolk.

"Zombie twins?" Gran Mosely asked.

"Desperately in need of brains," Mercedes explained.

"But you will be home in time to visit your mother this afternoon. Right?"

Mom. Crap. Third Saturday of the month. Nursing home day. The absolute low point of my social life.

It's not that I don't love my mom—I do. I really, really do. We were peanut butter and jelly. Ice cream and caramel sauce. More like best friends than mother and daughter.

We were gypsies roaming the wide plains of America in a station wagon, going wherever Mom had a singing gig. Or at least that was what we had done. Before the car accident that left her in a coma and me in the foster care system, living with Gran Mosely.

"I'll try, Gran. But I promised the other girls from the swim team I'd meet them to go dress shopping for the winter formal, so I might not be able to fit Mom in today."

"So we can go tomorrow."

"Swim practice," I said.

"Then next week we'll try to work something out," she said.

"Swim meet against Peters Township."

Gran Mosely sighed. "Well, perhaps the weekend after that?"

"Winter formal," I said quickly. "And swimming practices."

"Right. Well, about the winter formal. You and Winston are going together, aren't you?"

I looked over at the boy sitting silently at Gran's table, his dark skin flushed and his head bowed. "It's a group thing, Gran," he said quietly. "Not just me and Allie. It's not like a date or anything."

Yeah, because that would have been horrible. Really.

"Well," she sighed. "At least you'll be there to keep an eye on the girls in case any boy gets too fresh."

"Okay." I tried not to roll my eyes at the idea of any guy actually bothering to "get fresh," as Gran Mosely called it. I had a better chance of growing gills than being flirted with by some random guy. "Time to go now. Off to do homework. Yay homework."

Winston stood, his eyes still not meeting mine, and picked up his and Mercedes's plates as I took another bite of toast and tried to ignore Gran Mosely's searching gaze. She'd been trying to play matchmaker between Winston and me since I'd come to live with her, and I knew I wasn't the only one who felt weird about it.

The last thing I needed was to make a fool out of myself over a guy who was almost like a brother to me. It would be an absolute disaster. I wouldn't just *not* get the guy—I'd lose one of my best friends as well. No. Winston was definitely out of bounds.

"We'll see you later, Gran," Mercedes said, pulling me out of my thoughts.

"Right." Gran smiled first at me and then at my friends. "Have a good time today."

"Oh, it'll be a blast," Winston said, not even bothering to hide his sarcasm.

I quickly slid on a pair of black flip-flops and tried not to think about the fact that my feet looked like the human equivalent of hooves. Not that there was anything I could do about it. Swim practice six days a week made a pedicure pretty much pointless.

"We who are about to die." Winston picked up his own beaten-up black bag and slung it over his shoulder before ushering me out the door. "You know how it goes."

"Hail Caesar," Gran said before he closed the door.

"Come on," he said. "Or we're never going to make it out of this alive."

Chapter Two

Two hours later I was trying to figure out whether it was possible to actually use the shelves full of library books to light myself on fire. Wasn't there some kind of Chinese torture that involved a thousand paper cuts? Because I was willing to sign up for that if it just *made the stupid stop.*

Jesse was...well, he was what most girls would call absolutely gorgeous, and some part of me thought that should count for something. Anything. Instead it was like looking at a very pretty building and realizing that not only were there no lights on inside, but there wasn't *anything* inside.

He'd spent the first half hour trying to make sense of the project—even though I'd explained it twice already—and ever since he'd been trying to convince us that we'd be better off doing our project on a story with more pictures than words. Not that I didn't like comic books, but seriously?

Now I was at the point of snapping just because of the way his lips moved when he read. Which was why Mercedes and I decided to make one last run to look for books to use. Except there wasn't much left that hadn't been dismissed by Her Royal Highness Queen Heidi with a dismissive flick of her fingers and a nose-curling sneer before she went back to her magazine.

"Hurry up already, Allie," Mercedes hissed as she elbowed me in the ribs.

"I'm looking, but we're running out of books."

"Well, hurry anyway. If we don't go back to the table with something reasonable you know Jesse is going to try pitching his whole *comic books are really just fairy tales that don't suck* idea again, and Winston will lose it."

I winced. "Oh, God. I can't take another argument about the merits of comic books versus novels. I just can't. My brain is already throbbing from trying to explain to him that just because *The Avengers* had a woman in it doesn't make it a fairy tale."

"Mine, too. So, while I'd really love to watch Winston punch him and break into an old-fashioned throwdown, Mrs. Ath will bounce us out of here. Then we'll never get this project done, and we'll fail English, and then I will have to kill you."

"It's not my fault that we can't find a fairy tale that hasn't been claimed by another group already or isn't completely stupid—at least according to Her Majesty over there." I ran my finger over the edges of the thick books on the shelf.

Mythology. Cinderella. Scandinavian folk tales. None of them made it past Heidi's eye-rolling dismissal before she sent me back to the shelves to find something else. Nothing I found was right. Everything was too much work, or too boring, or simply too uncool. But she couldn't tell me what she wanted, so we were quickly running out of options. Unless we wanted to do a project on *The Avengers* or a critique on the fashion choices Disney had made when outfitting its princesses. The short version? Heidi thought they needed more couture and fewer ruffles.

"What about this one on folk tales from Africa?" Mercedes pulled a red leather-bound book off the shelf.

"She won't go for it," I said. "She'll say that folk tales are cliché. Besides, it will get her into another rant on clothes with clashing patterns, and dear God that makes the whole *Avengers* thing seem like a debate we'd be having during an Honor Society meeting."

"This from the girl who claimed a TV show was a totally modern version of fairy tales for people who were too cool to bother with reading books? We couldn't, I don't know, pitch them as a sort of ironic indie fashion statement thing?"

"Like I said, the folk tales won't work. What about this?" I grabbed a thick, dusty book crammed into a small space toward the end of the shelf, lying horizontal instead of standing upright like the rest. I flipped the book over carefully and looked at the royal blue cover. *The Chronicles of Nerissette.*

My jaw fell open. The book that inspired my dreams. Fate and her cloak of forgotten wishes. Kuolema and his brothers. My mother had read to me from this edition every night when I was a kid up until the accident, and when I'd gone back to our apartment to pack our things it had been gone.

"We'll use this." I shoved the book into Mercedes's hands and wiped my own sweaty palms on my jeans. I backed away from her, my eyes still on the book, and tried to ignore the queasy feeling in my stomach.

"Allie?" She quirked an eyebrow at me. "Are you okay?"

"Fine. This is the book we're using, and if Heidi doesn't like it then she can do the project on her own, and then we'll see what Mr. Brinnegar thinks of her fashion sense."

"Okay..." Mercedes followed me across the library cradling the book to her chest as the two boys in our group glared at each other. Heidi flipped through a cheerleading magazine, ignoring the rest of us as she had been for most of the meeting.

"How can you not watch the Steelers on *Monday Night Football*?" Jesse asked Winston, his blue eyes wide as he shook his golden-blond surfer fringe so that it flopped forward to cover one eye.

"I don't watch football," Winston answered. "It seems pretty logical to me."

"But it's all that our country stands for. Not watching football is—I don't know what it is. It's un-American. That's it. It's, like, communist or something. The terrorists win if you don't watch football."

"The communists aren't technically terrorists," Winston pointed out, crossing his arms over his chest. "Not that it matters because I still couldn't watch football. We don't have a TV in Casa Carruthers. The major says they rot your brain."

"You don't have a television?" Heidi lowered her magazine to glower at Winston, her pouty, pink mouth curled up in a sneer. "Isn't that like a crime or something? I'm pretty sure there's a law about it."

"You would think so," Winston said.

Mercedes and I came up behind him and took our seats on either side, across the table from our less academically inclined partners. I gripped Winston's clenched hand under the table. I knew the last thing he wanted to do was explain his father and the unconventional rules that he made them live by.

"But…" Winston uncurled his fist and gave my hand a quick squeeze before pulling away. "Try as I might, I can't persuade the Marine Corps to court-martial him over it."

"Oh, man." Jesse ran his hand up through his hair, pushing it back off his face, his eyes wide. "That sucks." He turned to me and smiled, a dimple flickering in his cheek. "Hey, Allie. Did you find something?"

"Um." I swallowed, and my heart started to pound again for no real reason. "Yeah. I found the book we're going to use."

"After I approve it," Heidi said.

"*I'm* the group leader." I turned to narrow my eyes at her and then reached out to get the book from Mercedes. "And I'm sick of you nixing all our choices. So this"—I dropped the book onto the table with a heavy *thud*—"is the book we are going to pick our fairy tale from."

Heidi sniffed. "Fine, but I get to choose what story we use."

"Whatever." Mercedes flipped the front cover of the book open. "Let's just choose something so that we can split the work up and get out of here."

"Fine." Heidi glared first at Mercedes and then at me.

"Fine." I gritted my teeth.

"I don't see why you all are making such a big deal out of this anyway," Heidi said. "Nobody else really cares about this stupid project. I don't see why you're making it such a thing."

"Because some of us need this grade," I said.

The snobby blonde rolled her eyes at me and twisted her lips into a sneer. Her normally hazel eyes looked gray and flat in the fluorescent lights, and I noticed she had a huge zit forming on her chin.

"Like Jesse, if he wants to stay off academic probation and on the basketball team," I said. "Or at least that's what Mr. Brinnegar told me when he put you on our team."

"And some of us have actual lives and really couldn't care less about anything as stupid as English class," Heidi snapped. "Besides, Brinnegar isn't actually going to kick Jesse off the team—they need him to win."

"What's this?" Winston asked, ignoring our bickering. He and Mercedes were leaning across the library table, their heads almost touching.

"What's *what?*"

"This." He pointed to a sketch on the inside of the front cover.

I leaned in for a closer look. The picture was of an old-fashioned room with a fireplace in the back and a table loaded with books. A small cauldron with tiny bottles and jars scattered around it was in the corner. In the very center of the table was a cat, peering intently into a crystal ball. A fancy ribbon was unfurled across the bottom of the picture with the words "The Fate Maker's Lair" in thick calligraphy. Smoke curled around the bottom of the picture's border.

"Hey." I goggled, bug-eyed, at the book and noticed that the picture seemed to have a lot more smoke than it had a second before, and, hold up—

"Is that picture moving?" Mercedes pulled the book toward her.

"What?" Winston yanked the book back, before glancing over at Mercedes like she'd lost her mind.

"Just a minute ago the cat was gazing in the crystal ball,"

Mercedes said. "I'm sure of it. The cat was on the table, staring into the crystal ball, but look at it now."

The lights flickered and thunder rumbled in the distance even though the library was still flooded with bright sunlight. I turned my attention back to the book and stared at the cat in question.

Mercedes was right. I'd seen that picture hundreds of times when I was younger. I knew that the cat was meant to be peering into the crystal ball, except that now it was sitting with its back straight, staring out of the picture at us with a wide, toothy grin.

"Don't be ridiculous." Heidi slammed her magazine down on the table and grabbed the book out of Winston's hands. "Pictures in books don't move. It's a *picture*."

Mercedes jabbed her finger at the cat on the page. "That picture moved."

"Pictures in books *don't move*," Heidi said, her voice crackling with irritation.

The book flew out of her hands, sliding into the middle of the table, and began to spin, its pages fluttering. The lights above us exploded, the glass from the bulbs tinkling against the sconces like the patter of rain on a roof. A cold wind tore through the library, throwing open the doors on the far side.

"Can't move, can't I?" a sharp, exotic-sounding female voice growled. I felt goose bumps prickle all over my body—I knew that voice. "Shows what you know."

Where the book sat open, no longer spinning, there was a black cat hovering in midair—glowering at us all. The same black cat that had been in my dream this morning. The one who'd said Fate was coming.

She blinked once and let her mouth stretch into a wide

smile, fangs glittering like they belonged in a toothpaste commercial.

"You...you...you can talk," I said. "You can actually talk. It's not just a dream."

"Either that or you've gone around the bend completely," the cat said.

She gave me a wicked grin, and I tried to tuck myself behind Winston, totally not caring that I was acting like a wuss by hiding behind a guy. If the cat from my dreams was here, then the dragon Kuolema might not be far behind—and if any one of us stood a chance against Death himself, I was placing my bet on Win.

"Either way, no time to waste." The cat's mouth stretched even wider into a maniacal grin. "You opened the book, and the die's been cast. Time to meet the fate you each so richly deserve."

Before any of us could respond, the cat blinked and the world lurched, pitching us toward the table and into the swirling black mass where the book had once been.

Chapter Three

We plummeted headfirst as cold, gray smoke rushed past us, and I clung to Winston with my left hand and kept flinging my right out to find Mercedes. My fingers brushed against something warm and I felt a reassuring tug. I couldn't see but I knew it was her.

The wind turned icy and a loud rushing sound, like being trapped underneath a waterfall, filled my ears before I landed on something solid—and dirty. At least it wasn't cold. Or alive. Mercedes landed a second after, halfway on top of me, and I coughed. Winston groaned at my other side, and I pulled away from him.

"Both of you have got to lay off the candy bars," he said.

I rolled over onto my back and opened my eyes. There were dirty brown rafters above me, and a large, ugly bird's nest in the corner. It looked like we'd landed in a room with stone walls, and I shifted—yep, I was going to be feeling that landing for a while.

"Oh, for the love of the stars," I whispered, my mother's favorite saying slipping easily from my mouth.

"Princess…"

That same female voice was back again, and I turned my head and saw the cat from the library staring down at me—actually alive this time—her very real nose twitching. She twisted her lips into another grin, and the black patch of fur around her eyes crinkled. She sat back and lifted one white paw, licked along the length of it, then used it to wipe her face.

I sat up and inched away from her on my butt, clinging to Mercedes and Winston again. "You get away from us. I don't know who you are or what sort of freaky trick this is, but you stay away."

"My apologies for the landing. The *Chronicles* positioned you too far to the right. It truly is a wonderful instrument but, well, even in life the book was never known for her aim."

"Her what?" I whispered.

"Just ask Tervalkien the One-Eyed Troll. Before their archery match he was just Tervalkien the Troll."

"Nope. No. No way."

"Yes, he was. And a rather handsome troll at that."

"No, this has got to be some sort of freaky prank. Like gas pumped through the vents at the library to make everyone hallucinate or drugs or—I don't know—*something* that Heidi came up with so she could have a laugh probably. This isn't real. You're *not real*."

The cat swung her head around to stare pointedly at the huge pile of fluffy pillows about three feet from where Winston had landed. "Then why didn't she arrange to land on the cushions instead?"

"What?"

"This," Heidi started. I looked over to see her and Jesse cowering behind a table in the corner. "Whatever the heck *this* is—I had nothing to do with it."

"Yeah, right." I glared at her.

"If someone drugged us then it was one of you weird, fantasy-role-playing nerds. And it's really not cool," Heidi said. "You *need* to fix this."

"I didn't have anything to do with it! How do you expect *me* to have pulled *this* off?" I asked.

"I don't know. You're one of those boring smart people. I'm sure you have your ways."

"Unlike some people, I don't live to torture others. If anyone is behind this it's the cheerleading squad. This has *you* written all over it, Heidi Spencer. Nobody else would come up with a prank this over-the-top dramatic."

"We'd steal your clothes while you were in swim practice or fill your iPod with twenty hours of people yodeling, but causing explosions and kidnapping people? Not really our style."

"Allie." Winston tugged on my hand and my gaze locked on his. A shiver ran up my spine. I shook it off.

"Heidi and the rest of the cheerleaders aren't smart enough to pull this off," he continued. "I don't even know what it is that happened, and if I can't figure it out, you know Heidi couldn't have done it."

"What?" She narrowed her eyes at him. "Are you saying you're smarter than me?"

"Yes, and there is no way that you managed to pump the library full of hallucinogens, cause an explosion, and somehow manage to transport us to some weird prop room that's been made to look like a castle dungeon."

"But how did it happen, then?" I asked.

"He's right," Mercedes said, her voice trembling. "Heidi can't spell explosion, much less make one. There's no way she could have pulled this off. Whatever *this* actually is."

"Just because I have better things to do with my time than hang out in a chemistry lab doesn't mean I'm an idiot," Heidi snapped. "And for the record? I'm smart enough to not end up with mint-green highlights when I do my roots. So there."

"Heidi." I turned to glare at her. "Did you do this somehow?"

"No, duh, but that's not the—"

"Like I said"—the cat stepped closer so that she was standing next to my foot, her tail extended into the air like a flag—"*I* brought you here...with the help of the book, of course."

"*The Chronicles of Nerissette*? You're saying that a *book* brought us here?" I asked.

"Yes, the book. The one you picked up in the library. Remember that one? Blue cover? Slightly oversized and a bit pretentious in her bindings? More than a bit familiar to look at? Maybe it even reminds you of a book that once sat on your bedroom bookshelf?"

I swallowed. "How did you know that?"

"Miss I-Need-to-Be-in-Royal-Blue-Leather helped me bring you here, but she aimed too far to the right so you missed the rather soft pillows I had laid out for you," the cat said, ignoring my question. "Like I said, she always did have a lousy aim."

"Uh, well, thanks?" I shifted on the hard floor, trying to find a comfortable spot to sit. "I mean, for the pillows. It's the thought and all when it comes to that sort of stuff. Or at least that's what my mom always said…but we really shouldn't be here."

"Yes, she did." The cat looked at me shrewdly. "They do… mothers, that is. They always have those silly sayings like 'it's the thought that counts' and 'never count your mice before they're digested.' Things like that."

I bit my lip and stared at the cat. I was pretty sure my mother would have freaked out if I even considered eating a mouse, and she definitely wouldn't have given me any tips on their digestion.

"Look, as nice as it was for you to put out pillows for our landing, maybe you and the book could possibly come up with a way to—"

"To?" The cat's tail waved back and forth like a particularly curious S.

"Take us home? Because whoever you think we are, we aren't the people you want. None of us are rich or important or anything else. Kidnapping us won't help you."

"Who said anything about kidnapping?" The cat tilted her head to the side, and I tried to control the tremor that was rushing through me as her lips curled upward into another smile. "Princess, I didn't kidnap you. I brought you home."

"I'm…uh…" I scooted backward on my butt, trying to get away from her.

"Hey, look, you." Jesse stood up from behind the table and came around to stand in the middle of the floor, facing the cat. "I don't know who you think you are but this is seriously not cool."

"I'm Esmeralda," the cat said, "one of the creatures in this world who loves the princess the most. The one who would give up everything if it would keep her safe. The one who would bargain with Fate herself."

"Look, whatever sort of whacked-out hallucination this is"—Winston slipped in front of me—"it ends now."

"Hallucination?" the cat asked.

"Whoever you are, whatever you think Allie knows or has or—I don't know—you're wrong," Winston said. "You've got the wrong girl, and you need to take us home now before things get any worse."

"I can't." The cat sat back on her haunches and stared up at him. "You're here, and until Fate has her say none of you can leave. Not if you want to stay alive, that is. Fate must have her due."

"Well, if you can't get us home then I will just get there myself." Heidi pushed past Jesse to stare down at the cat. "I'm not going to sit here and let you just kidnap me, you furry little...little..."

"Little?" the cat asked.

"Freak. You furry, disgusting *freak*. Allie may not have the backbone to tell you how it is, but if you don't get out of my way I'll dropkick you all the way back to Bethel Park and straight into one of those chambers where the vets put cats to suck their lungs out of their chests."

"Actually, that's not how animals are euthanized," Mercedes said quietly.

"Shut up, you." Heidi stalked over to the wooden shutters set in the far window and shoved them open. I gasped.

Outside was...it was...well, it wasn't home. There weren't commuter train tracks across the street or the Bethel Bakery standing cheerily nearby. There were no cars on South Hills Road.

There was no South Hills Road.

Instead, there was a long expanse of grass the color of Granny Smith apples and probably longer than four football fields. Beyond that were trees. Huge trees. Trees that stood higher than the skyscrapers in downtown Pittsburgh.

I pushed myself up and stumbled to the window, shouldering Heidi aside. We were up high. I looked out and down, trying to judge just how high we were. Six floors up, maybe seven. And the trees, with their gnarled black trunks and their brilliant, dark-green leaves, had to stand at least a hundred feet higher.

I turned my head to the left and had to take a deep breath. There was a low, red crushed-rock path winding away from whatever building we were in, and there were fewer trees— shorter trees with bloodred leaves—beyond.

I licked my lips and gazed out into the distance again. There they were: two enormous white stone hands raised heavenward, a clear gleaming crystal the size of a…

"A billion wishes and unanswered prayers," I said quietly, remembering the line that had described it in the stories my mother had once read me.

"You know what it is," the cat said.

"The Hall of the Pleiades with its great guardian. Her white hands raised to the stars, holding the hopes of a thousand untouched worlds in her hands," I whispered.

"Yes," the cat said.

I looked back at her, still sitting in the middle of the room, studying me. "So, it's true? All of it? The crazy stories that my mother used to read me that no one else had ever heard of? The dragons and the men who ate fire and called down the sun?"

"The Firas," she said. "They're real."

"And the grasslands with the hunting parties who ride great fanged beasts as they hunt giants and trolls? They're real, too?"

"The Veldt." The cat kept her eyes fixed on mine. "All true."

"And the nymphs? The fairies? The spirits of the trees? The mermaids? The woodsmen who can become one with the shadows?"

"All true."

"And the Lost Rose of Nerissette? Trapped inside a mirror and left to die? What about her? Or the warrior princess who would save the world from darkness?"

"The Rose may be lost," Esmeralda said. "But we rejoice at the return of our princess." She smiled at me as best a cat could.

I jerked my head back and forth. "No. No way."

"Allie?" Winston and the rest of them were gaping at me. "What's going on?"

"It's a fairy tale. All of it. Nerissette. The world on the other side of the mirror. The place where things that can never be are real. The World of Dreams."

"And we're what? We're in that world?" Mercedes asked. "Why? How?"

"Because we need you," Esmeralda said. "We need all of you."

"For what?" Jesse asked.

"You've reached your six thousandth day," Esmeralda said, still staring at me. "It's time for your debt to Fate to be paid."

"My what?"

"Your debt. One way or another, Fate must get her due. You can give it willingly, or she can send Kuolema to collect in her place."

I swallowed. If this cat wasn't talking total nonsense then that meant if I didn't obey the will of Fate I'd die. "And them?" I nodded toward the other four members of my group. Just because I was trapped here didn't mean they had to stay.

"They're here to make sure that you do not fail. Because if you fail, well…just don't. No matter what. Don't fail."

"Esmeralda!" a deep, thundering, male voice roared.

"What happens if I do fail?" My heart pounded in my ears, and before I could move—or she could answer—the heavy wooden door in the corner flew open and bounced hard against the wall. There, in the doorway, stood a man about my mom's age who towered over me. His shoulders filled the frame, and he was at least a foot taller than my own five foot six. He was even taller than Winston and Jesse, who were each over six feet.

The man was dressed in midnight-colored robes with silver symbols stitched into the fabric that seemed to writhe as the folds moved around his legs. "I felt a disturbance in the ether. Someone is using mag—"

He stared at me with bloodred eyes, the centers filled with coal-black flames. His dark hair stood in shaggy waves around his pale cheeks. "*You.*"

"No." I stepped back, plastering my hands against the rough stone wall behind me. "You're not real. They banished you."

"Your Majesty—" the cat said.

"No," I interrupted. "The King of Nightmares was trapped inside one of the great trees, then they chopped it down and broke his body before throwing it into the waves of the Sea of Nevermore and trapping his soul inside the Bleak."

The man froze and stared at us each in turn. He glanced over at the cat and then back at me. Then back at the cat. He opened his mouth. No sound came out. "I…"

"Alicia Munroe, Crown Princess of Nerissette," the cat said, her voice ringing with an authority that would make even my most hard-core high school teacher jealous. "Meet the Fate Maker of Nerissette. The grand high wizard, leading practitioner of magic, and one of your *most trusted* diplomatic advisers. He's protected your kingdom for you until you came of age and has guarded this land with his magic. Protected us from trolls and giants and from the scheming of Bavasama."

"Bavasama?"

"The queen across the mountains who would have taken your throne. The Queen of Nightmares. He's cared for your kingdom because he's *devoted* to you and your rule." She hissed the last bit and I wasn't sure if she was explaining it all to me or reminding him.

"You, you, you." He stared at the cat, his now-pale eyes wide. "Why?

"She has reached her six thousandth day, and it is time we place our rightful ruler on the throne."

"I should have been consult—"

"It must end here. Fate must have her say."

"But the *Chronicles* end with—"

"All things end," Esmeralda said. "It is the only way for new things to begin. Now you must do the spells."

"But I can't just—"

"You must. It is how the end was written."

"The *Chronicles*—"

"Will begin again, but first you must do the spells."

"Look," I said. "I don't know what's going on here but I

think you've made a mistake."

"You are Alicia Wilhelmina Munroe," Esmeralda said. "The Last Golden Rose of Nerissette. You must bring about the end of this age so that life can begin again for our people."

"No," Heidi said, her voice biting. "I don't know who you are or why you think *Allie,* of all people, is some sort of warrior princess, but you need to take us home. Right now!"

"The end must come, girl, and only then can any of us ever be free."

"I'm telling you, Allie is not a princess," Heidi said.

"Fate," Esmeralda said sternly, her eyes fixed on mine, "must be paid. Only then can you go home."

"Allie?" Mercedes's eyes were wide and filled with fear.

"Now." Esmeralda fixed her gaze on the Fate Maker. "Do the spells and let us end the Time of Waiting."

Chapter Four

"Wait, wait." The Fate Maker held a hand up. "This, the prophesies inside *The Chronicles of Nerissette*, all of it…just wait."

"Fate doesn't wait, no matter what a wizard might believe," Esmeralda said. "Not even the wizard who the prophecies declared the Guardian of Nerissette may question Fate's motives. We do the will of Fate or we die. There is no in between. And there is certainly no *bargaining*. For any of us."

"But she hadn't told me that this is meant to happen now," the Fate Maker snapped. "She would have spoken to me. She would have told me it was time. I'm the guardian of this land. Touched by Fate herself. She would have told me."

"So you think that means Fate is required to get your approval?" Esmeralda shot back.

"There has been nothing in the mirror, nothing in the Orb of Fate. Nothing," the Fate Maker said.

"Have you actually looked? Or did you not want to know?"

Esmeralda asked.

"Look, I don't know what you two are going on about," I said, "but you're really starting to freak me out. Whatever this Fate thing is, and six thousand days, and I don't know what, but it has nothing to do with me."

"She's not fit for this role," the Fate Maker said.

"Finally someone gets it." Heidi crossed her arms in front of her chest.

He held a hand out toward me. "She's a child. They're all children. *The Chronicles of Nerissette* says that the Last Great Rose will be a warrior queen."

"She'll become the queen she needs to be."

"No, the *Chronicles* say she'll march a great army into Bathune and claim the Land of Nightmares as her own again, then she'll banish magic and rip the world apart. You think this *child* can do any of those things?"

I glanced over and saw Jesse and Heidi huddled together as Winston and Mercedes moved closer to me, pulling me into a protected position between them.

"She'll bring peace," Esmeralda said. "Thousands of years of peace will come."

"At what cost?" The Fate Maker threw his hands up in the air. "The death of magic? The end of everything we know?"

"If that is what it takes," she countered.

"She could bring a thousand years of peace by wiping us out of existence. All of our kind. An empty world is a peaceful world, isn't it?" The Fate Maker shook his head as he spoke.

"Then that's what must happen," said Esmeralda.

"But this can't be her. This can't be the Last Great Rose. Even if the Time of Waiting must come to an end, it won't be brought about by *her*." He scrunched up his face in disgust.

"I think he might be right," I said. "I'm not a warrior or anything, and I don't know how to invade anyone. I don't even want to. I just want to go home. My mother's there, and she's sick. She needs me."

I swallowed. We were trapped here, on this side of the mirror, and my mother was on the other. I hadn't gotten to say good-bye. I hadn't even bothered to go see her in three months, and now I was here and she was there—alone. I had to come up with a way out of this. A way back to her.

"It is her," Esmeralda said, ignoring me as she stared at the Fate Maker. "You and I both know it's her. It always has been her. That's why we did what we did those years ago."

"We were protecting our home," the Fate Maker said angrily. "If she would have stayed the results would have been disastrous."

"If who would have stayed where?" I asked.

"This girl is a child. What you're asking is madness."

Esmeralda ignored him. "Now Allie, step in front of the mirror."

"What mirror?" I asked.

"The Mirror of Nerissette. That one. In the corner." She nodded her sleek, black head toward a large mirror in a plain, dark wooden frame. "Step in front of it, and then run your fingers across its face."

I walked slowly toward the large mirror and stared into it. I looked at my reflection and then lifted my gaze to Mercedes, who was huddled against Winston behind me.

The mirror began to hum like a swarm of bees, and I focused on my own reflection again. My brown eyes stared back at me, but instead of reflecting the still, wide-eyed and terrified version of myself, the reflection smiled, her teeth gleaming. And then she winked.

"Wait a second."

"Stay close to it," Esmeralda instructed, now sitting by my feet.

I glanced down at her.

"Don't look at me. Keep your eyes fixed on the mirror. Tell it what you want to see."

"I don't see anything. It's just black."

"Tell it what you want to see."

"I want to see my mother," I said quickly. "I want my mom."

The mirror filled with smoke, the humming getting louder, and then it went black again. I was staring into nothing but darkness. The mirror was no longer a mirror but a window into my nightmares, a portal to where the dragons waited.

"No." I shook my head.

"Keep your eyes on it," Esmeralda said, her voice stern. "Don't let your focus slip. You're in control of it."

"I want to see my mother," I said selfishly, sounding like a whiny two-year-old when my voice began to tremble.

The darkness began to lessen, and suddenly, there was a burst of bright-pink light, and the mirror filled with flowers of every imaginable color, petals unfurling like fireworks.

"Stay strong," Esmeralda said. "You're almost there."

"Show me my mother right now," I said through clenched teeth. "Whatever this trick is, stop it. Stop it, and let me see my mother."

Then I saw her, holding me as a baby, singing on stage, dancing around our kitchen, cheering at my swim meets, sitting in the waiting room during my judo classes and the fencing lessons she'd insisted on. All of those memories flew past like the frames of a movie, blurring together as if the mirror were a television screen and my mother's life was a movie on fast-forward. There was a birthday cake on a passenger seat of a car, and the sound of the radio, and then a horn, and the mirror went black again.

"No." I beat my fist against the mirror. "No, give her back to me. You give her back to me."

"I told you she's not the one," the Fate Maker said, his voice hushed.

Light flickered in the mirror, and then my mother filled the glass again. Her hair was spread out on the pillow, and her cheeks were pale. Even in a coma she was one of the most beautiful people I'd ever seen.

"Mom." I dropped to my knees in front of the mirror and ran my hand over her cheek. "Oh, Mom."

"This doesn't mean anything," the Fate Maker said.

"She can control the only remaining relic. If we had the Dragon's Tear or the First Leaf she would be able to use those as well," Esmeralda said. "She could use the portals."

"There's no way to know that," the Fate Maker said. "It could be a residual connection. She's a girl who asked to see her mother; the emotional bonds alone would be enough to make the mirror take pity and show her what she asked for."

"The Mirror of Nerissette responded to her touch," Esmeralda said.

"The connection was shaky. She had to travel through the woman's unconscious. That's hardly proof," the Fate Maker said.

I felt an arm wrap around my shoulders, pulling me close. "Allie?" Winston's touch was warm, comforting. "Come on, Allie. It's okay."

"That's my mom." I held on to the mirror, unwilling to let

my mother go, as he scooted closer to me.

"I know." He let me lean my head against his shoulder as I kept stroking her cheek.

"There is another way to check," Esmeralda said. "A way that would remove your doubts."

"She's a child," the Fate Maker said. "If you're wrong, think about the damage you'll do, the pain you'll cause her."

"I'm not wrong, and do not pretend that you care what happens to the children. We both know that compassion isn't something found in your character."

"Forget my character. If you are wrong she could be crippled."

"If I'm wrong we'll send them back home. No one will ever be the wiser."

"You can do that?" I turned to her. "You can send us home?"

"If…" Esmeralda sighed. "If I'm wrong, then there is no reason to keep you here. So I could send you home, but I must warn you, Princess, I'm not wrong. I'm not."

"You could be, though? You could be wrong. This could all be a mistake." I clung to the idea that this was all some sort of weird, cosmic misunderstanding.

"No." She shook her head.

"Yes." The Fate Maker's voice sounded hollow. "She could be wrong. She could have misinterpreted the will of Fate, but the test she wants to do…it's brutal. If she's wrong you could be seriously injured."

"Will it tell you for certain, without a shred of doubt, whether or not I'm your lost princess?"

He nodded.

But it all kind of made sense. The stories, the judo and the fencing, the way Mom was always somehow *different* from other adults… But I couldn't be a princess. It made sense, but it wasn't right because no one, no matter what world they lived in, would look at me and see royalty. Which meant the cat had to be wrong. *She had to be.*

Now I just had to prove that whoever their lost princess was, I wasn't her. "Then let's do it," I said, my voice sounding braver than I actually felt.

"Are you certain? When I say the test is dangerous I'm not trying to scare you," he said.

"I'm trapped in a world that isn't my own. Things are already dangerous. Let's do it. I'll prove I'm not your princess, and then you can send us home."

"As you wish, then." He turned away from me and made his way to a large wooden chest in the corner of the room. He waved his left hand and the chest's lid flew open.

He held his hands out, palms down, and golden light began to pour from his fingertips. His lips moved but no sounds came out, and his hands shook.

A black box with golden roses carved into it slowly floated upward, hovering beneath his hands. Light seeped through the cracks in its lid. He stepped away from the chest and turned toward us.

"Come to the table," he said, his voice strained. "Let us finish this."

Winston helped me to stand, and together we walked slowly toward the table where the Fate Maker had stopped, the box just barely floating over the tabletop.

"*Avautua*," Esmeralda said quietly.

The lid slid backward. I stepped closer, and my breath caught as I saw the glowing, twisted, metal crown inside.

"Touch it," Esmeralda said. "If you are the Golden Rose you'll be able to touch the Rose Crown."

"But what if I'm not?" I asked. "What happens then?"

"The crown will mark you. A pain that will sear itself into your very bones," the Fate Maker said. "A wound that will forever scar you—that is, if it doesn't simply kill you in a horrible, intensely agonizing death instead."

"What about our families?" I looked over at the others. "What about them?"

"I don't understand," Esmeralda said.

"What happens if I am your queen? What happens to them, I mean? Are they forced to come here?" Would they bring my mother here? Would she be trapped here along with me? Would Gran Mosely?

"Of course not," she said. "They're of no use to us."

"But don't you think they'll worry? You took us from a public library in a flash of smoke. Someone will have seen. People will be freaking out. You can't just steal people's kids and expect nothing to happen."

"But nothing will happen," Esmeralda said. "Because nothing was seen. You weren't seen."

"But—"

"For the World That Is, none of you exist," Esmeralda said.

"Wait." Heidi held up a hand. "What? We don't exist?"

"You have been erased from their world. No shadow of you remains there. There are no memories, no dreams, no one to notice that you're gone."

"But what happens when we go back?" I asked. "Then we're what? Just strange, homeless kids?"

"Of course not." She looked up at me, her eyes shining. "You'll slot back into the world as if you never left. They'll remember you, and the time you were apart will be nothing more than a dream that none of them can quite remember."

"But that—us going home and slotting back into our lives—can't happen unless you're sure that I'm not actually your queen?"

"No. We must know if you're the Rose."

"Right. Okay."

I held my hand out toward the crown, and my shoulders started to tremble. I took a deep breath and then stopped. What if I wasn't their lost princess? I'd be burned, scarred.

But if it didn't kill me we could all leave. I could go home and back to my normal, boring life. I didn't want to hurt myself, but if it was that or being forced to stay here forever, then perhaps a bit of pain was worth it to get home. To make sure my friends got home. To be with my mom again. "Oh, this is so stupid," Heidi said, breaking me out of my own thoughts. "It's just a crown."

She stalked forward and shoved me out of her way and farther into Winston's arms. "If all it takes is picking up the stupid crown to become queen, I'll do it. I'd be a better queen than Allie anyway."

She reached out for the crown, and it started to buzz a low, discordant note.

I grabbed her wrist to stop her. The idea of Heidi touching that crown—*my crown*, a tiny voice in the back of my head screamed—made my skin crawl.

She jerked her hand away from mine. "What are you doing?"

I bit my lower lip, and then let go of her hand. "Don't touch it. It's not meant for you."

"And it's what? Meant for you? Let's be serious. If anyone

here is a lost princess it's me, not you."

"I hope you're right. Then we can go home. Either way, why not let me touch it first?" I closed my eyes, and my hand dropped to the top of the crown. It was warm, and I could feel it vibrating against my fingertips, almost like it was purring.

"Oh crap." Heidi swallowed, her wide hazel eyes meeting mine. "If I would have touched that…"

"Yeah." I shrugged. "You're welcome."

"All hail the Last Great Rose of Nerissette," Esmeralda said, her own voice quiet. "May the stars save us all."

Chapter Five

"But I don't want to be queen," I said softly. "I'm not cut out to be a queen."

"You don't have a choice," Esmeralda explained. "You *are* queen."

"What if I refuse?" I asked desperately. I *could* refuse. I could tell them no and order them to send me home. They could find some other queen to run the place.

"If you rebel against the will of Fate, then chaos will descend. Everything we know will be destroyed. People will die. Fate will take a revenge upon our world that will devour us all, and Kuolema will come for you to devour your bones."

"That sounds bad." So much for refusing, then.

"She is a vengeful master," Esmeralda said. "If you defy her there will be consequences."

She padded over to the Fate Maker and glared up at him. "You need to do the spells now. Now that there is no question of who she is, you must do the spells."

"We could still send her back," the Fate Maker said. "We're the only people who know she's here. No one would ever find out. We can keep Nerissette safe."

"We can't. This is the will of Fate."

"We could wait until she's older. When we've had more time to prepare, when we know what will come next."

"Fate waits for no one," Esmeralda said. "She comes in the time of her choosing."

"But the girl's not ready. What if she destroys everything we've built?"

"When the time comes she will be ready," Esmeralda said. "And we've always known the end of our ways was coming— and soon. Now, you *must* do the spells. No more excuses, no more delays. The Time of Waiting is at an end, and we all have a part to play."

"The things to come will be terrible," the Fate Maker said. "The end of everything."

"I know." Esmeralda's voice seemed defeated for the first time. "But we are the servants of Fate, and we cannot oppose her. Otherwise, there will be grave consequences."

He closed his eyes and grimaced. "Fine."

He let his hands drop, and then the box clattered onto the table, its lid sliding shut so quickly I barely had time to get my fingers clear before the lock snapped back into place.

"Stand back, Princess," Esmeralda said. "Away from the others."

"Why?" I looked at her and the wizard standing across from us, and then at my friends, clumped together.

"Because they are not of this world, and they must be brought into the fold of Fate's cloak," the Fate Maker said, his voice dark and hoarse.

"And what about me?" I asked.

He opened his eyes and stared at me, his red eyes fathomless and unreadable. "Fate knew you as her own before the first winds blew over the Veldt. Like all of us, you've been sealed to her whims since before the first star was born in the sky."

"And them?"

"They're from the World of Waking," Esmeralda said, her voice a low, throbbing whisper. "They are the children of her brother—Free Will. Now step back so that the Fate Maker can do the spells that will make them her own. Otherwise they can't stay."

"But if they can go back," I said, "shouldn't we let them?"

"They can't go back."

"If they can't be here and can't go back…"

Winston grasped Mercedes's hand, his chocolate eyes fixed on mine. He nodded once, silently.

I swallowed. I couldn't send them back, and they couldn't stay. To keep them safe I was going to have to kill my friends. "Will it…"

"No," Esmeralda said. "It won't hurt any of them. A flash of light and some noise and then it's done."

Winston pushed forward. "I'll go first."

"Perhaps one of the others?" the Fate Maker said. "An easier transformation."

"I said, I'll go first." Winston moved closer to him. "So do it. Whatever it is, just do it."

"Right." The Fate Maker nodded at him. "It seems Fate chose well with you, Winston Carruthers." He looked up at the rest of us. "You'll all need to stay back. This particular spell is…" He grimaced. "Messy."

"Messy?" I asked.

Instead of answering, the Fate Maker pushed back the long, billowing sleeves of his robe and raised his hands, his eyes fixed on Winston. He mumbled a low, hissing chant that I couldn't understand, and red sparks flew from his hands.

There was a sharp *snap,* and the spot where one of my closest friends had just stood was enveloped in blue-black flames. The air crackled, and heat billowed around us as the flames licked at the wooden rafters above our heads.

There was a sharp, anguished scream from inside the flames, and I watched the shadow where my friend had been, glowing, inside the dark fire. He writhed against the heat. The figure shimmered once, caught in the flames, and then crumpled to the floor.

"Winst—" I lunged forward.

The Fate Maker threw a hand out to stop me. "Give him a second to become accustomed to the change."

There was a loud, agonized roar—the howl I had imagined would come from one of the fanged beasts that I'd thought were only fairy-tale monsters. The howl turned into a high-pitched wail as the flames folded in on themselves. Slowly, they disappeared into the huddled form of the broken boy lying on the floor in front of me.

I stared intently at the still, silent body. "You said it wouldn't hurt him."

Winston's shoulder twitched, and then his back heaved as he made a sudden gasp for air. He sat upright like he'd been jerked awake by nightmares.

My heart pounded. "Winston?"

"Okay, that was weird. Those sparks came out of your fingers, and then it got really hot but nothing happened,"

Winston said. "And now I just feel strange. What happened?"

"Man…" Jesse pointed at him. "You were on *fire*. Like real fire. Flames, poof!"

Winston looked at the rest of us.

"Try it out," the Fate Maker said. "Close your eyes and focus."

"Focus on what?"

"You'll know once you try."

Winston pushed himself to his feet and licked his lips. He nodded and shut his eyes, focusing as instructed. He started to shake, sweat beading on his forehead, and the room darkened. Suddenly he seemed to waver, like that image of water you see on the highway when it's really hot. One second he was there and the next he was a shimmery mirage.

The image shattered then, and Winston screamed again, another agonizing wail that made me clench my eyes shut and cover my ears with my hands to escape the sound. The range of his voice changed, and the scream became a roar, so loud that I couldn't block it out. Tears slipped down my cheeks without my permission.

By the stars, what had I done bringing my friends into this nightmare with me?

I felt the Fate Maker's arm around my waist, and he reached up to pull my hands away from my ears. "He's fine. Open your eyes and see how glorious he is. Truly my best work yet."

I cracked my eyes open and my jaw dropped. Where Winston had stood there was now an enormous black dragon with smoke curling out of his nostrils and heavy blue-black wings outspread from his back.

"Win?" I stepped forward when the dragon lowered its

head toward me. "Are you in there?"

The dragon snorted and dipped its snout to sniff. I tried not to giggle at the feel of his hot breath on my neck—right now didn't really seem like the best time to break out in hysterics.

"Are you okay?" I asked. The dragon snorted against my neck again.

"Very good, Winston." The Fate Maker clapped his hands once. "You will make an excellent Queen's Champion. You were born to fly."

"Yeah, well, I have to say the wings help," Mercedes said.

"Now." The Fate Maker rubbed his palms together. "You're taking up quite a bit of space, and we've got some more magic to make. Would you mind going back to your two-legged form? Same process as before, only in reverse. Close your eyes, concentrate, and I'll take it from there since we're in mixed company."

"What does that have to do with anything?" Mercedes asked.

"The dragon is magical. His clothes, unfortunately, are not." The Fate Maker glared at her, and we all looked at the ground at Winston's feet, staring at the destroyed clothes littered there.

"You mean he's going to be—" Jesse shook his head. "Aw man, that's not cool."

"I can conjure some new ones as he changes shape," the Fate Maker said. "Now, everyone be quiet and let's continue. We've quite a bit to do still."

The large dragon stood upright and flapped its wings experimentally before closing his eyes. Flames erupted again, but this time there was only a quiet groan from inside them.

The flames died away, and Winston kneeled where the dragon had been, clutching his head and wearing clothes identical to the ones he'd destroyed. "*That* is brutal."

"Oh my God." I hurried forward, and Mercedes and I wrapped him in a hug. "Are you okay?"

"Fine," he said, his voice hoarse. "If you can get over the fact that every single law of physics has just been violated, I'm completely fine."

"Leave it to you to be worried about some stupid laws a couple of dead guys came up with." I hugged him tighter. "You were a dragon—*a dragon*—with wings and a tail. You even had smoke coming out of your nose."

"Did I at least look cool?"

Mercedes put a hand on her hip. "If you think looking like a giant black dragon is cool."

"You were amazing," I said.

He smiled, glancing up at me, and I smiled back. He pressed his shoulder against mine, and my breath caught at how close he was, how warm he still felt from the flames. Mercedes cleared her throat, reminding me that we weren't alone, and I jerked my gaze away from his while he did the same, making me feel even more awkward than usual.

"For a reptile, I mean." I tried to collect myself. "How are you feeling?"

"Not too bad." He shifted, and I let him rest some of his weight against me as I helped him stand. "You know, for having just been a mythical creature that isn't supposed to exist."

I followed Winston to one of the benches next to the table Heidi and Jesse had been hiding behind.

"Now." The Fate Maker turned to Mercedes and smiled.

"The brilliant Miss Garcia, it's your turn."

"You know what?" Mercedes backed away from him, her hands up in front of her. "I'm good without any special powers, thanks. I've got my girl Allie's back just the way I am. Always have. No special powers needed."

"Come now." The Fate Maker raised his arms again, pushing the robes up past his elbows. "I promise this is a much gentler spell. You'll hardly feel a thing. A little tingle, and it will all be over."

"I don't think—"

The Fate Maker ignored her, pointing his hands in her direction, green smoke curling out of his fingers. There was a muffled *pop*, like the first kernels of popcorn in the microwave, and the smoke twisted around my best friend, hiding her inside its tendrils. I heard a loud cough and then saw a hand batting away the smoke.

"Just because I don't want to be turned into a dragon doesn't mean you have to gas me," Mercedes said, coughing again. "Haven't you ever heard of lung cancer, you creep?"

"A creep?" the Fate Maker asked, his voice a low grumble. "Like I enjoy doing these spells? I expend my energy, and you call me a creep. I thought teenagers in *this* world were disrespectful. It shows you how gratitude works among the Otherkind."

"Yeah, well, I like breathing, so a little warning would have been nice, thanks." Mercedes flapped her arm at the smoke again, clearing it.

"Oh crap," Winston voiced for us all. I just stared. If I'd thought I was shocked to see Winston turn into a dragon that was nothing compared to this.

She was green. The same pond-green color her hair had

been this morning in Gran's kitchen. But *all* of her was green. Her skin, her nails, even her clothes, had turned green. The only things that weren't green, strangely enough, were her eyes and her hair. Both of them had turned a sort of silvery color, glinting in the light of the room. Her hair had also grown, draping over her shoulders and crackling around her head like a halo instead of lying in its normal short, messy bob.

"So what happened?" Mercedes asked. "I mean, besides the smoke?"

"You're green."

"I'm what?"

"You're green," Winston said. "And not in an environmentally friendly sort of way."

"I don't think I quite understand you," Mercedes said slowly. "What did you say?"

"For God's sake." Heidi pulled a red plastic compact from her jeans pocket. She opened it and held it up in front of Mercedes. "You're green."

"Oh man," Mercedes said, her voice wavering.

I looked over at the Fate Maker and narrowed my eyes. "Fix this."

"Fix what? I turned her into one of the most powerful dryads Nerissette has ever seen. Don't tell me that you're upset she's because she's not a more popular shade of green."

Mercedes stared at him. "You've turned me into a tree sprite? Why? What makes you think I want to be a tree sprite?"

"Fate doesn't care about your wants. She sculpts you to her needs."

"But a tree sprite?"

"Besides, will it really be such a hardship? Don't you like

to make things grow?" he asked.

"That is entirely beside the point," Mercedes began.

"That is Fate sculpting you to her design."

"How did you know about that, though?" Mercedes looked straight at him. "I mean, with the growing things?"

"You were formed by Fate to become the tool she most needed. It only makes sense that she would give you a love for growing things."

"So, you were guessing?" Mercedes asked.

"I was making an educated assumption."

"Either way, I'm a dryad now? I can't trade?"

"No." He shook his head. "And you wouldn't want to. Dryads are a powerful race. Some of the greatest magic in this world resides inside them."

"What sort of magic?" she asked. "Tell me what it is that I can do."

"Why don't I show you instead?" The Fate Maker grabbed a pot of dirt off the table. It had one flower in it, and I recognized it from the picture. It had been next to the crystal ball Esmeralda had stared at. "Touch the dirt."

Mercedes took the pot from him and touched the soil inside it with one finger. The plant shook, and flowers began to rapidly bloom, spilling over the side of the pot.

"That is so cool," she said.

"Touch one of the timbers," the Fate Maker urged next.

"The timbers are dead." Mercedes took her hand away from the plant and stared at her palm. "They've been cut down and turned into lumber."

"Trust me on this. Wizard, remember?"

"Right," Mercedes said before walking over to one of the timbers and slapping her hand against it.

Green vines curled out of her fingers and began traveling up the length of the wood, white flowers sprouting along the vine as it twisted around the room. I looked up and saw that the entire ceiling was covered in tiny white and pink flowers. One tendril of the vine was creeping along the stone walls toward the mantelpiece, and another crept across the floor, wrapping itself around the wooden table leg. Within seconds the room was covered in flowers and not an inch of stone could be seen anywhere besides the floor.

"Now, you were complaining about being green?" the Fate Maker asked.

Mercedes shook her head, mute as she turned circles, looking around the room. She held her hands up again and wiggled her fingers, staring at them with wide eyes.

"Good." He flicked his fingers at the door, opening it by magic alone. "I've got a kingdom to run, and I've wasted enough time on this."

"What about us?" Heidi asked. "What kind of superpowers do we get?"

"Superpowers?" The Fate Maker narrowed his eyes at her. "Who said I was going to give you superpowers?"

"But to stay here," Jesse said, "you have to change us, too. Don't you?"

"Or I could let you die." The Fate Maker shrugged.

"No." I hurried over to slide myself between Jesse and the Fate Maker. "No one dies."

"They're spares. Debris that got sucked into the vortex. We don't need them here."

"Too bad. Do the spells that can make them stay."

"But—"

"Do the spells," I said through gritted teeth. "No one is

dying."

"But they're worthless. They serve no purpose."

"Then find them one."

"Fine." He sighed and then looked over my shoulder at Jesse. "What do you want to be?"

"I'm thinking a giant flying bird. Yeah, I could rock the whole enormous bird with golden wings look. Or a knight. I'd be an awesome knight," Jesse said.

"I think not," the Fate Maker said. "You don't have the makings of a Queen's Champion. Battle is best left to those who Fate calls to it. Besides, I find that I may have need of you and your particular skills."

The Fate Maker narrowed his eyes at Heidi and then at Jesse. He brushed past her, coming face-to-face with the boy. He tilted his head to the side and stared. "I've always wondered why Fate chose what she did for you. Handsome enough but not very bright. Not what I'd expect a warrior princess to need as she faces the end of the Waiting, but Fate knows her business."

"I don't understand," Jesse said. "Did you just call me dumb?"

The Fate Maker put his hands on Jesse's forehead and rolled back his eyes so that only the whites could be seen.

There was a sharp *crack* and Jesse's eyes widened as his body jolted forward. "What are you—"

"There." The Fate Maker pulled his hands away and nodded. "Prince Jesse Harper. Royal consort to Her Majesty, the Princess Alicia. Now, do us all a favor and don't screw anything up. I'll have need of you later. You, out of everyone here, will be most essential to me."

"Wait," Winston said. "What? He's what?"

"Royal consort to Her Majesty," the Fate Maker repeated, his voice quiet.

"Wait a second." Heidi grabbed the Fate Maker by the shoulder and turned him to face her. "He's *my* boyfriend."

"Yeah." I nodded quickly. "What she said. He can't be my prince consort."

"Why not?" the Fate Maker asked.

"Well, he's nice enough, I guess, but Heidi's right. He's her boyfriend."

"Not anymore." The Fate Maker narrowed his eyes at Heidi, ignoring me entirely. "Though I must say, you've shown me exactly why Fate has given you the future she has."

He pressed his hands onto her forehead, and I stood behind Winston, his arm blocking me from the rest of them as she began to shake.

Her hair began to dull, no longer its normally brilliant, bouncy blond. Now it hung limp, a dishwater blond. Her skin flaked as angry red spots began to speckle her face.

The Fate Maker pulled his hands away and stepped back. "Heidi Spencer, I give you the fate you so richly deserve."

"What?"

I gasped, stunned at the change in the girl staring back at us. Her normally fabulous figure had thickened, and her skin looked like she'd been sick for weeks. He'd turned her...not ugly. No uglier than anyone else had been at least once in their life. She wasn't scarred or anything. It was worse—he'd made her plain. Average. *Normal.*

"Your face now matches your soul. And now, I name you as maid to Her Majesty. To clean up after someone whom you've treated like nothing more than dirt."

"What?" she shrieked.

"Welcome to your new life." He turned his back to her and focused his bright eyes on me before bowing his head in a sharp nod.

"You…" I gasped, trying to work out exactly what he'd just done to the girl who'd tormented me from my very first day in Bethel Park. He'd changed her into my what?

"Yes?" he asked.

"I don't want a maid. The idea of someone following me around and doing stuff for me is weird."

"I did as Fate required. Now, I think it's best if all of you take the remainder of the day to rest, before there is no longer a chance. Semanchia will take each of you to your quarters. If that meets with your approval, Your Highness?" He raised an eyebrow, and I realized he was talking to me.

"Oh, yeah." I nodded. "I think we can all take the rest of the day to get, um, settled? Yeah, settled is a good word for it."

The Fate Maker nodded again and stalked toward the open door, not once looking back at us, huddled in the middle of room with absolutely no idea what sort of weird nightmares waited for us outside the tower.

Chapter Six

"Oh my God!" Heidi pointed one of her now-unmanicured fingers at the pink fairies that flew through the door the Fate Maker had walked out of. "What are those?"

"Fairies." I bowed my head in greeting to the tiny creatures with their petal-pink skin and golden wings that were now hovering in front of me.

"If you'll follow me, please, Your Majesty. You may bring the maid as well," the fairy on the left said, her voice high and tinkly, like the sound of jingle bells.

"The rest of you come with me," the fairy on the right said, her voice the same high, musical sound.

"Allie?" Mercedes asked, her voice shaky.

"They're peaceful. At least I think they're peaceful. The book always said they were peaceful."

"And we're going with what the book says?" Mercedes asked.

"You have any other ideas?" I asked.

"No."

"The *Chronicles* always said that fairies were helper sprites. They won't hurt you. So I'm going to trust that they aren't going to kill us and eat us."

"Never hurt," the first fairy said. "We live to serve Your Majesty in all things. Never would we bring harm."

"Now, follow, please," the second said. "Food and warm beds are waiting. A chance to get clean. Come now."

"It'll be okay," I said.

"We'll find you afterward," Winston said.

"Food and beds. Hot baths," the second fairy insisted. She flitted closer to Winston and poked at his nose with one of her tiny fingers. "Sleep for dragons and sleep for queens. Fairies keep watch. No harm to come. Follow now."

"Promise me," he said quietly.

"No harm to come, dragon. No harm to come to the queen."

He nodded and then let her lead him out of the room, the rest of them trailing behind them as Heidi and I stood with our own fairy, watching them go.

Once they'd disappeared from the doorway I turned to the fairy. "And us?"

"To Rose's Tower. Warm bath and a nice rest." She flew closer and began to run tiny fingers through my hair. "Warm and happy Rose. Beautiful Rose. Take you home now."

"What about me?" Heidi asked. "If anyone needs a bath, it's me. Did you see what that wizard did to me? I'm disgusting."

"Will find bucket for the maid," the fairy said.

"What?" Heidi yelped.

The fairy ignored her and let go of my hair before flitting

back to where she'd been a moment before, hovering in front of my nose. "Come, Rose. Sleep now. Fate will seem kind after resting."

"I am *not* a domestic," Heidi said loudly. "And I'm not your maid. I refuse to be your maid."

"Fine," I said. The fairy flew out of the room and I hurried after her. If I was going to figure out what the heck was going on here and then find my friends, I needed to get out of this room and learn the layout of the castle. Then we could all meet up and figure out how to get out of this mess.

"I don't care what that wizard freak says, I'm not your maid. I'm not going to be a servant."

"That's great, Heidi, you do that." I quickly turned to gawk at the mile of paintings that seemed to litter the walls and then hurriedly turned my attention back to the tiny wings of our flying tour guide.

"Are you even listening to me?" Heidi asked.

I waved my hand at her impatiently, trying to keep up with the fairy, who kept veering off down corridors without warning. Now was not the time to hash out Heidi's problems. "You're not my maid. I don't care. Whatever makes you happy."

"What do you mean you don't care?" she shrieked. "I bet you love the idea. You think you're going to be able to order me around, and we'll all have to pretend to like you because some guy sticks a crown on your head."

"I couldn't care less," I said over my shoulder as I picked up my pace. I turned the corner the fairy had disappeared around and noticed that the next hallway looked exactly like the last. Great.

"Oh right," Heidi said. "You couldn't care less. As if."

"Like I told the Fate Maker—the idea of someone rooting around in my stuff is just *weird*. So don't worry about being my maid. I hate the idea just as much as you do, so we can just forget about it, and no one ever has to know."

"Who said I wanted to root around in your stuff anyway? It's not like you have anything I want. I mean, really, where do you get your clothes? A charity store or something?"

"Hey." I spun around and jabbed my finger in front of her face, heat flaring in my stomach. I couldn't believe that she would take now of all times to say something about the fact that most of my clothes were secondhand. "There is nothing wrong with my clothes. They fit, and they're fine. Just because I didn't max out my foster mother's credit card on a new pair of jeans doesn't mean there's anything wrong with what I'm wearing."

Heidi flipped her hair over her shoulder and sneered. "It sounds like you're just looking for an excuse to explain away the fact that you have no sense when it comes to clothes."

"Screw you, Heidi." I tightened my hand into a fist. Punching her in the nose would feel so great right now, but I knew it would disappoint Gran Mosely and my mom. They really believed that violence didn't solve anything. Personally, I thought it might not cause any more problems in Heidi's case.

"Your Majesty," a tiny voice said close to my ear.

I ignored the fairy. "You know what you might want to think about, Heidi? I'm the only one who knows anything about this place."

"So?"

"So you might want to try being a little bit nicer to me and my friends because, from how I understand it, I'm your only way home. And if you make one more crack about me—or my clothes—I might forget to take you back."

Esmeralda appeared around the corner and sat primly at my feet. "Or we could throw her in the stocks. Wait, I know! We could execute her. That always gets the population's attention. A good execution to show them there's a new queen in town."

"What?" Heidi stepped back from us, her hands in front of her throat and her eyes wide.

"We're not executing anyone." I shook my head at the cat. "Not even Heidi."

"Oh, come on," Esmeralda said and then sighed. "A beheading would really get the people in the spirit for a new coronation. It's the perfect event to start the festivities."

"We're not beheading any—" My words cut off as a portrait on the wall caught my attention, and I started toward it, suspicion clawing at my chest. I was the lost princess of Nerissette. The ruler, now that their queen was no longer able to rule. And the person inside it looked exactly like—

"The people love a good beheading," Esmeralda continued and hurried to plant herself in front of me. "For only from death can the lands truly be reborn."

"No beheadings," I repeated and moved to step around her.

"It always draws a large crowd when we have an execution. Besides, I'm close with the executioner. As a favor to me he could arrange to do it before dinner."

"What?" Heidi had wrapped both hands around her throat and had dropped her chin, trying to hide her neck from the cat's piercing gaze.

"A few last words, a drumroll, then *ker-chunk*. Head in a basket, and your first day is off with a resounding success."

Esmeralda twined herself between my ankles so that I couldn't move.

"Allie?" Heidi's eyes were wide and filled with fear.

I tried to hide my smile before dropping my head to stare at the cat now curled in a figure eight around my ankles, licking the tip of her own tail. "I don't think that's such a good idea."

"Are you sure? He's very good. Excellent really."

"I'm sure," I said sternly. "Now, if you could tell me where my room is, I would really like to go take a nap and try to wake up from this craziness. That fairy was supposed to take us there but she seems to have disappeared."

"Fairies…" Esmeralda gave me a one-sided grin and tilted her head. "What can you do? They never can be trusted with any sort of important task. Now, what do you want me to do about the maid since you won't let me behead her for public entertainment?"

"I don't know." I looked at the cat, ignoring Heidi, and shrugged. "Can you put her in a room somewhere else and just let her be? Give her a magazine to read or something so she stays out of my hair until we can work this out."

"This is her role." Esmeralda uncurled herself from around my ankles. "This is what Fate thinks she deserves."

"But my maid? Really?" I bit my lip at the look of horror in Heidi's now-squinty eyes.

"You cannot go against Fate," Esmeralda said. "Not without even graver consequences."

"Grave?" Heidi asked. "As in bad?"

"Very bad. Deadly even," Esmeralda said darkly.

Heidi crossed her arms over her chest and turned to me. "Consider me your own personal tutor in how to be cool then."

"Whatever you want to call yourself," Esmeralda said. I shoved my hands in my jeans pockets and tried to keep from smiling. It was like they were each arguing with a brick wall. "Either way, come, and I'll show you to Her Majesty's suite."

"What about my suite?" Heidi asked. "She's not the only one who's tired."

"Your cot is in Her Majesty's smaller closet," Esmeralda said. "Now, follow me. I have other places to be, believe it or not, and I don't want to waste any more time than necessary explaining all of this to you."

"I have a cot?"

"Not listening to you anymore." Esmeralda turned and started back in the direction we'd just come from. "I know a better way to get to where we're going."

We followed the cat down the hallway and into an identical one before climbing a grand staircase and turning left. We went down *another* hallway and climbed *another* staircase—a stone one this time that spiraled up the inside of a tower. At the top, Esmeralda nodded toward the door. "*Andefangen.*"

The door creaked open and I stared at the cat. The door was on a voice command? Yeah, that wasn't going to be difficult to remember. Especially since it sounded like a foreign language.

"Did you just speak German to the door?" I asked.

"Spritling," she said.

"Spritling? It sounded like German," I said.

"If they sound similar, and you know this German that you speak of, I would give it a try," Esmeralda said. "The door refuses to speak the common tongue and won't take any of our commands unless they're in the sprite language. Rather than argue, I just humor it."

"I'll keep that in mind." I silently hoped that a year and a half of high school German would be enough for me and the door to muddle through a basic understanding of each other.

"Wonderful," Esmeralda said. "Your room is through there. Clothes are in the closet. Please change into something appropriate for dinner. The assembled nobles joining you tonight are a bit stuffy about those things."

"Okay, but um…" I crossed my arms over my chest to hide the way my hands were shaking at the thought of dinner—with nobles—in the World of Dreams. Somehow I thought I was probably way out of my league.

"What?" Esmeralda was slinking toward the stairs but she stopped and turned to face me.

"Where's dinner being served?" I asked.

"The formal dining room. Obviously." Esmeralda's eyes were wide, and I got the impression that if the cat could she would have rolled them at me.

"Yeah, but how do I get there?" I wrinkled my nose and hoped she'd take pity on me and my cluelessness.

"I'll send one of the footmen to retrieve you," she said with a sigh. "He'll bring your maid a tray."

"Personal tutor in cool." Heidi flounced past the cat and into my bedroom. "And I've got dibs on that bed. Allie can sleep in the closet."

"You can try, but I don't expect you shall succeed," Esmeralda said haughtily. The cat nodded her dark head toward me. "I'll bid you good afternoon, Your Highness. Rest well."

"Right." I took a deep breath and tried to push down the

urge to seriously freak out. At least until I was alone.

"Agh!" Heidi screamed.

Obviously the door wasn't the only piece of furniture in my room that had an attitude problem. The mattress had rolled up around her and was bouncing against the wooden slats across the bottom of the bed.

"Get me out of here!" she wailed.

"Stop!" I ran into the room and grabbed for the mattress. "Stop already. She'll get off you, but let her go first."

The mattress began to spin, levitating over the bed frame.

"It's not working," Heidi shrieked. "I'm going to throw up."

"What's the German word for stop?"

"I don't know. I took French because Madame Sullivan let me skip every day since she was the cheerleading coach."

"Crap." I tried to remember the vocabulary I'd learned in freshman German. Gran was right—I should have paid more attention to Frau Bittner in third period.

The mattress quit rolling and bounced up and down, slamming itself against the wood. The bed frame began to creak, the mattress hitting it so hard that the floor vibrated.

"Hurry up," Heidi moaned.

"*Gestopt*," I said.

The mattress bounced harder.

"I'm seriously going to throw up."

"That wasn't it. I know it's close, though… Wait a second. *Stoppen*! *Stoppen* right now!"

The mattress landed hard on the frame and ceased its antics. One end unrolled slowly, settling down before the other side unfurled and released Heidi. She stood and pushed her hair back from her face. "So much for dibs on the bed."

"I think things here respond differently depending on who

they're interacting with."

"What do you mean?"

I walked over to sit down on the edge of the mattress. Instead of attacking me, it started to warm underneath me, supporting my weight. "Well, it's my bed. So, if anyone besides me tries to sleep in it the bed attacks them."

"So you're saying if I try on one of your superspecial princess outfits it's going to strangle me?"

"It might."

She watched me warily, her hair standing up on end and the neck of her shirt torn. The other side of the mattress curled angrily, and I laid my hand against it, trying to be soothing. The last thing I needed was it attacking my new roomie—again.

"Your bed just tried to kill me." She said it slowly, as if trying to convince herself it was true.

"Yep." I stared up at the ceiling, which was covered in stars. Correction: the ceiling was painted a dark blue to look like the night sky with *diamonds* scattered across it in the shape of constellations. Big diamonds.

"Aren't you going to—I don't know—*do something about it*?"

"Right." I plumped one of the pillows and dropped it back on the mattress. "Bad bed. No eating people. That cover it?"

"That's what you're going to do? You're going to scold it?"

"What do you want me to do? Ground it? It's a bed."

"It's a homicidal killing machine. You need to be stern with it or else it's going to go on a murder spree, you wimp."

"It's letting me lie on it just fine. So maybe you should just stay away from each other, then if the bed gets hungry again it'll hunt dust bunnies instead."

"You're unbelievable," she said. "I'm going to go check out your clothes. If you hear me screaming that your closet is trying to kill me, maybe, if you're feeling helpful, you could come try to save my life."

"Sure thing." I yawned and rolled over, burying my face in a pillow. "You scream, and I'll come running. As soon as I've gotten some sleep."

Chapter Seven

"This is the best of the bunch," Heidi said.

We both stared at my reflection in the mirror, and I couldn't help but sigh. This was not good. On a scale of one to a pop quiz in Chemistry, this was possibly finding out the quiz was worth most of your semester grade. This dinner was going to stink.

And apparently there were no jeans in my new wardrobe, only dresses. *Gowns* if you wanted to be picky about it—lots and lots of long, flowing gowns. The one I had on was deep ruby-red velvet with thick gold embroidery down the front. Brilliant gold vines tangled along the hem and climbed up the front of the dress to bloom into three golden roses at the neckline.

"It brings out the highlights in your hair."

"Really?" I looked at my reflection again and turned my head slightly.

I wasn't fond of wearing dresses, no matter what the

occasion, but if Heidi said this was the best of the bunch, and I had no choice anyway, then I might as well give it a try. As long as I didn't trip over the skirt and fall face-first down a set of stairs in front of a bunch of strangers, I'd consider the night a success.

"Yeah, I mean, if you like looking like you've got streaks of blood in your hair instead of highlights," Heidi said. She shoved me toward an antique-looking dressing table with a gold-filigreed mirror that had rosebuds trailing along its sides.

"Thanks. For a second there I thought you were actually going to pay me a compliment and that would have just been too weird today."

She pushed me down onto the padded bench. "Here, let me fix your hair. You can't go out looking like that. Every other girl in the kingdom will use you looking like crap as a chance to steal my boyfriend."

"Wait, why does my hair have anything to do with your boyfriend?"

"He's supposedly your prince consort, right?"

"Right."

"Well, if you look all frumpy, some pampered brat in a fluffy dress will try to take him from you. And then I'm out a boyfriend. So they need to think that they can't get to him through your laziness. Now sit still, and let me do your hair."

"I don't think whether or not my hair looks good is going to matter when it comes to your boyfriend. Even without the flirting noble girls involved."

"Look, one thing I've learned from two years of high school popularity is that every queen needs a court full of hangers-on to lord it up over. And every single one of them would like nothing more than to knock you off your pedestal."

"That's sort of sad."

"It's the life of a princess. If you don't have people to torment with your superiority, then what's the point?"

"I don't know, to be a leader? To help people improve their lives?"

"No. It's about popularity." Heidi started pulling the brush through my hair, not bothering to be gentle about it. "That's the only reason to sign up for a gig like this one. Royalty gives you ultimate popularity. No one, and I do mean no one, steps on your toes if you've got a tiara sitting on top of your head."

We stared at each other in the mirror, and she jerked her eyes away from mine. "You wouldn't understand," she said quietly.

"So, let me get this straight…" I fixed my eyes on hers in the mirror and tried to keep my head still while she tore the brush through my hair. "You want to make me pretty so if your boyfriend is inclined to flirt with someone he'll flirt with me?"

"No, I want you to be gorgeous so that no other girl even thinks about flirting with him because they're afraid to go up against you. That way you're still in charge, and my boyfriend is safe. Got it?"

"You're not concerned that I might, I don't know, try to steal him from you? I mean, you're basically asking me to flirt with your boyfriend."

"Of course not. I'm asking you to go in there and be my wingman because you got me into this crappy mess in the first place, and you owe me. Besides, I know you wouldn't try to steal my guy." She jerked the brush through my now-smooth hair a final time and then began weaving it into an elaborate braid at the back of my scalp.

"Why not?"

"One, you're you, and as much as you annoy me, basically all the time, you aren't a boyfriend-stealer." Heidi tied the bottom of the braid off with a piece of ribbon, then tugged on the ends of it and tucked it underneath somehow so that the bottom part of the braid was hidden, leaving my entire neck exposed.

"Two, I sleep in your closet. So let me explain something to you: I'm a base during cheerleading stunts, not a flier. Do you know what that means?"

"Uh, no."

"I might look cute and sweet, but I've got the upper-arm strength to hold another girl up over my head. *By myself.* That means if you mess with my man I will end you. You got me?"

"I got you." I nodded, and tried to seem like the type of girl you would trust your gorgeous—possibly prone-to-flirting—boyfriend with.

She picked up a large, milky-white stone on a golden chain and dropped it over my head so that the pendant nestled in the hollow of my throat. "But even though I trust you, I don't trust him, and I'm not just going to sit here and twiddle my thumbs while he goes out and cheats with some duchess. Even if I am nothing but a maid."

"Being a maid shouldn't matter. No one deserves to be cheated on."

"Whatever." She rolled her eyes at me in the mirror. "Deserving has nothing to do with it. Give a guy half a chance to move up the popularity ladder with a new girl, and he'll drop you like *that*." She snapped her fingers for emphasis.

"Not every guy," I said, thinking about Winston. We'd never talked about relationships, but I knew him well enough to know that if he were with a girl, he wouldn't go out and flirt with another one.

"Every guy cheats if you give him the chance."

I shrugged. I wasn't going to win that one, so I stood and made my way to the door, then tugged on the heavy gold handle. The door creaked and opened slowly.

"Finally," Esmeralda said from the doorway. "What took you so long? Did your maid die at the hands of the furniture or something?"

"Sorry," I said. "I didn't know anyone was waiting out here. Besides, didn't you say you were going to send a footman with food for Heidi?"

"Her tray will be here after the main dinner has been served. But the cook says that after tonight, when your maid wants food she'll have to eat in the servants' kitchen with everyone else." Esmeralda stood, her tail high, and gave me an appraising once-over.

I glanced back at Heidi before the door closed behind me and saw her wince, her face screwed up into a grimace like she'd just drunk spoiled milk. Because if there was anything worse than the humiliation of the most popular girl in school becoming a maid for one of the Honor Society nerds, it would have to be other people seeing her in her new role. "Well, I'm sorry to keep you waiting," I said.

"I won't be waiting after tonight," Esmeralda said. "You can find your own way after this. I'm not a tour guide."

"Right. Of course." I picked up my heavy skirts to rush after her as she scampered off. "I just don't know how I'm going to manage. Every hall is identical."

"That's why you find the signs," Esmeralda said, not bothering to slow down. "They tell you where you are, and if you know how to use them they can take you there as well."

"What signs? And what do you mean they can take me there?"

"The signs on each corner, silly. How do you think I keep from getting lost in this place? If it's all the same to someone your size, how do you think it looks from down here? Besides, could you imagine how tired I'd be if I had to walk everywhere?"

"I hadn't thought about that." I wrinkled my nose. "I still don't see the signs, though. Where are they?"

Esmeralda stopped at the next corner. She smacked one of the bricks near the bottom of the wall with her paw, and I noticed a complicated series of scratches on it.

"I thought those were just scuff marks."

"You have to get close enough to look instead of rushing past like every other biped in this place. See, that brick has three Es and then a five scratched into it."

I knelt down on the floor beside her and looked at the brick in question. Dead center of the brick was carved "EEE5." "So, what does it mean?"

Esmeralda hit the brick again. "It means that you are in the East Wing, third floor, and this is the fifth corridor. The dining room is in the main hall, so you'll want to go all the way to EEE1 and then down to the first floor."

"Okay?" I stared at the runes. "Then if I want to come back here after dinner?"

"If you want to come back you just rub the carving and tell it where you want to go. But don't try it right now. You don't want to get sick before your first state dinner, and the runes are a bit dodgy the first few times."

"Right, *o-kay*." I nodded. "That's ingenious, Esmeralda. Did you come up with it?"

"No, a giant named Krumpwaither did. He thought it would be a convenient way for twelve-foot ogres to get around the castle." She did that almost-eye-roll thing again. "Of course I came up with the idea. Just because I've taken on the appearance of a house cat doesn't mean I'm a complete idiot."

"Sorry."

"Apology accepted, Princess," Esmeralda said. "Next time you assume I'm just a cat, though, I might have to sharpen my claws on your skirt…while you're in it. Now, you know how to get yourself to the dining hall, and I have a dinner of my own to catch."

Instead of waiting around for me to answer, Esmeralda turned on her heels and ran back in the direction of my suite. Obviously I was on my own. Great.

All I had to do was follow the signs she'd pointed out and it would lead me to the dining hall. I turned down the corridor that read "EEE4" and kept going. I turned down three more identical hallways and found myself in the middle of a large, open-air space topped by a stained-glass dome designed with elaborate pictures of not only humans, but a variety of different creatures. Above me was an image of two mermaids hugging while dragons circled overhead. Next to that was a group of women with branches for arms. And at the top of the dome was an enormous golden rose, its vines sprawling out to form frames for each of the scenes below it. This had to be the main hall. I looked up at the stained-glass rose again and took a deep breath. *Here goes nothing.*

I turned and walked down the wide staircase, clutching the rail and trying not to trip over my own feet. The last thing I needed to do was to fall down the stairs my first night in the castle—that would really convince people I'm their magical warrior princess.

"You look beautiful."

Jesse's voice caught me off guard, and I froze, looking up from my feet to stare at him. Somebody that popular couldn't be talking to me...could he? He'd never known I existed before unless he needed help with his homework. I glanced behind me to see if Heidi had followed me down to dinner, but I was alone on the stairs.

Jesse was dressed in a severe black suit with the jacket buttoned all the way to his neck. His left shoulder was embroidered with the same gold roses that were on the neckline of my dress. His hair looked damp and was combed back neatly, like he'd just gotten out of the shower.

"What?" I asked.

"You look...wow, Allie. Really. Wow."

"Seriously?" I felt my cheeks get warm. "You don't think I look..."

He raised an eyebrow.

"Like a complete dork?"

"You look different." He held his hand out to me and smiled. "But it's a good different. Not that you didn't look good before or anything. You just look nice tonight. In that dress you're just, wow. You look gorgeous, is what I'm trying to say. Very princess-like."

"Thanks," I said. I couldn't help smiling back, and I came down the last two steps to stand in front of him. "You look nice, too. We're both wearing the same roses."

"This goblin with these huge ears, who lives in my room apparently, said that they're the crest of Nerissette's royal house. Your symbol, I guess, since he keeps referring to you as Her Majesty, the Golden Rose of Nerissette."

"Wow, that's a mouthful," I said. "I was hoping we could go with just plain old Allie. You know, be a bit modern with it."

"I thought it fit, actually," Jesse said, moving close enough that we were almost nose-to-nose. "But I can still call you Allie if you want? Since I'm your prince consort and all, maybe we should keep things more *informal*."

"Right." I took a step back from him, trying to focus on what I had to do, rather than the boy currently standing way too close to me. "I'd like that."

"Guess what I found today while you were napping?" He pulled back from me even more, and suddenly I could breathe. "Well, I should say guess what I found after I talked with the Fate Maker?"

"You spoke to the Fate Maker?"

"Yeah, he stopped by my room for a bit."

"What did he want?"

His eyes went blank for a second and then he shook his head. "He didn't want anything. He just told me to make myself at home and go explore if I wanted. Then he explained a bit about Nerissette and the history and some stuff about my role as your consort."

"What stuff?"

"Nothing major." He shrugged. "Just that the whole World of Dreams is always ruled by women from the same family and that their consorts are advisers and the power behind the throne. That sort of thing. Anyway, guess what I found out?"

Excuse me? Jesse was going to be the *what* behind the *where*?

"Allie."

"What?"

"Guess what I found out."

"What?"

"You'll never believe it," he said, his eyes sparkling.

"Then tell me." I grinned at the look of wonder on his face, even if he was being majorly annoying.

He leaned closer so that we were almost touching again and smirked mischievously. "A mermaid pool," he whispered.

"Mermaids?"

"Yes, mermaids. I told them that the new queen was a swimmer, too, and they can't wait to meet you. I promised I'd bring you to say hi after dinner."

"You told them about me?" I asked, stunned that he would go out of his way to do something nice for me. Jesse Harper never did anything nice for anybody.

"Of course I did," he said. "Who else would I bother trying to find a pool for? I can't do more than dog paddle, and Heidi never actually wants to swim. All she wants to do is work on her tan."

Jesse squeezed my fingers and didn't let go. Instead, he tugged me toward a large set of double doors and turned to smile at me.

"That's..." I wasn't sure what to say. Jesse Harper had found me a pool full of mermaids? Just because? "That's really sweet of you."

"I know you like to swim," he said. "I mean, you're on the varsity swim team, and if this is creeping the rest of us out I figure it has to be weirding you out the most with the whole... well, you know."

"Fact that I'm apparently the lost warrior princess of a fairy-tale world?"

"Yeah. So, I thought it would help." He shrugged.

"What do you mean help?"

"Maybe if I could find you something normal—something from your old life—maybe it would make things feel less weird or something."

"That's really considerate." I tried to subtly untangle my fingers from his. It was great that he was being nice and all, but this touching stuff was not going to happen. Especially not after that whole *power behind the throne* crack.

"So, anyway, once you finish letting all these stuffy old people kiss your butt and call you Her Royal Highness, the Golden Rose of Nerissette, we'll go see it. I'll even let you teach me to swim if you want."

"Okay, but it's just Allie, remember? We're modernizing this royalty thing."

"After you then, just Allie." Jesse pulled the door open. He stepped aside so that I was standing alone in the doorway.

The room in front of me had six huge crystal chandeliers hanging over a table that could have fit every single person who lived on my street with seats left over. It was loaded with food, more food than I'd ever seen in one place in my entire life.

My head jerked up at the sharp scrape of chairs being pushed away from the table, and I stood there, dumbfounded, trying to take every bit of it in. There was a sharp cough, and I let my eyes wander to the people around the table, all of them in fancy clothes and dripping jewels, staring at me like I was an animal in the zoo. These must be the "hangers-on" that Heidi had been talking about.

"Her Royal Highness, the Golden Rose of Nerissette, the Crown Princess Alicia," a gravelly voice said from my side.

"Um…" I looked at Jesse and then back at the room full of fancy-dressed hangers-on. I lifted my right hand and sort of wiggled my fingers at them. "Hi?"

Chapter Eight

There was a light touch on the back of my hand, and I glanced away from the now-standing nobles to stare at the wrinkled, green creature with floppy ears that came up only as high as my knee. It would have reminded me of my neighbor Mrs. Tucker's beagle if she'd pierced the dog's ears and put gold hoops through them. I glanced at Jesse and raised my eyebrows.

"Goblin," he mouthed.

Great. Because today couldn't get any stranger. I glanced down at the creature again, and when it looked up at me with its bugged-out eyes and pushed-in nose I smiled and tried to keep from grimacing or pulling away from its scaly hand.

"Thank you," I said, my voice squeaking. I hoped the goblin didn't take offense at my surprise. I wasn't exactly sure how I was supposed to act around them. Goblins, I mean.

Then again, Mom had always told me to be nice to everyone I met until they did me wrong. *We're all same underneath the skin, Allie.*

Did that apply to goblins? I was pretty sure it did, but maybe she'd only meant humans? It was probably best to just assume that she meant all creatures and leave it at that. Besides, did I really want to know what was underneath his leathery skin? Ick.

"Princess Alicia," a smooth voice said.

I raised my head and stared at the group of nobles—who thankfully all looked human—still standing around the elaborate table, studying me.

The Fate Maker came forward, wearing a long, black robe with silver flames curling up its length. He held his hands out to me in welcome, acting like we were the best of friends and my arrival here had been all his idea. Or that he'd at least been told about it first.

"Would you care to come and sit?" he asked.

"Who are all these people?" I asked quietly.

"Your royal court, Princess," he murmured in my ear. "Now, smile and look interested. Let me handle everything, and we'll be fine."

"Right." Smile and look interested. Just like World History class.

I followed him to the front of the room, and he pulled out a chair at the head of the table for me. "Milady," he said, bowing low over the chair.

I sat while everyone else stood. Jesse was standing at the other end of the table, facing me. On my right was another man with dark hair and black eyes, wearing long, crimson-colored robes.

"Your Majesty," the man said. "It is a pleasure to meet you."

"Thanks." I stuck my hand out for him to shake, and he lifted an eyebrow at me questioningly.

"I am Melchiam, first of my name, Rach of the Firas." He took my hand gently and brought it to his lips, brushing them across my knuckles.

The Firas. Okay, I remembered the stories about them from the book. Tribes of wandering desert-dwellers that worship the gods of fire. Right. Okay. I could handle this.

"My mother used to tell me Firas stories when I was younger. My favorite was one about a princess who'd fallen in love with a bard, but her family wouldn't let them marry. Then her brother killed the bard, and she fed her brother to a dragon in revenge."

"I know this story well, Your Majesty." He let go of my hand and smiled. "Nasa and Dragon."

"Really?" I used to imagine I was Nasa, and that I could feed my brother to the dragon. I didn't have a dragon, or a brother, but when we lived in Florida my neighbor had a brother, and we used to threaten to feed him to their iguana.

"Nasa was my great-aunt," Melchiam said. "It was my grandfather she fed to the dragon."

"Oh." I swallowed—probably not the best story to mention, then. "I'm sorry."

"Not nearly as sorry as the dragon," the man on my left said.

"What?" I turned, my mouth hanging open, trying to take in all of his enormous form. Easily seven feet tall with long, shimmering blond hair hanging to his shoulders, the man could probably arm-wrestle a giant and win. Easily.

"Valtual said your grandfather had such a long beard that he was hacking up hair balls for a week. And he got indigestion." The man chuckled.

Melchiam smirked. "I'm not surprised. He was most likely trying to tunnel his way back out."

"But…" I gaped first at Melchiam and then at the other man. "Wait a second. You knew the dragon that ate his grandfather?"

"We are clanmates," the man said. "I am Ardere, head of the gold dragon clan and the current Drakos of Dramera."

"So you're related to the dragon that ate his grandfather?" I glanced over at Melchiam. "And you're okay with that?"

"I've more pity for the dragon, honestly," Melchiam said. "From the stories I've heard, my grandfather was a difficult man. His sister wasn't the first to try to kill him. She's just the one who succeeded."

A trio of fairies flitted over to us with a silver platter crammed with goblets balanced between them, and they lowered it slowly to the table. Both of the men took goblets and Ardere handed one to me as well. "Dragon's blood?" he asked.

"Excuse me? You want me to drink what?"

"It's a juice, Your Majesty. A rare delicacy pressed from the flesh of the ember fruit."

"Oh, well, as long as it's not…you know."

"Of course not, Your Majesty. I'm not some sort of cannibal, drinking the blood of my own species. That would be barbaric."

"Yeah." I gave him a tight nod. "Barbaric is a word for it."

"Although, since we're talking about barbaric delicacies, I do believe that tonight we're having authentic gold-wing soup for dinner. Made from the old recipe."

One of the fairies stiffened and swooped close to his face.

"May your wine turn rancid and all your eggs open empty."

Ardere laughed and there were amused chuckles from others at the table. "No worries, little sprite," he told her reassuringly. "I'm sure the gold color comes from the tanpaoli used to make it sweet."

"*Hmph*," the fairy huffed and then flitted away, dipping low so that she caught her bare toes in his goblet and then kicked the contents at him.

"Touchy things," Ardere said.

"What's gold-wing soup?" I asked.

"It used to be a delicacy in Nerissette," a tiny, blonde woman with miniature hummingbirds in her hair explained, her voice high and tinkling. "We were quite famous for it in the Veldt. My mother's recipe was superb."

"And it's made with…tanpaoli?" I asked. "What's that?"

"It's what you call sweet potatoes back in the World That Is," a younger man with curly dark hair said. His voice lilted musically with what sounded like James Bond's accent…if James Bond had left Britain and had been living somewhere else for a long time. Faded somehow.

"Okay, so fairies don't like sweet potatoes?"

"No. Then again the original recipe called for boiled fairies instead of sweet potatoes. That's where it gets the name—the boiled wings would turn the soup a gold color."

"Eww." I wrinkled my nose, and he grinned.

"That's what I always thought. Thankfully they don't serve that version anymore." He nodded his head toward me. "Rhys Sullivan. Lord general of your army."

"*You're* the leader of the Army of Dreams?"

He straightened his shoulders, his back stiff, and narrowed his eyes at me like a giant bird ruffling its feathers. "Yeah, what of it?"

"You're a kid."

"I'm nineteen. That's older than you."

"Yeah, but…" I stopped.

"I'm sure the Rose was wiser on her first day than you are on your seven thousandth." The tiny blonde next to him glowered in his direction, the silver hummingbirds in her hair chirping as they rubbed against each other.

"It's just Allie," I said.

"My apologies, Princess Allie." She nodded toward me. "I never thought Lord Sullivan was mature enough to take control of the Army of Dreams, no matter Fate's decree. Much better the role goes to someone strong and decisive, someone like my son Gunter."

"Now, Lady Arianne," the Fate Maker said. "We've discussed this. Fate has decreed that Lord Sullivan is in charge of the army."

"But the oldest son of the steward of the Veldt has always led the Army of Dreams."

"Then let him learn to protect the Veldt instead of making war inside of it," the Fate Maker suggested. "If he manages that, which I doubt he will, then we can discuss more responsibility with the army."

"You're from the Veldt?" I asked.

"Yes, Your Majesty," she said. "I am Arianne, Lady Steward of the Veldt."

I had loved the pictures of the Veldt in my book when I'd been a child, but the woman sitting near me looked nothing like the great stewards the pages had shown. The stewards had been depicted as giant women in golden armor who rode enormous black beasts known as narva to spear rampaging trolls. But this lady looked more like my seventh-grade English teacher in a Halloween costume.

"She's also mother to a boy who once bombed their own palace," a pale-haired man with deep iron-gray eyes added. "Or did you forget the time he turned his catapult the wrong way and tore down your walls?"

"That was an accident, Woodsman," she hissed. "At least my son would apply himself to the art of war. Yours would rather stay in his trees."

"The men of the Leavenwald may prefer the woods," Rhys said, "but we've never failed to come when this kingdom is in need. Each of Sir John's men is easily worth a hundred times his weight in gold."

I focused on the woodsman. "Are *you* Sir John?"

"Your Majesty." The man bowed his head, his strange eyes never leaving mine.

"You can talk to the animals. And you have a mouse that traveled with you. Sir John the Gallant."

"A mouse?" he asked.

"Gallant?" Lady Arianne asked.

"You've got a pet mouse?" Rhys asked. "You don't feed it at the table, do you?"

"I don't think so," Sir John said. "Then again I don't remember ever keeping a rodent as a pet."

"So, Eamon isn't real?" I asked.

The men at the table burst into loud roars of laughter as Sir John's cheeks turned pink.

"Eamon? A mouse?" Rhys beat his hand against the table.

"It would explain so much," Lady Arianne said between giggles.

"I'm sorry?" I asked.

"Eamon, Your Highness," Sir John said stiffly, "is my son."

"Oh." I was really going to have to quit bringing up the fact that the only things I knew about this world had come from a storybook. "They were really great stories, though. He was an exceptionally brave, clever mouse."

"Eamon as a mouse," Rhys chuckled. "That's just bloody brilliant. Thank you, Your Highness. That alone has made my evening complete."

"Allie," I said.

"Allie?" Rhys asked. "You want us to call the future queen of Nerissette *Allie*?"

Okay, this guy was strong and had a gorgeous accent but apparently was not bright. Not that I was particularly surprised by it, but what did Muscles-for-Brains think was wrong with calling me Allie?

"It is my name, and I happen to like it. Do you have a problem with that?"

"No," he laughed. "No problems at all. Allie. I like it. But you are the future Golden Rose of Nerissette. Don't you want to be known by something more dignified? Throw a couple of fancy titles in there for effect?"

"I think I can manage without them, thanks."

"Whatever you say, kiddo." He winked at me.

The Fate Maker coughed, glaring at Rhys. "Perhaps the new crown prince would like to make a toast?"

We all shifted in our seats, waiting for Jesse to stand up as he stared in our direction, completely oblivious that the wizard sitting on his left was talking about him.

"Your Highness?"

"Huh?"

"A few words?" the Fate Maker asked, jaw clenched. "A

toast?"

"Oh, God, I don't know. We're not really religious at my house."

I grimaced. He really was an idiot. But then again he was an idiot who'd found me a swimming pool. Besides, I knew from experience, there's nothing worse than finding yourself stuck in the center of attention with no idea what to do.

"I'll do it," the man on the Fate Maker's other side said. He stood, his pale hair dull in the candlelight, his white robes glowing softly around him like flames.

"Thank you." The Fate Maker gave Jesse a grim look, and Jesse sank back in his chair, silent, visibly wilting under the other man's hard stare.

"I am Sarai, Your Majesty, Ambassador of Bathune," the man began. "In the kingdom that stands near the Sea of Nevermore, the place where lost dreams die, we stand as the sentinels of the great forests of sadness."

The Land of Hopeless Dreams. Where all you wanted but could never have stayed forever out of your reach. I'd always hated when my mother had told me about the remote strip of land that stood separated from the rest of Nerissette by the White Mountains of Anguish.

"Her Majesty, Queen Bavasama, bids you welcome and asked me to tell you that she awaits the day you bring about the end of the Waiting. May your reign be long and prosperous, Your Majesty." He raised a glass and everyone else followed suit.

I took a small sip of the sweet apple-juice-like liquid and smiled. "Thank you."

The Fate Maker picked up his wine goblet and held it toward me. "To Her Majesty, the Golden Rose of Nerissette, the Crown Princess Alicia Munroe, first of her name. May your counsel always be wise, your laws always just, and your reign both long and happy."

"To the crown princess." The other nobles raised their glasses to toast again.

I tried to look pleased, but if I had my way my reign wouldn't be long at all. Whatever it is they needed me to do I wanted to get done and then make Esmeralda send my friends and me back home. We couldn't stay here. We had lives to get back to that didn't involve castles or dragons or anything of the kind. Besides, who would take care of my mom if I never returned?

Although now that I thought about it… "Excuse me, does anyone know where my friends went?"

"Your friends?" Melchiam asked. "What friends?"

"The hatchling Winston is in the aerie," Ardere said, his voice echoing in the large, mostly empty room.

"Why isn't he here?" I asked.

"He's busy working with the head of the Royal Mews, Lord Vestriera, learning how to control his new powers. After all, we'd hate for him to burn down part of the castle if he sneezed."

Right. That would be bad. I hadn't thought about Winston hurting himself or someone else when he was in dragon form. Or that he'd need help learning how to control his powers.

My palms began to sweat at the thought of Winston accidentally hurting himself. The worry must've shown on my face too, as Ardere continued with encouragement.

"He'll be fine. A few days at most, and he'll be back by your side, only handsomer this time. In ways only a dragon can be."

"That's, well, um..." I stopped, my cheeks on fire, and Ardere grinned.

"What about Mercedes?" I asked hurriedly. "Is she around? She didn't get lost, did she?"

"The new dryad?" Rhys asked. "She came here with you?"

"Yeah, have you seen her?"

"She's with her tutor as well," the Fate Maker interceded. "There are quite a few new things for her to learn, new powers that she must master before she can be allowed to practice her craft."

"Oh." My throat went dry, and I swallowed a sip of my drink.

"You'll see both of them soon. Perhaps we can discuss all the details at a later time. There is much to be done before the coronation, after all, and we don't want to get bogged down with silly details like your friends." The Fate Maker bowed his head but kept his eyes fixed on mine.

"Sure. Maybe I'll stop by and see them tomorrow at lunch. We can eat together and then compare training notes."

Two small, blue pixies flew toward me with a golden plate full of food hoisted over their heads. They sank lower and lower until they were nearly facedown on the table. Once they were lying flat, they gently set the plate down in front of me, a bowl of golden soup balanced in the center.

"I don't know if that's a good idea, Princess," the Fate Maker said.

"You don't know if I can see them?"

"They need to concentrate on mastering their new powers, and so do you. You should wait until you're all more settled to go running around *comparing notes*."

"Right, but it's just lunch."

"Your Majesty." The Fate Maker brought his fist down on the table, making all the goblets shake. I jumped in my seat, stunned to see that his face turned a deep purple. Which was a bit of an overreaction.

All of the nobles had their eyes fixed on their plates, and their shoulders were tense. Every single one of them acted like the unpopular kids did when Heidi walked into the cafeteria. I could feel the table shaking as the fairies trembled, still facedown next to my plate. There was a sharp rasp as Arianne sucked in a breath. Even Sir John wouldn't meet my eye.

"I must insist that you listen to my suggestion and leave your friends to their studies while you focus on yours. I have defended this kingdom in your name for the past six thousand days, and I must demand you listen to my counsel. There isn't long until your coronation, and you have a lot to learn between then and now."

"Fine." I picked up my spoon and scooped up a bit of soup, accepting that for the time being it was in my best interest to do what the Fate Maker said. "I'll wait until their tutors say they're ready to hang out."

"Wonderful." The Fate Maker took a bite of his bread. "I'm pleased you can see that I have only your—and your friends'—best interests at heart."

"Of course." I bit my lower lip to keep from arguing. I glanced up from my plate and saw Rhys staring at me, the left side of his mouth lifted in amusement, while Jesse sat at the end of the table glaring at the annoying lord general.

The rest of dinner was silent, and everyone ate quickly. Once the Fate Maker wiped his lips, he stood and bowed low before me. "I wish you a good evening, Your Majesty. If you have need of my guidance you'll find my tower in the West

Wing. Good night."

"Good night."

The two pixies lifted my plate and began to fly away carefully as another pixie picked up my goblet and followed. Well, obviously dinner was over when the Fate Maker had finished, regardless of whether anyone else was done. And that included the princess.

I stood and everyone else did the same a moment later, looking at me curiously. "Well, it was nice to meet all of you. Thank you for coming to dinner."

They watched me expectantly. Without moving. Like there was some sort of ceremony before I could leave. What was I supposed to do now? I couldn't throw them out. I felt a tug on my skirt and found the goblin from earlier standing by my side. I leaned down and tried not to gag at the smell of onions on his breath.

"They're waiting for you to leave, Your Majesty. Some people in this palace still know the proper way of things," the goblin whispered. His eyes were narrowed as he glared at the door out of which the Fate Maker had just left.

"Oh." I nodded and let him pull my chair out with a wave of his fingers and a few muttered words I thought might be magic of some type. "May the dreaming be sweet for you, Your Majesty," the goblin said as he bowed low.

"Thank you." I reached down to pat the back of his head—it was the only part of him I could reach.

I walked down to the end of the table and joined Jesse. I smiled at him gratefully, and he walked me out of the room, close enough that his shoulder brushed against mine. I was willing to forget the fact that he was Heidi's boyfriend for a minute and just be happy that I had someone there with me. Jesse was the only familiar face and right then my entire reality had gotten so crazy I needed to be near something at least relatively normal.

"You okay?" he asked when we were outside the dining room and in the main foyer. I looked up at the glass dome and tried to relax.

"Not really," I said. "This place is really weird."

"But cool. I mean, where else are you going to find goblin doormen and pixie waitresses?"

"Yeah, but then apparently there are people who have been eaten by dragons, and I accidentally called Sir John's son a mouse. Not to mention wizards with major control issues."

"So he's a bit intense. The rest of them were nice. Besides, I think he's just trying to watch out for us. You know, sort of like a substitute parent to keep us from getting hurt."

"Right. Anyway, those people expect me to be a princess." I shook my head.

"You are a princess."

"No, a *princess* princess."

"And that's different from a normal princess how?" he asked.

"They want me to be a princess who makes decisions and stuff. I have no idea what I'm doing, and even worse, nothing anyone said tonight has given me any idea of how to get us out of here."

"Right now"—he smiled and took my hand—"you are going to take a big breath and relax. Shake out your fingers and let it go, like Coach says."

"Okay." I took a deep breath and exhaled slowly, shaking my fingers along with him.

"There you go. Now. We're going to forget about all those

weirdos and go check out some mermaids. Or did you forget about them?"

I laughed. "Who forgets about mermaids?"

"Come on, then." He grabbed my hand and tugged me toward the back of the foyer, underneath the stairs, and toward what I thought might be the back of the palace.

"Your Majesty!" Rhys called after us. "Your Royal Highness, the Golden — Oh, forget it. Princess Allie!"

I spun around and felt Jesse tighten his grip on my fingers, which was sort of nice, if a bit strange for a guy who had never really paid me any attention before I suddenly became a princess.

"Rhys?"

There was a *clomp* of boots against the marble floor as he ran toward us and slid to a stop.

"What's up?" I asked.

"What's up?" he asked. "It's been a long time since I heard that — five years at least. Man, I miss the real world."

"The real world?" Jesse asked. "You mean you're from our world?"

"Yeah, idiot." He grabbed my other hand. "Where did you think we all came from? Opened the book in Brighton, fell through the hole in reality, woke up here. Now, where are you two sneaking off to?"

Chapter Nine

I was stunned. "You fell through the book and ended up here, too?"

"Yes." He crossed his arms over his chest and let his eyes trail over both of us.

"Tell me what happened," I said. "How did you end up here?"

"The same thing that happened to you, I'll bet," Rhys said, his eyes still fixed on Jesse. "Opened the book, out popped the cat, and next thing I knew it was smoke and a hard landing in the middle of the Fate Maker's chambers."

"Where?"

"The Fate Maker's chambers," he repeated. "Where else are you going to land?"

"No. Where were you from before?"

"Like I said, I was from Brighton. It's in England. But why does it matter now?" he asked. "This is where we are now, and there's no getting back."

"Yes, there is," I said. "And I'm going to find it. When we go back we can take you with us."

"There *is* no way back," he said. "And even if there was, that world has nothing for me. I was brought here and trained for war. There's no place for me there."

"But it's your home," I said.

"This is my home. Our home. Fate wanted me here to lead a great army in your name and protect you. Here I have a purpose. There? I'm another kid that somehow got lost and was never found again—there are legions of us here."

"Seriously?" I asked.

"An army. All willing to die to protect you. Now, where were you two sneaking off to? It's late."

"We're not sneaking anywhere." Jesse pulled me closer to him, away from Rhys. "I'm taking the princess to see her mermaids. Not that it concerns you."

"Actually..." Rhys glared at Jesse. "You might want to reevaluate that idea. The grottos are no place to go at night alone."

"Why?" I asked.

"You might get lost in the dark."

"But there are mermaids," I said.

"Whom you could see in the morning. When the sun's shining."

"But the Fate Maker is going to make me do lessons or whatever tomorrow. You know he won't let me out of it to go see mermaids. He's too much of a stick-in-the-mud."

"You need the lessons," Rhys said sagely. "You can't just pick up elemental magic all on your own. Or learn politics for that matter. You have a serious job, and he's trying to train you to take it over."

"I know." I rolled my eyes. "But there are mermaids. Real live *mermaids*."

"Fine." He sighed and shook his head. "You're worse than my little sister ever was. Come on." He started toward the back of the castle. "Let's go see the mermaids."

"We can handle this on our own," Jesse said. "We don't need you to supervise or anything."

"Right," Rhys said, not slowing down. "So you know all the things to do to keep from offending the mermaids? How to keep them from drowning the princess, for example?"

"Why would they want to drown me?" I asked.

Rhys walked along with us. "Mermaids are touchy creatures. Very independent-minded. If they think you're taking liberties, they might react badly."

"Allie is the princess," Jesse scoffed. "They'll be honored to have her come visit them. She's going to be their queen."

"Uh-huh." Rhys pushed open the glass doors that led outside. "I wouldn't tell them that if you want to keep her breathing air and not water."

"Are the mermaids really dangerous?" I asked.

"Nah." Rhys gave me an impish grin. "Like I said before, you've just got to know how to talk to them. The mermaids have a lot of pride, and they're touchy about living here in Nerissette. Especially Talia."

"Who's that?" I asked.

"The Mermaid Queen," Rhys said. "Well, she would have been the queen if the mermaids still had their own lands. Now, she's meant to be some sort of queen in exile, acting as your ambassador for their species."

"What happened?" I asked. "Why is she in exile?"

"Their sea was lost, and her mother died," Rhys said

matter-of-factly. "She ended up here with the last of their tribe. I wouldn't bring it up if I were you."

"I won't," I said, thinking about how much it hurt to talk about my own mother with strangers. And she was still technically alive.

Rhys led us into a path of thick hedges. It looked like one of the mazes I'd seen at the botanical gardens when Gran Mosely had taken me to see all those colonial plantations on our summer vacation to Virginia last year.

"How did their sea get lost?" Jesse asked from behind me.

"It got sick," Rhys said, "and then one day it died."

"And Queen Talia's mother?" I asked.

"It was her home, and she refused to leave it to die alone. She stayed and was lost along with the sea."

"Sounds loony to me," Jesse said.

I turned to glare at him over my shoulder in disgust. I knew he wasn't the most sensitive of guys, but *really*?

"Anyway," Rhys said. "When the queen realized the sea couldn't be saved, she had the Fate Maker transport Talia and the rest of her tribe here, to a special pool where they could live for the rest of their days."

"Oh." I blinked. "So instead of the sea they live in, what? An aquarium with people gawking at them all day?"

"It's a decent-sized pool," Rhys said. "And no one watches them. The dryads grew a maze around their sanctuary so that they could keep people away and live in peace."

"Then why are we going there? Shouldn't we leave them alone?" I asked. After all, if I were trapped inside a maze I wouldn't want someone coming to stare at me in the middle of the night.

"The maze is to keep other people away." Rhys guided

us around another fork in the maze and along another long corridor that looked identical to the last.

"Exactly," I said. "We're other people."

"Yes, but you're also the future queen of Nerissette. The mermaids would be offended if you didn't come and pay your respects. Although I'm sure they expected you to come during the day."

I worried my lower lip. "We could wait."

"Nah." Rhys smirked at me. "We're almost there."

We went past two turns and kept moving straight toward the center of the maze. Rhys veered left and then quickly took a right. At the end of the corridor a solid green wall stood at least twice as tall as I did.

"Remember, Talia doesn't consider herself your subject, so she'll see this as a meeting of two queens, not as a visit from a queen to a subject." Rhys led me toward the dead end and then stopped.

"If she's expecting to meet a queen tonight she's going to be disappointed, isn't she?" I tried not to be nervous. Which was harder than it sounded. I was supposed to meet the queen of the mermaids and not make a fool of myself? Or start some sort of war? Yeah, this was going to be interesting. The only thing we probably had in common was our ability to do the breaststroke, and I was pretty sure she could kick my butt in that.

"Why would she be disappointed?" Rhys pushed back the greenery to uncover a door carved into the wall.

"Because I'm not much of a princess, and she's queen of the mermaids. A creature I didn't know even existed before dinner."

"Did you know about goblins before you saw Timbago?"

He ducked through the door he held open for me.

"Is that the goblin from the Great Hall?"

"That's him. *Master* Timbago, head butler of the Crystal Palace," Rhys said, staying on the other side of the shrubbery.

"He was nice." I smiled at the thought of the gnarled-up, but helpful, creature.

"He's a bit stuffy, but trust me, that pat on the head tonight earned you a loyal friend for life," Rhys said.

"I was just being nice. And it was the only part of him I could reach without taking the chance of tripping in this darn dress."

"Goblins aren't accustomed to kindness from other races here in Nerissette. They look strange, and people think that gives them the right to treat the goblins like they don't matter," Rhys said. "So any kindness they receive is always welcomed."

I shook my head in disgust. "Everyone matters."

"That is why you'll have no problem meeting with Talia, Your Royal Golden Roseness." Rhys let the door close between us, trapping me on one side, and him and Jesse on the other.

"Now, you," I heard him say as the door clicked shut, his voice low and dangerous. "I think we need to discuss when and where the crown princess goes without an armed escort. Especially if she's going there with you."

"Oh, for the love of…" I grumbled at the wall between me and my stubborn lord general. "Forget it. He won't listen to me anyway."

I turned away from the shrubbery to find myself face-to-face with a woman I was guessing was Queen Talia. She sat on a large, moss-covered rock in the middle of a pool filled with shimmering blue water, her pink tail flipping idly, making small waves around the rock.

Okay, pink tail, human-looking body, pink-seashell bikini top. So far, so good. Nothing too strange besides the fact that she was a mermaid.

"I don't frighten you, do I?" a husky voice asked. I looked into deep black eyes surrounded by a calm face crowned with flowing golden hair. Apparently our world had gotten the beautiful-mermaid stereotype right.

"No." I shook my head nervously and stepped closer. "I mean, no, Your Highness."

"The Golden Rose of Nerissette?" the mermaid asked, raising her left eyebrow at me.

"Queen Talia?" I rubbed my sweating palms on my skirts.

"I've waited so long to meet you, child. So very long."

"Really? But I just got here…"

"Your arrival was foretold. Now come, and let's dispense with the titles for now so we can get to know each other, queen to queen."

"Okay." I came close enough to sit on the bank beside her pool. "Are you sure? I mean, I was told to expect you to drown me, and now you want to chat."

"Drown you?" She began to howl with laughter. "Why in the name of the great seas would I want to drown you?"

"I don't know." I shuffled my feet. "Disrespecting you, insulting you somehow by not knowing the proper way to bow, general stupidity on my part? That sort of thing."

"I think, for tonight, you're safe. Now sit with me, child. I promise there will be no drowning."

"Sure." I clenched my fingers in my skirt to hide the way they were trembling. "So, I'm Allie."

"Allie?" she asked. "How do they say it in your world? It is a pleasure to meet you, Allie. I am Talia. Fifteenth bearer of my name, daughter of Mavalle, ruler of the Lost Sea of Gallindor."

"I'm just Allie. It's nice to meet you."

"And your mother?" Talia asked. "How is she? Excited to see her only daughter take her rightful place as princess?"

"I'm sure if she had any idea what was going on she'd be great about it. Mom always loved a party, even if she had no idea what it was for. But the thing is she's…"

"I see. I am so sorry. You must be so alone here, without your mother and father. I, too, have lost my parents."

"I haven't exactly lost them. I never knew my dad," I said. "And Mom's not dead, she's just…"

There was no good way to explain about Mom that didn't make people uncomfortable. If I told people that she'd been trapped in a coma for the past five years, being kept alive by machines, they just sort of got silent. Not that I really blamed them. Who knew what to say in that sort of situation? I didn't, and she was my mom.

"She can't take care of me right now because of her injuries," I said lamely.

"Well, I'm sure wherever she is, you'll make her proud. Now, when your consort visited us earlier he mentioned that you are quite an accomplished swimmer. A champion in your world. He seemed very impressed."

"My who? Oh, you mean Jesse? He's not mine. He's actually my maid's boyfriend. Or he was. Now he's—" I ran a hand across the back of my neck in frustration. "Never mind, I don't know why I'm telling you all of this."

"Because I want to listen," she said. "Indulge me, young

queen."

"But—"

"Let me treat you like the daughter I'll never get to have. Now, unburden yourself to me."

I nodded slowly and then gave her the lowdown on the drama that was currently taking place with Heidi and Jesse and the whole "Heidi being turned into a maid" mess.

"That is…complicated. What will you do about this boy and this girl who's now your maid?"

"I don't know. Nothing? If it weren't for the fact I was a princess, he would still be paying no attention to me. It's not me he's interested in—it's the title."

"Is it?" she asked.

"He didn't even know I was alive before. Not that it's really surprising because the girls on the swim team aren't exactly ruling the school if you know what I mean."

"Do they not?" Talia grinned at me, her eyes twinkling. "Yet, here we are. Two born swimmers who are now queens when the most desired girl in your world is now a chambermaid. Perhaps Fate knows her business after all?"

"Maybe," I said. "Or maybe this is all a mistake."

"You are the rightful Rose, and while I would guess that your new friend is perhaps not as noble as you'd first thought, he might actually like you. The stars have seen crazier things happen when young men finally wake up and face the day."

"I don't think I want him to like me, no matter how crazy the stars decide to get with their matchmaking. Suddenly I'm a princess, and he's telling me how pretty I am? Which I can tell you right now is going to be one heck of a surprise to my maid."

"I imagine many things will come as a surprise to your

new maid," Talia said. "Just as I'm sure that there will be many things that will shock you, as well. But you are welcome here any time, queen of the land dwellers. My people will sing of the Rose who rests upon the water for one hundred times the length of your reign."

"That's really nice of you," I said, "but I don't really think I'm going to be here that long. Esmeralda told me that I'm here to end of this thing called the Time of Waiting and then that's it. Then they'll let us go home."

"Home?"

"Well, yeah. I don't know how to run a country, and everyone says you've got a Lost Golden Rose somewhere out there. So, once I help with whatever it is, then she'll come back, and I can go home."

"Queen Allie...when we say that the last Rose was lost, we mean that she will never return. You are the Rose now."

"But why me? Someone's had to run this world since she left. Someone had to do the job. Didn't they?"

"The Fate Maker has been acting as regent until Fate decreed it was time for you to come."

"See?" I held my hands out toward her. "He's been running the place, and I haven't seen a lot, but it doesn't seem too bad. So I say we let him keep doing it. Trust me. You're all better off that way."

"It's not too bad here?"

"Well, I haven't been out of the castle yet, but it seems like he's doing an okay job ruling Nerissette. Better than I would."

"Excuse me?" Her eyes widened. "You don't intend to *rule*?"

"What does it matter? It's just a show, isn't it?"

"A show?"

"Like the whole thing with the Queen of England. I'll let them put a crown on my head and call me Your Highness, but in the end, the government makes all the decisions, and I just nod and smile."

"I do not know how they do things in this England of which you speak, but I can assure you that the Golden Rose of Nerissette is not meant to be a figurehead. You are the government. You are Nerissette, and your word is law. The only law."

"But the Fate Maker has been ruling for who knows how long."

"Only because you, our true queen, had not reached your six thousandth day. When our last queen was lost, Bavasama—the Queen of Nightmares—threatened our lands, and Fate declared through her orb that the wizard was meant to keep the throne safe for your return."

"How did she threaten you? With a war?"

"No." She shook her head. "She would have marched on us but instead the Fate Maker challenged the Grand Vizier, the head wizard of Bathune, to a battle of magic and the winner would rule Nerissette. For three days and nights they fought, each of them conjuring spells, and in the end, the Fate Maker was victorious. Nerissette was safe and he became regent. But the Fate Maker's regency was never meant to be a permanent solution for governing Nerissette. The people need you. Their rightful queen."

"They really don't," I said. "I have no idea how to even start trying to be a queen. None."

"That's irrelevant."

"I can't even manage to keep my swim class kids in line without someone else around. So, trust me, I am definitely not the person for this job."

"To do the job properly you must accept that who you are doesn't matter. What matters are the people you've been tasked with protecting—and they are the only thing that matters."

"Except I can't protect these people. I'm just the stupid girl who picked up the wrong book in the library. I'm not a warrior, and I'm most definitely not a queen."

"Whatever you may think, you, Alicia Munroe, were born for this. There is no other queen who can save the people of Nerissette from the darkness that is coming for them."

"What darkness?"

"No one knows what will come when the *Chronicles* end and the Time of Waiting is over. We don't know what comes next. Fate has left us blind as newborn kittens, and you are the only one who can save any of us. All of us. You have been foretold."

"I'm just a girl. If darkness is coming then you need someone who can truly protect you from it, and I'm not her."

"What was it you told Rhys before you entered our grotto?" Talia asked. "Before he left you on this side of the maze and closed the door?"

"That everyone matters," I said. "No matter who they are, everyone matters."

"Does that include maids who may have hurt your feelings before you fell through the book?"

"Everyone matters. Even Heidi."

"Then it sounds like you know more about being queen than you give yourself credit for," Talia said. "But it is late now, Golden Rose of Nerissette, and you'll have much to learn tomorrow. I have only one piece of advice to share with you."

"Just one piece of advice?"

"A true queen never allows herself to become a figurehead. She always works to do what's best for her people. Now, go and rest. Come back and enjoy our pool whenever you like. Before the end of your prophecies, and ours, are reached, you may need it."

Chapter Ten

"So," Rhys asked as I pushed the door open and joined him and Jesse on the other side of the hedge wall. "How did it go?"

"She invited me back to visit whenever I want," I said.

"That is good." Rhys nodded once, sharply, and then started down the maze, not bothering to wait for us. "Watch your step."

"I think we'll be fine," Jesse said as we hurried to keep up.

"I'll see you and your prince back to the castle so you don't get lost along the way. I'd hate for one of the dragons to mistake you for a snack—especially the crown prince. That would be tragic," Rhys said, completely ignoring Jesse.

"No one would hurt us," Jesse said, panting slightly as we rushed after the long-legged lord general.

"How do you know?" I asked.

"This is your palace, and you're going to be their queen," Jesse said, his eyes gleaming in the darkness. "No one would attack you."

"Am I?" I looked between the two of them. "Going to be their queen? Do you think that they'll all just go along with it?"

"The Fate Maker and that cat both say you're the queen," Jesse pointed out. "Everyone in the palace is bowing whenever you walk in the room. You're in charge. No one is going to go against you. They'll do whatever we say."

"Do you think if I ask the mermaids to follow me against Talia they will?" I asked. "Or do you think they would side with her?"

"Very clever, little Princess." Rhys waved his free arm out in front of him, gesturing me forward before he let his hand rest on the hilt of his sword again.

"I wouldn't say that," I said. "I mean, she didn't seem really happy when I told her that once the prophecy was fulfilled I was going to go home and let the Fate Maker run Nerissette again."

"What?" Rhys's face paled. "You're going to do *what*?"

"After the prophecy thing is over. We talked about this. I'm going to let the Fate Maker run the country again so I can take my friends and go home."

"And what do you think will happen here in Nerissette, Your Majesty?" Rhys sneered. "What happens if you go home? If we all just pack up and leave?"

"Nothing. Everything will go back to normal. It'll be like nothing changed."

"Do you know what normal is here?" He was yelling then. "Normal is living in fear of the wizards. Normal is waiting to have your children taken away from you or your home burned down."

"But why would they do that?"

"Normal," Rhys said, ignoring me. "Normal is waiting for a war that may never come to pass. Normal here is a nightmare like nothing you could ever imagine. Nothing that you could have dreamed about in the World That Is could have prepared you for what's normal here."

"That's why he should be in charge and not me. The Fate Maker knows how to keep all the bad stuff from happening. I don't."

"He's the one who keeps making the bad stuff happen!" Rhys shouted.

"Why would he ruin his own country? A country that he's supposed to be protecting?"

"Because he's a wizard, and that's what they do," Rhys said. "What do you think comes after the Time of Waiting? What do you think it is we're waiting for?"

"I don't know. Talia said that once the waiting was over, then darkness would come, and no matter what's going on here, it can't be worse than that."

"The darkness is already here," Rhys said. "What you're bringing is the spark."

"What spark?" I asked.

"War. Rebellion. A chance to take Nerissette back from the wizards and finally be free. The rule of Fate ends with the *Chronicles*. Now that you're here and the prophecies are going to end, we can finally rule ourselves—free of Fate and the wizards and everything that ties us down."

"But Talia said that he defeated the wizard of Bathune to keep Nerissette safe."

"For him! He defeated the Vizier and let the people place him on the throne as regent, then he turned out to be just as evil. He crushed the people underneath his feet as surely as Queen Bavasama would have. The same suffering, just a different dictator."

"So why haven't you fought him before? Why didn't you stand up to him?"

"Because we're ruled by Fate, and Fate decreed that the Fate Maker was meant to be regent."

"So overthrow him anyway."

"If we go against her we'll die. She will kill us all, and it will be for nothing. So we bowed our heads and we waited for the day you would come and conquer Fate. The day you would set us free."

"But I have no idea how to do that!" I wanted to shake him. No one was listening.

"Then you better figure it out, because I'm sick of watching people suffer while we sit and do nothing, waiting for *you* to save us."

"You're not listening to me. I don't know how to save you."

"I lost everything, gave up my life to keep people safe, and now that you can change things you're just going to run away because it's not convenient for you? Some queen you turned out to be."

I stood there with my mouth hanging open as he turned on his heel and stalked away from us.

"Allie?" Jesse took my hand in his and squeezed my fingers. "He's full of it, okay? He's a crackpot. Or jealous. Maybe both."

"Jealous?"

"Yeah." Jesse began tugging me down the winding passageways of the maze. "He's jealous because you're going to be queen, and he's stuck playing army man. So he'll say whatever he can to make you feel bad about it. That's what people like him do." Jesse tightened his grip.

I slid out from underneath his arm. "Well, he's kind of right. And what do you mean, people like him?"

He let go of my hand and wrapped his arm around my shoulders, pulling me into his side. "Look, people get crazy jealous when you've got something they don't, especially when they think they deserve it more than you do. The Fate Maker warned me about things like that here."

"Maybe he does deserve to be in charge, though. I mean, what makes you think I deserve to be some sort of queen?"

"You do deserve it, more than anyone else I know. You're smart, and you're pretty. The mermaids seem to like you, and most important, you're really nice to people, even people who haven't earned it."

"Like Heidi?"

He stopped walking and looked over at me. "Yeah, I guess Heidi probably fits that description, but that's just on the outside."

"Is that much different from the Heidi on the inside?" I asked skeptically.

"Once you get to know her she's not really the same person she is at school. She's different, but the thing is she's got all these expectations on her. All these things she's got to live with. She's not like you are."

"You don't think I have expectations I have to live up to?" Bitterness tinged my voice. "It's not like Gran Mosely and I are rolling in money like Heidi's family. My entire future depends on my grades and how quickly I can swim across the length of a pool."

"Yeah, but Heidi has stuff, too."

"I'm sure her worries about her nail polish and how popular she is at the moment are right up there with world hunger on the list of important stuff."

"That stuff is pretty superficial," Jesse said. "Not world hunger but the popularity stuff. But you don't understand what it's like for Heidi."

"No, sorry, I don't know what it's like to be rich and beautiful and spoiled. Why don't you tell me how horrible that is for her?"

"Did you know she watched her dad walk out on her mom because he said she wasn't pretty anymore? Heidi's new stepmom is, like, twenty-two, and her dad already has another girlfriend. One of the seniors from last year."

"You're kidding." I felt a mixture of revulsion at her dad's creep factor and sympathy for Heidi. What was with this day? Now I was pitying *Heidi Spencer*? Of all people?

"No, it's really gross. So, Heidi just sort of realized that if she makes sure she's the prettiest and the most popular then she won't get hurt. Her parents aren't like yours—all they care about is how she looks. They've taught her that's all that matters."

"So that's why she's a witch to everyone then? Because we don't live up to her beauty standards? She thinks she has the right to trample on people because somehow she won a genetic good looks lottery?"

"It's all about image with Heidi," Jesse said, "but what you don't get is that she has to be that way. Without the image she's just a girl whose dad doesn't want anything to do with her. A jerk who walked out of her life like she was no big deal."

"Yeah, well, she's not the only one whose parents aren't

around anymore." I pulled away from him and hurried toward the exit of the maze. "At least she's still got a mom."

"Crap." Jesse grabbed for my hand. "I didn't mean it that way. Well, I guess I meant it that way, but I didn't think about how that sounded when I said it."

I turned back to look at him and sighed. It wouldn't do me any good to be annoyed with Jesse. He wasn't smart enough to get how insensitive of a jerk he happened to be. "It's fine."

"I didn't mean your grandmother is wrong for caring about your grades and stuff," he said lamely.

"Gran Mosely isn't my grandmother. She's just—" What was she really? Sure, she was the woman who took care of me for the state foster care system, but she was so much more than that. She was like family but not. "It's complicated."

"She loves you, and she takes care of you," he whispered, leaning closer. "And I'm really sorry. I shouldn't have said anything about your parents."

"Forget about it."

He leaned his forehead against mine and wrapped his arms around my waist. I froze, trying to figure out the best way to get away from him and put some space between us. He was too close, especially for a guy who was dating someone else. And way too close for any guy who had made a habit of ignoring me before now.

"We should probably go back inside," I said quickly. "You can come back to my tower and hang out with Heidi if you want."

"Why would I want to hang out with Heidi?" Jesse asked, his forehead still pressed against mine. "I'm already here with you."

"Because she's your girlfriend?"

"Not really. We go out and stuff, but it's not like we're boyfriend and girlfriend or anything. The only reason she wants me around is that she thinks it will help her become the junior princess for the winter formal court." Jesse's face was so close to mine that I could smell the onions from our dinner on his breath.

"That's not what Heidi told me earlier." I tried shifting backward to get out of his arms, but he tightened his grip on me. "She said the two of you were together."

"Only until the winter formal's over," Jesse said. "But now I think we've all got bigger things to worry about than some silly dance, don't you? Unless being pulled through a book and into a different world is how you normally spend your Saturdays."

"No. I thought this was your idea of a good time." I jerked away from him, hard enough this time that he didn't have a choice about letting me go. I tried to pass it off as some sort of really weird joke instead of just being massively, uncomfortably awkward.

"So what would you like to do?" Jesse asked as he stepped closer again.

"I think we should go back inside," I said, my voice unnaturally high.

"Really?"

"I'm tired, and I think I bruised something when I landed on that floor earlier. I should really rest. Tomorrow's a big day. A really big day. Got to learn how to run a kingdom and all. Maybe do some magic or something. Who knows, huh?"

Jesse reached for my hand. "I'll walk you to your door."

"That's okay," I said, my voice cracking on the last syllable. I spun away from him and grabbed my skirts so I could run without falling on my face. Things were awkward enough. "I'll tell Heidi you said hi."

"But I didn't," Jesse yelled after me as I bolted across the lawn.

"'Night," I called out when I reached the door, not bothering to turn around and see where he was. I pulled the door open and hurried inside.

"Good night, Princess," I heard him say, his voice sounding amused while I slid the glass patio door closed. I turned to see him standing in the middle of the grass, his hands in his pockets and a stupid grin on his face.

He gave me a jaunty wave, but instead of waving back, I turned and sprinted toward the stairs. I ran back to the main foyer and hurried up the winding staircase. The third floor of the East Wing, fifth corridor. Now, if only someone had left the lights on so that I could see Esmeralda's signs. I didn't even know which way east was.

I stopped at the top of the steps and looked around. When I'd first seen the dome above me I'd turned right and went down the stairs. That must mean the East Wing was to my left. I turned and tried to figure out what I'd done next. I had to be in the first hallway on the second floor. I ran toward the end of the corridor and found myself at a fork. Which way had I gone?

I leaned down and brushed my hand against the bricks, trying to find the one with the carving on it. Why didn't people leave lights on around here? Okay, so it wasn't environmentally friendly, but couldn't they come up with something? I couldn't be the only person who got lost around here at night.

I felt the edge of a carving and kneeled to get closer look.

Two Es and an eleven. Why was there an eleven? My tower was at the end of the castle and it was only at corridor five. Where was the eleventh corridor supposed to be tucked away then? Were there hidden corridors or something? Somehow I wouldn't be surprised if there were.

"Why isn't it ever easy?" I ran my fingers over the carving again.

Wait, Esmeralda had said something else about using the stones to get where I wanted to go. Tell them where I wanted to go, and they'd show me?

Worth a shot.

"All I want to do is go to Three E Five," I said, hoping that whatever it was they were supposed to do would happen.

Green light burst out of the wall and surrounded me as I sucked in a mouthful of smoke. Coughing, I waved my hands in front of my face to clear the white clouds. I opened my eyes and realized that I was no longer in the same dark hallway. Instead, I was kneeling in front of my own double doors, a torch burning merrily away beside me.

"By the stars," I said, my voice wheezing.

The freaking cat had a teleport built into the castle. When she said they'd take me where I wanted to go I thought they'd have a map or something that popped up. This was just too much.

I stood, brushed the dirt off the front of my skirt, and turned my head, trying to see how much mud I had gotten on the back of my gown while I'd been talking with Talia. Oh well. Even if it were caked on I was pretty sure whoever did the laundry would have some sort of magical powder to get the stains out.

"I have no idea what I'm supposed to say to you." I waved

my hands at the door. "And I'm way too tired to remember German. Any chance you could help me out? Please?"

The door opened with a creak and I slipped inside, patting its main panel as I went. "Thanks."

The door squeaked once again as it shut, and I felt it warm against my palm.

Inside the suite all the candles were lit, and there was a roaring fire going in the fireplace. Heidi was sitting on a wooden, straight-backed chair like the ones in the library, dragging a comb through her newly dull hair.

"Have fun?" She slammed the comb down on the small table beside her and stalked over to me so that we were face-to-face, my back to the door.

"It was okay, I guess. I mean, except for the fact that I think I may have insulted some—well, okay, most—of the royal court."

"So flirting with my boyfriend is only okay?"

"Uh…" I felt my jaw drop open, and I instinctively tried to step backward, but there was nowhere to go.

"Little hint," Heidi said, her breath ghosting over my face. "If you're going to try to steal someone's boyfriend, don't do it standing where anyone looking out of the tower can see you." She motioned to the open window.

I walked over and looked straight down onto the maze where Jesse and I had been earlier. Uh-oh. Hopefully all that stuff about holding girls over her head earlier had just been a bluff. "I wasn't trying to steal… Jesse was the one who was flirting… I told him that the two of you were dating," I said. Even to me it sounded weak.

"The stupid jerk. We've been dating since eighth grade and he tells you it's a dance thing."

"I knew he was lying," I said. "I didn't flirt back. He's a jerk."

"Yeah, but he's a fabulous-looking jerk, so you might as well have kissed him. You're the princess. He's the handsome prince. I'm a *maid*. I may not be in all the accelerated nerd classes like you, but even I can figure out what that means."

"When we get back to Bethel Park he'll realize he was being an idiot and want to get back together with you," I said, trying to be reassuring.

"Jesse Harper can find another cheerleader to drag him along behind her." Heidi's shoulders straightened, her chin lifting higher, as a familiar sneer graced her lips. "I'm nobody's second pick."

"Right. Good. Good for you," I said.

"Maybe I'll try my luck with Winston," she said. "I bet having a dragon for a boyfriend could have some definite advantages."

"You don't want to date Win," I said maybe too quickly.

"Why?" She raised an eyebrow. "Are you two together?"

"No." Ugh, how stupid was that? Sure, he was handsome. And funny. And smart. And the only guy who it didn't completely suck to talk to. But we were definitely just friends. No matter how great he was and how much I wouldn't have minded us being more than friends.

"So what's the problem with me going after him? If you don't want him…"

"Just…" How could I explain that the last person I wanted to see with Winston was Heidi? There was no way she was good enough for him. "You don't have anything in common."

"So?"

I looked around the room, desperately trying to find a way to find something to change the subject to. My eyes landed on the hard chair she'd been sitting in, perched right next to a large, overstuffed one with velvet cushions.

"Why don't you want me with Winston?"

"Why were you sitting on that hard chair?" *There. Ignore the question.* "With all the comfy things in here, you're sitting on that?"

"The other chairs are in league with the mattress. This is the only one that will let me sit in it."

"Oh."

"Now, let's talk about Winston and why you don't want him dating someone else."

"Let's not."

"So what else do you want to do? As far as I can tell it's talk about Winston or take the chance of letting me give you a makeover so that you actually look like you deserve to be a queen."

"How much of a makeover?"

"Think reality television."

"What do you want to know about Winston?"

Chapter Eleven

I woke the next morning before Heidi and pulled on the same clothes from the day before. They weren't my favorite running clothes, and I was going to have to go barefoot since I couldn't run in my flip-flops, but they were better than a ball gown. Maybe, if I was lucky, one of the fairies could find me some clothes to wear later so I wouldn't feel like a total idiot running five miles in a pair of dirty jeans?

I opened my door to the Fate Maker waiting outside, a grim smile on his lips. "Your Majesty," he said. "You've risen early."

"I was going for a run like I do every day."

"A run? Why would you want to run? Aren't you happy here in the palace?"

"The palace is lovely, but I want to get out and get some exercise. I don't know how long we're going to be here kicking off this whole End of the Waiting thing, but I need to stay on top of my swim training for when we go home."

"I don't think that would be wise." The Fate Maker glared at me. "There's no need for you to run about the countryside exposed. Someone might harm you. Or even worse, kidnap you and hold you for a ransom we can't afford. You make a rather appealing target."

"So I'll take Winston with me. He's a dragon now. He can protect me," I said, my hands clenching into fists.

How dare this guy tell me I couldn't go for a run? I'd run every day since I was nine years old. Mom had been a marathoner, and even though I didn't love it like she did, it was always the time we'd spent together before the accident. I didn't care what the Fate Maker said. I was going for my run.

"He's still not safe on his own yet. The dragon isn't a reliable escort."

"Then I'll take…" I wasn't going to take Jesse, and if I couldn't take Winston along, who could I take? Someone so annoyingly responsible that even the Fate Maker couldn't complain. "I'll take Rhys Sullivan. He'll keep an eye on me."

"Lord Sullivan is busy overseeing the army. He doesn't have time to cater to your whims, Your Majesty."

"He can't take the day off? Or, here's an idea: he can bring the army along with us. They could all probably use a run."

"The men are not dressed for such strenuous exercise." The Fate Maker grabbed my arm, his grip tight.

"Then they can change." I jerked my arm away and glared at him. "I want to go for a run."

"You'll go back into that room." He pointed at the door behind me. "You will change and you will get these ridiculous ideas about running out of your mind."

"Going for a run isn't just some stupid idea."

"It isn't safe, Your Majesty, and besides, there's no reason for you to worry about keeping in shape."

"But when we go back…" My stomach clenched, and I tried to keep my knees from knocking together.

"Your fate is here, not there, and you'll put these silly ideas of going home behind you, too."

"But once Fate's rule has ended then we'll go home. Me and Mercedes and Win and everyone else who's from that world. You'll send us all home, and these people can rule themselves."

"You listen to me, you spoiled, ungrateful child. Fate's not giving up her rule on this realm."

"But I thought her time was over. I thought the prophecies said that her rule was at its end."

"And I am her loyal servant. I will give her this world to feast upon. Now we can all play along with this whole prophecy to make Esmeralda happy, but let me be very clear—this is my world, and I am not going to let you destroy it."

"I—"

"You're the one who's going to give me this world. You're going to rededicate Nerissette to the whims of Fate."

"And if I refuse?"

"I'll have you kept in chains until the day the head of the Dryad Order drops that crown on your little head. Now, do as I say," he ground out.

I straightened my spine, trying to look braver than I felt. I hated feeling weak, and after years of being bullied by Heidi and her crew of brain-dead sycophants I knew that cowering away from him would only give him more incentive to be cruel.

"I will turn your friends into hostages, and let you

watch while I break them," the Fate Maker said, his voice a low, angry growl. "Now, change your clothes, and come to breakfast. Or I might have to stop by the aerie to see how Winston is faring."

Instead of waiting for me to answer he snapped his fingers and disappeared. I stood, trembling, and watched the smoke clear. My knees wobbled, and I had to fight against the sudden wave of nausea that flooded through me.

I turned to the door and narrowed my eyes. The door didn't even hesitate; it opened without a sound and began to hum like the chattering of a swarm of bees.

Heidi stumbled into the room from the closet, her hair sticking up in all directions. She rubbed her eyes and looked at me, oblivious to the smeared mascara underneath her eyes. "Is everything okay? I heard yelling."

"How much did you hear?" I slunk over to my bed and flopped down on it.

"The dorky dark wizard from yesterday is basically psychotic, and we're now his prisoners. You don't do what he says, and he'll throw you in the dungeon in chains and torture the rest of us."

"That about covers it, yeah," I sighed.

"So basically we're screwed," Heidi said, her voice dripping with condescension. "I'd like to say I told you so but somehow that doesn't seem like it's going to help."

"No, it doesn't." I sat up. "So what do we do?"

"Well, my dad always says if you can't make the other person's legal team see that you're right then you take them out at the knees," Heidi said. "So, that's what we do. We find out how to hurt him, and we do it."

"What?" I looked at her with wide eyes. "Your answer to

this problem is to go club a wizard in the knees? I don't think that's going to work. Besides, I've never actually hurt someone before. Not physically or anything."

"No, stupid." Heidi rolled her eyes at me. "We find out what he needs and take it from him. Psych him out. Look, you're on the swim team. You do those swim meets or whatever."

"Yeah? So?" I wrapped my arms around myself, trying to fight the chill that lingered from my encounter with the Fate Maker.

"So, have you ever done something to psych the other swimmers out before you compete? Like hide their iPods? Move their towels? Say something nasty right before stuff gets started? Anything to give you an advantage by throwing off their game?"

"That's a crappy thing to do. If I'm going to beat you in the pool I'm going to do it because I'm faster, not because I somehow ruined your race. I don't need to cheat to win."

"Well, now you do," Heidi said. "Because you can't win by playing fair in this game. Now, we're going to get you dressed for breakfast, and you'll go down and play nice with the Fate Maker. Get him to relax and think that you're going to do things his way."

"Then what?"

"Find out what his weakness is. Once you know it, we'll use it to destroy him and get back home because I was right and you were wrong, and this is not a place we are supposed to be."

"I thought you weren't going to say I told you so?"

"I lied." Heidi stood and flounced into my closet. She left the door open while she rooted through the dresses and grabbed one.

"Great. Thanks for that."

"I told you so, and now we're trapped. You'll just have to find some way to get us out of this mess," Heidi said. "Now breakfast. What are you going to wear?"

"I'm not hungry." I peeled off my shirt before I reached for the waistband of my jeans. I felt weird about the whole getting naked in front of Heidi thing, but I didn't see where I had much of a choice since we were sharing a room.

"Tough." Heidi waited until I'd kicked my feet out of the jeans and then handed me a purple dress with silver flowers embroidered on the skirt.

"Why do you care if I eat breakfast anyway?"

"My dad always says that an army fights on its stomach. I'm not sure what that means exactly, but I'm pretty sure it has something to do with eating breakfast every day."

"I didn't know your dad was in the military." I slipped on the dress and turned so she could button it.

"He wasn't," Heidi said, her fingers flying over the buttons along my spine. "He just likes watching all those documentaries on the Military Channel. That doesn't mean he isn't right. I'm sure Winston's dad would tell you the same thing, and he *is* in the army."

"Marines, but yeah, I know what you mean. We could really use Winston's dad right about now." Major Carruthers was a pain in Winston's neck most of the time, but he'd know what to do. He'd know how to get us home safe.

"Yeah? Well, he's not here," Heidi said as she buttoned the last button at my neck. "So, let's hope all that time without a television means his son learned something, because if Dragon Boy can't help you get us out of this, we're in real trouble."

Chapter Twelve

I walked to the dining room a half hour later, my knees trembling.

"Your Majesty," the goblin from last night said. What had Rhys said his name was? Tim, something…Timberfield? Timpani? Timbago! That was it. "I hope your sleep was pleasant."

"It was wonderful, Timbago, very comfortable. How was yours?" I tried to keep my voice even. It wouldn't do for the goblin to know that I was terrified. Not until I knew where his loyalties lay.

The goblin looked up at me in surprise. "My sleep was excellent as well… Thank you for asking, Your Majesty. May I escort you to your seat?"

"I'd like that." I rested my palm on the back of the wrinkly hand Timbago held up for me.

The goblin led me to the front of the room, his head held high and his large nose quivering. He waved his fingers again, and the chair I'd sat in last night slid out for me.

I sat and looked over at him. "Thank you."

"The pleasure is most distinctly mine, Your Majesty," Timbago said, two bright spots of red appearing on his cheeks.

"Allie," I said, knowing that it would drive the Fate Maker insane to hear the palace staff calling me by my first name instead of by my formal title. It wasn't much, but any battle that I could win right now would go a long way in showing that he couldn't defeat me with just a few threats in the hallway.

He may want me to become a queen who lived under his and Fate's joined thumbs, but there was another way. If I could convince the people to follow me, then I could fight back; I could do all the things Rhys said last night. I could free us all, and then my friends and I could go home.

"Allie," he said, his voice cracking. He ran one of his long, talon-like nails under his shirt collar and swallowed. "May I ask what you'd like for breakfast, Your Maj—Allie?"

"Could I have some toast with cream cheese and a glass of orange juice? Wait, does Nerissette have cream cheese and orange juice? If you don't, I'll eat anything."

I didn't want to seem like I was spoiled and demanding, and it wasn't like it really mattered to me.

"If we do not have it, Princess Allie," Timbago said, his voice stern though his face was cherry red, "I will personally fight my way through the Bleak and defeat Kuolema himself to go into your world to find it for you. Every day if need be."

"That's not—"

The goblin clapped his hands and disappeared in a cloud of smoke. So much for putting a potential ally at ease.

I set my chin in my upturned palm and started picking at

the tablecloth with my other hand. What was I supposed to do now?

"Ah, Princess." The Fate Maker swept into the room with his long black robes swishing behind him. "How kind of you to be prompt, and may I say you look much better than before?"

"You may say it, but that doesn't mean it's true." I didn't look at him, knowing that I wouldn't be able to keep the disgust off my face if I did. Better for him to think I was pouting or something. Just a silly teenage girl who didn't get her way.

"Now, Princess." He sat down beside me and took my hand, patting the back of it. "I do hope that we can put the unpleasantness of this morning behind us. You must see that your safety is my gravest concern."

"You threatened to arrest me when all I wanted to do was go for a run," I said, trying to keep my voice low and petulant.

"I will admit I overreacted, but you cannot blame me for being concerned. After all, what would your dear mother say if she knew I let her precious child come to harm when I could have prevented it? She would never forgive me."

What was it with these people and my mother? Sure, I was almost positive she'd known more about Nerissette than she'd told me before, but why did they all care so much? It wasn't like she'd actually been their queen. I'd have thought that was something she might have told me about at some point if she were. Wouldn't she?

Then again, this was Mom. She didn't tell me that she forgot our pet hamster when we moved from Seattle to New York when I was nine. So anything was possible.

"My mother was, I mean, she is—"

"Not well, yes." The Fate Maker patted my hand. "I still

doubt she would approve of my careless handling of her only child. So, out of respect to her, it's best if we keep you safe."

"Safe isn't what I'm—"

"I would have no quarrels between us," he said, talking over me. "After all, we will be spending quite a bit of time together from now until your coronation. There's much you need to learn about your new kingdom. So many things we're going to have to discuss so that you know what to do when it comes time for the prophecy to be fulfilled."

"Okay." I grimaced at the idea of having to deal with him for the rest of the day. Wasn't there someone else who could teach me? Then again, who better to learn from than the guy you were trying to beat?

Besides, maybe he could explain exactly what was going on with my mom. "What happened to the last queen? How did she die?"

"The last Rose didn't die."

"But Talia said she was lost. If she isn't dead then why don't you just find her and bring her back to rule instead of me?" I could feel my heart sinking into my toes. If the last queen was alive and couldn't come back that meant Mom had lied to me about a lot more than my hamster Biggles.

"When did you see Talia?"

"We met last night, and she told me that being lost was how you referred to death."

"It is, Your Majesty, but it also means anyone that we can no longer touch. People who are still alive but trapped away from this realm."

"So, where is she, then? If she's not here she's got to be somewhere. Can't you just pull her through from that other realm like you did me? Heal her?"

"It's more difficult than that, Your Majesty. I can't heal wounds of the mind and the body. It's beyond even my powers and..."

"And?"

"Fate has decreed that it is your time to rule. The old queen was lost, and when a Rose next returns to the throne she will be the princess."

"How? I haven't met Fate yet. Where is she? How do you know this is what she wants?"

"Fate is a goddess. She lives in the spirit realm with the rest of the Pleiades and doesn't mingle with the mere mortals of Nerissette," the Fate Maker said. "She speaks to us through a chosen wizard."

"You?"

He nodded. "Me."

"That's how you became regent. You're her wizard, so when the queen was lost Talia told me you fought against the Grand Vizier of Bathune in a battle of magic. And when it was over you were declared regent."

"That—"

A loud *crack* tore through the air, and we both froze, turning to the red-faced goblin standing in the middle of the room. Smoke wrapped around his feet, and he clutched one of Gran Mosely's good china plates in his left hand and a crystal goblet full of orange juice in his other.

"Your Majesty," Timbago panted. He bowed low again and presented me with my food. "I hope I have not kept you waiting for too long. Your request was a bit more complicated than I first expected."

"You didn't actually go through the Bleak to get me breakfast, did you?" I asked. "I could have had something else for breakfast. I mean, seriously, you could have gotten hurt."

"Absolutely not," Timbago said, his neck flaming with color. "Your Majesty's every trifling desire is my most fervent command. I have sworn upon the relics."

"The relics? What are those?"

"They are…" Timbago stared, his eyes wide, and I turned to see the Fate Maker glaring at him. "I should return to the kitchens. We have much to do for tonight's banquet."

The Fate Maker smiled at me indulgently. "Perhaps your time here will not be as confining as you first thought this morning, Your Majesty. After all, we're having a ball tonight in your honor. Just a small thing to introduce you to the kingdom before all the coronation business starts."

He turned to Timbago and snapped his fingers. "Two griffin eggs, poached, and a glass of dragon's blood. Warmed, of course."

"Of course." Timbago clapped his hands and disappeared.

"The juice, that is," the Fate Maker said, turning his attention back to me. "No worries, Princess, your friend hasn't become part of my breakfast. At least not this morning. Although, my guess is that Timbago won't be delivering my food personally. That's the problem with goblins, really. They're horribly insolent creatures."

"He seemed nice to me." If I were Timbago I'd have spit in the Fate Maker's food if he'd talked to me that way. "You know, saying *please* and *thank you* never hurt anyone."

Two fairies appeared in front of him, a silver plate balanced between them. The two creatures lowered the meal in front of him, lying facedown on the table, not daring to look in his direction.

His lips curled into a sneer. "Yes, but it's so very inconvenient."

"You should be nicer to people. You'd get further with them."

He looked around the room, making sure that we were alone before he gave me a cruel smile. "But why should I worry about being liked when I could just make them fear me instead?"

"Why should anyone be afraid of you?" I asked, my voice trembling. "It's not like you can do anything to them now that you're no longer regent. Or at least you won't be the regent once I've been crowned."

"You may be the future queen," he said, his voice low and angry, "but I am still the high wizard of Fate herself, and this is my world to control. Do you want to know what I'll do to anyone who tries to get in my way?"

"What?"

He picked one of the fairies up by her leg, dropped her onto the floor, and stomped. I heard a dull *crunch* and closed my eyes. The other fairy let out a high-pitched squeak and trembled on the tablecloth.

"I'll crush them," the Fate Maker said, his voice cold. "No matter who they are."

I swallowed. "The nobles, the people, they won't let you—"

"They'll do whatever I say. I suggest you do the same."

"If they know what you're doing, though, they won't just stand by."

"They have for this long. That's the power of fear, Your Majesty. Once you've cultivated it, no one gets in your way. Now, finish your breakfast and then find something to amuse yourself. Something quiet."

"I thought you were going to teach me how to be queen after breakfast."

"Can you say 'whatever the Fate Maker thinks is best'?" He stood and smirked down at me. "Or do we need to bring in some more fairies to help motivate you?"

I shook my head vigorously, my eyes wide.

"Good." He narrowed his eyes at me. "Go practice that until you think you won't forget. It's your answer to everything. No matter how trivial. Are we understood?"

I nodded again.

"Answer me."

"Yes."

"Say you understand."

"I do."

"Say it."

"I understand."

"And the answer to any question is?"

"Whatever the Fate Maker thinks is best."

"Good. Now, go find your precious pet dryad and stay out of my sight. Otherwise, tomorrow morning my dragon's blood may be a bit more...*fresh.*"

He stalked away from the table and toward the door.

My knees beat together underneath the table and my hands shook. I couldn't bear to look underneath the table at the creature hidden below. My stomach lurched, and I had to fight the nausea as tears welled up in my eyes. He'd killed a fairy just to prove a point. To keep me in line.

When he reached the door he stopped and turned back to me. "I have only one other *request*, Your Majesty."

"What?" I asked.

"Don't leave the palace grounds. Otherwise, I'll be forced to send the army after you, and what will the people say if I have to return you to your rooms in chains?"

"You wouldn't dare," I said, my voice choked, knowing that he would probably love to lock me up if I gave him half a chance.

"Never doubt what I would dare. And just so you know, if you're in chains you won't need a maid. What will we do with her? What was her name? Heather?"

"Heidi."

"Right. I'm sure we could find something to do with her. If nothing else I could turn her into a battle dummy for Lord Sullivan's army to practice their swordplay on, for a few hours at least."

He swept out of the room, and I slowly pushed my chair back and got to my feet. That had not gone well. I looked at my barely touched breakfast, and my stomach lurched. There was no way that I could eat now. Not after what he'd done.

I peered under the table at the broken, pink body and shuddered. I wanted to throw up, but I didn't think I could. Instead, I backed away from the table, my eyes fixed on the fairy, and started toward the door.

"Your Majesty?" a small goblin in long, brown skirts asked as I backed out of the room. "Are you all right?"

"There's been an..." I couldn't meet her eyes.

"I see." She lowered her own head for a brief moment and then lifted her chin. "You go on. Get some fresh air. I'll handle it."

"But she—"

"I'll handle it." The goblin took my hand and gave my fingers a brief squeeze. "Now go on. Try to put whatever unpleasantness it is out of your mind."

"Do you know where the aerie is? Where the dragons train?" I asked. If anyone could figure out a way to get us out of this before the Fate Maker killed anyone else, it would be Winston. "I have a friend who's with them, and I'd like to see him."

"The new black dragon? He's with Lord Sullivan."

"With Rhys?"

"Yes, Your Majesty. If you hurry you might catch them." She pointed toward the back of the castle.

"Thank you."

She shooed me away. "Go."

I started toward the back of the castle where she'd pointed and tried not to cry at the thought of the fairy underneath the table. I glanced around, trying to see if there was someone who could tell me where to find Winston and Rhys or where they would go. I needed to find both of them and then track down Mercedes. The four of us needed to figure out how to get free of the Fate Maker, save the world, and then get the heck out of here before anything else happened. No matter how much Rhys Sullivan disagreed with me about it.

Chapter Thirteen

I pushed open the doors to the back lawn and found Rhys and Winston striding toward a large tower detached from the main palace. A large red bird was perched on Rhys's shoulder, its talons digging into the black leather coat he was wearing.

"Winston! Rhys!"

Both boys spun around.

"Allie?" Winston started toward me at a quick walk and then broke into a run.

When he reached me he pulled me into a tight embrace. "I was so worried about you. Rhys came and found me this morning, but he wasn't sure we'd be able to get to you. He said something about the Fate Maker maybe trying to keep you locked away in the castle with Jesse."

"Oh my God," I said against his shoulder. "It's so good to see you. The Fate Maker is—"

"Evil, I know."

"They don't intend to let us go, either. He and Esmeralda—

they want to keep us here forever."

"I know. The dragons told me. They say that you're supposed to rule for one hundred years. According to them, we're stuck."

"What are we going to do?" I asked.

"We'll figure something out."

"I've told him there's no way out of this," Rhys said. "Fate has forced you to come here."

"I'll find a way," Winston said, and let me go. "Fate can just stuff it as far as I'm concerned."

"I'm telling you, there's no way home," Rhys said. "I've tried. The magic that brought all of us here can't be replicated. The spells are lost except to the people who know them and—"

"So we find someone who knows the spells," I said.

"The only person who knows them is the cat, and trust me," Rhys said bitterly, "she's not talking."

"But if there was—" I said.

"There's not. You have to face that this is your life now. Fate has decreed that you are queen, and so queen you shall be." Rhys patted the creature on his shoulder absently. "Now, forget about Fate and trying to get home or anything else. We'll worry about all of that later. Right now, I've got something more interesting to show you. You're not the only one with a flying pet."

"Hey!" Winston said. "I'm a dragon, not a pet."

"Sure you're not." Rhys raised an eyebrow before focusing on me. "Just remember to take him for regular walkies, Princess. Dragons are notoriously hard to housebreak."

"I'm going to housebreak you," Winston said, taking a step toward Rhys. I couldn't help smiling.

"You can try." Rhys smirked. "It's been a long time since

I beat the crap out of a dragon. Might be a good way to kill some time. That is, if you can quit cuddling with Princess Allie long enough to face me."

"I wasn't cuddling—" Winston started.

"Enough. No one's housebreaking anyone," I said. "Now, what is that bird on your shoulder? He's enormous."

"Princess Allie, this is Balmeer, a miniature roc who allows me to hunt with him and call him friend. Balmeer, meet the Princess."

The roc dipped his head low in front of me, his eyes fixed on mine. I bowed my head in return, and the bird made two clicking sounds before straightening and pulling his far wing up to hide his face. "He's a miniature? Are you sure?"

"He is. A full-sized roc can grow to almost twelve feet tall with a twenty-foot wingspan. It's said that in ancient times, when the roc colonies migrated, they blocked out the sun."

"He's beautiful. How did you get him for a pet?"

"Rocs are common here in Nerissette," Rhys said, taking my arm and leading me away from the castle. "But Balmeer isn't actually a pet. He was separated from his family and has allowed me to foster him. We are friends and comrades, but he is his own creature, not something that I own."

"How did the two of you meet?" I asked.

"Darinda, the head of the Dryad Order," Rhys said. "She was helping him to find a new home and thought that I might need a companion in the north. It seems that he had made a nest in her tree and made a bit of nuisance of himself."

"You know where to find the dryads?"

"Of course. Why?"

"I want to find Mercedes."

"Mercedes?" Rhys asked.

"One of my friends who fell through the book with me and ended up here. The Fate Maker turned her into a dryad."

"Yeah," Rhys said. "You mentioned your friend the dryad last night, but I didn't catch her name. Mercedes? I like it."

"I need to see her as soon as possible," I said, ignoring his comment about her name.

"Well," Rhys said, "lucky for you, I know where Darinda and the rest of her order spend their days. It's near where Balmeer and I were going to take Winston to teach him how to hunt. You and the dryad should join us. If you'd like, perhaps I can teach you a bit of swordplay? Just in case."

"I'm not going to go watch someone else kill innocent creatures just because he can. That's how I spent breakfast, and I don't need you to teach me how to swordfight. I already know how to fence. My mother made me take lessons when I was a kid."

"We don't hunt for the fun of it," Rhys said. "Rocs can only eat food they've hunted for themselves once they've left the hatchling nest. Balmeer must hunt if he is to survive."

"What?" Winston asked.

"I said we don't hunt for the fun of it," Rhys said.

"Not that." Winston put his hands on my shoulders and stared deep into my eyes. "What did you say, Allie? About killing innocent creatures?"

"I…" I wrapped my arms around my waist, holding myself upright as best as I could.

"Allie?" Winston asked.

"Princess?" Rhys said. "Are you okay?"

"The Fate Maker killed one of the fairies during breakfast. He just picked her up and threw her on the ground and stepped on her. Like she was nothing," I whispered. "He just killed her."

"Oh, Christ," Winston said, disgust in his voice.

"I told you he was evil," Rhys said. "Now, what are you going to do about it? How do you intend to stop him?"

"I told him he couldn't just kill other people, or creatures, or anything. They have the right to live without being stepped on one morning because he feels like squishing something during breakfast."

"And?" Rhys asked.

"And what?" I asked. What did he expect me to do? The guy had everyone in his grasp. Wasn't it enough that I'd stood up to him?

"How will you enforce it? You've told the man that he cannot do something. Have you told him what the consequences will be if he crosses you?" Rhys asked.

"Then I'll—" Winston started.

"You'll fight all her battles for her?" Rhys asked. "You'll go in front of the Court of the Silver Thorn and tell them they *must* do everything her way or you'll breathe fire on them? You'll show the world she can't fight for herself? They'll never believe she is a queen if you do that."

"But—"

"Now." Rhys stepped forward and lowered his face so that we were eye to eye. "How will *you* enforce your ban on murder?"

"I ordered him to stop killing."

"You ordered him to stop killing *or else what*? Will you hold him to his oath with a sword at his throat?"

"I…"

"The race of man only obeys laws because there are consequences if they don't. If you ask a man not to do something he may agree out of respect to you, but when you order a man to do things he will only comply out of fear. He must know that no matter what horror faces him for obeying your order, it pales in comparison to what will happen if he fails."

"Yeah, well, if you haven't noticed he's bigger than I am, and he's a wizard. What can I do to scare him? Threaten to be mad? Stab him? Violence isn't the answer."

"Sometimes it's the only answer," Rhys said. "But no, you don't stab him. You use your army to be the force behind your commands. Then, if anyone defies you—even the Fate Maker—you send us to enforce your judgment without mercy. Humiliate and destroy him where everyone can see. Show that your rule is without question."

"How is that different from me stopping him?" Winston asked.

"Because she has to be the one seen to give the order. She has to be the one to order the men out to possibly die in her name," Rhys said.

"That's barbaric," I said.

"I never said it was a civilized manner of ruling, but I've often found that even the most cultured men can only be persuaded to do something they don't like because they are threatened by someone else."

"I can't order people to their deaths," I said quietly.

"One day very soon, Princess, you may not have a choice." Rhys stepped back. "Now, come along. You're in shock from your fall through the book yesterday, and now, after the Fate Maker's antics, I think you could use some air."

"But—"

"Is there anything you can do, right this moment, to stop the Fate Maker?" Rhys asked.

I shook my head. "No."

"Then come along." He motioned toward the forest and then started walking, leaving Winston and me behind.

"It'll be okay," Winston said as we entered the woods, the dark tree trunks soon hiding the palace from sight. "We'll find some way to stop this and get home."

"Do you really think so?" I asked.

"I do." He slipped an arm around my shoulders, and I couldn't help snuggling into it, enjoying the feel of him beside me, more than I should have.

"Why?" I asked. "Why are you so sure that we can get back?"

"Because I don't believe in Fate," Winston said. "According to the dragons, no one has seen her since the Pleiades disappeared into the sky. She's a legend. The only one who's ever even talked to her is each generation's Fate Maker and that horrible cat. For all we know, Fate doesn't exist."

"Then how did we end up here?" Rhys asked.

"Magic. Crazy cats that wield magic and want to control the world but lack thumbs? I don't know how she does it, but it's not some magical god in the sky. It's just the cat being insane, and the wizard using her craziness to control everyone."

"So, you don't think she even *might* be real? Fate?" I asked.

"If she is, she can come down here and force me to do her will," Winston said. "Because I don't intend to just roll over and give up without a fight, and I don't care what Fate has to say about it."

"What about you, Rhys?" I asked as he pushed his way farther into the forest, holding branches out of the way while we followed him. "Do you believe in Fate?"

"I believe that we're here and there's no way home so we don't have much choice left. But any time it's possible, I try to decide for myself."

"And what can you decide for yourself here?" I asked.

"Where my loyalties lie." He pushed back another low-hanging branch covered in silver leaves, and I found myself in the middle of a clearing. Looking around I saw that we were surrounded by dozens of women, all of them sitting cross-legged in front of the trees, singing songs while roots grew out of their fingers and intertwined with those of the tree in front of them.

"And where is that?" I asked, my eyes fixed on the women in front of me.

"With you and the throne," Rhys said softly from beside me. "Always. Now please, Princess Allie, allow me to introduce you to the Order of the Dryads."

Chapter Fourteen

"Allie!" Mercedes sat in front of a tree, its roots wrapped around her like some sort of weird, living blanket, and all I could do was stare at her in shock.

"Oh my God, Allie. Where have you been?" She disentangled herself from the roots and hopped up before running toward me. She threw herself into my arms, and I stepped back, bumping squarely into Rhys's chest.

"In the palace," I said, breathless. "Where else would I be?"

"Where else wouldn't you be?" She laughed and squeezed me tighter before looking up at the guy holding us both upright.

"Hello? Who are you? And why are you so touchy-feely with my best friend?" She turned to Winston. "Win, barbecue him. He's getting all grabby with Allie."

"Rhys Sullivan." He let go of me before stepping aside and bowing his head to her, his face a blank slate. "You must be the new dryad our queen has spoken so highly of. May you have much luck in finding your tree."

"Rhys Sullivan." A new, richer feminine voice spoke then, her tone reminding me of dirt and forest and all those things.

I turned toward the voice and found myself facing a woman with skin the color of grass. She towered over me in her bare feet, standing even with Winston's six-foot-two frame. She was broad-shouldered with thickly muscled legs that resembled the trunks of sturdy trees and arms that looked strong enough to rip one of those giant California redwoods out of the ground by its roots. She had a large gnarled tree branch in her hand that she was using as a walking stick. But with the way she held it, I could tell that the woman in front of me would have no problems using it as a club against my head if she wanted to.

She narrowed her eyes at us but bowed her head low, her gaze never leaving mine, though she spoke to Rhys. "Why have you come to my forest, Iron Lover? Do you wish to die?"

"I have no fear of dying at your hands, Darinda." He bowed.

She waved her stick at him menacingly, but she smiled. "Then perhaps you would like to give up your iron-mongering ways and join us?"

"While I have nothing but the greatest respect for your trees, we both know that the way of the forest is not meant for me," Rhys said.

"So?" she asked. "Why are you here? And who are the tiny leaves you've brought along in your wake?"

"This is the crown princess. It seems your newest sapling is her friend."

"*Best* friend," I said before reaching out to grab Mercedes's hand.

"Best friend." Rhys bowed his head to me. "My apologies."

"I expected the Fate Maker's newest toy to be smaller. The last one was so tiny, after all."

"Sorry to disappoint." I glared first at Rhys and then at Darinda. "But this is the size I come in. I can slouch if you prefer, but either way, I'm not the Fate Maker's plaything."

"Are you not?" she asked. "The last Rose was. She simpered and preened, but in the end she did what she was told, no matter who was harmed."

"Well, that was her, not me," I snapped.

"You'll be different? You're just a girl."

"And you're nothing more than an overgrown tree sprite," I shot back. "One that crumples at the merest touch of iron."

"And you'll be the one to wield that iron?"

"If I have a choice? No. But if I'm queen here then things are going to change, and I'll do whatever's necessary to stop anyone who gets in the way."

"Change, will they? And what does the Fate Maker say to this?"

I glanced over my shoulder, hoping not to see anyone following us. I highly doubted the Fate Maker would try something with the lord general right there, but then again, I was pretty sure that the wizard was completely insane, so who knew?

"I didn't ask his opinion."

"You're either exceptionally brave, my future queen," she said with a grudging smile, "or incredibly stupid. Let's hope it's the former."

Darinda clapped her hands, and the dryads seated around her shifted onto their knees, bending over so that their heads touched the ground, their hands outstretched, palms up in front of them.

White flowers bloomed from the other dryads' hands, and Darinda's began to sprout golden roses.

"Wow," I murmured.

Darinda lifted her head, and the sides of her mouth twitched upward for a moment before she carefully schooled her features. "Wow, indeed, Princess. Now is there anything I can do for you? Or did you simply wish to peer at some of your odder subjects?"

"I…" What should I say? If I were Darinda I would hate having some teenage girl showing up to dictate orders to me in my own forest. Heck, I hated the guy giving me orders inside my castle, and I hadn't been on the job nearly as long as Darinda had.

"Yes?" She raised a feathery, silver eyebrow at me.

"Would you mind if I spent some time with Mercedes today?"

"Mercedes? If the queen requests to spend her time with a dryad sapling, then who am I to refuse her?"

"Thank you," I said quietly.

Instead of waiting for Mercedes to respond, Darinda turned and clapped her hands once more. The clan of dryads rose off the ground and returned to the forest, Darinda following.

"Well, that was interesting." I grimaced as I watched them disappear into the shadows of the forest.

"She's been really nice to me," Mercedes said. I glanced over at her and raised an eyebrow. "But they've all been a bit jittery since they learned about a new Rose being brought through the book. They seem to think you showing up is a bad omen."

"Tell them to join the club," I said. "It seems like everyone's either freaking out or trying to find a way to use me to their advantage."

"Then we have to make sure that you're in control of the situation," Rhys chimed in. "Make sure that the advantage is still yours."

"That might be easier said than done," I said. "I'm not even supposed to be out here. The Fate Maker told me that if I left the palace grounds he'd have me dragged back in chains."

"Yeah, but I'd be the one holding the chains," Rhys said.

"And that makes it less dangerous for me?" I asked.

"No." He shook his head. "But the best thing we can do is figure out how to prepare you, and everyone else, for what the future might bring."

"And how do you propose we do that?" Mercedes asked.

"We make her a warrior queen," Winston said, a hint of mischief in his eyes.

"Precisely." Rhys turned to Mercedes. "We take your princess, and we forge her into a leader so fierce that even the Pleiades tremble in the face of her wrath."

I shivered at the intensity of his expression and tried to stay calm. Whatever he thought, I highly doubted that I'd ever be much of a warrior.

I could see Mercedes worrying—she knew I wasn't a warrior, too. It was like the day she'd accidentally set the science lab on fire, and we'd both been sent to the principal's office for it. We were in way over our heads, the look seemed to say, but at least we're in it together.

"So, Rhys?" Mercedes said, her voice overly friendly, almost perky as she tried to change the subject.

"Yes, sapling of the Dryad Order?"

"Who are you? And why do you keep calling me sapling? Only the other dryads have called me that, and my guess is, from the sword you're wearing, you're not a worshipper of the Tree of Life."

"I'm not, but that doesn't change the fact that you are a sapling, an honored novice of the Dryad Order, and I am Lord Sullivan, defender of Her Majesty's northern border and lord general of the Army of Nerissette."

"Oh, yeah." I nudged her shoulder. "Rhys has a thing for titles. He thinks everybody needs one."

"Because everyone has one," he said, "of some sort or another, even if it's just farmer or peasant or exalted mother, but both of you have distinguished titles. You should be proud of them."

"Yeah, well, blame it on being from Pennsylvania, but we're not really big on the pomp and circumstance."

"Ah yes, Americans. The accent should have been a tip-off."

"Americans?" Mercedes asked. "How did you know that? I told three other dryads that I was from America, and none of them knew where it was. They kept asking if it was one of the lands over the mountain. One thought it might be where fever dreams come from."

"Rhys is from our world. England, actually."

He nodded. "Brighton."

"Brighton?" she parroted.

"Like the princess just explained, it's in England. Anyway, I fell through the book about five years ago," Rhys said, "and ended up here, running an army of my very own."

"Crap, you've been here five years?" Mercedes asked. "Why?"

He led us out of the underbrush and started across the grass. I picked up my heavy skirts and trudged along after him. My best friend's shorter skirt didn't give her nearly as many problems—leaves were apparently more versatile than velvet.

"The same reason you're here," Rhys said. "My father bought the book at some shop in London when he went there for a business meeting, and then one day I opened it and *boom*, here I am."

"If your dad bought it, why didn't it pull him through?" I asked. "It would have made more sense to take a grown-up to lead the army."

"The book did take him," Rhys said, his jaw tightening and his eyes focused off into the distance. "When I was three."

"Wait, so one day he was just *gone*?" Mercedes asked.

"I never even knew he existed. One day he was there, and the next it was like I'd have a vague thought about Dad but everything except the word itself was sort of hazy. Mom never mentioned him, and I just sort of forgot he existed. Then I came here, and they explained it. He wasn't some hazy memory anymore; I could remember everything, like he'd never left."

"So, your father is here?" I asked. "He's been in Nerissette this entire time?"

"He was," Rhys said. "But he died fighting a troll. Then the Fate Maker's cat claimed that it was to clear the way for my own disappearance. She took me the next day."

"You never got to see him again?" Mercedes asked, uncharacteristic tears welling in her eyes.

"It wasn't like I would have had much to say to him," Rhys said stiffly. "We didn't even know each other. All I had were the memories of a three-year-old."

"That's horrible." She reached for his shoulder, but he jerked away from her.

"Anyway, we're here." He stopped and motioned to Winston. "They said at the aerie that you can manage your change now?"

"I can."

"Good. There's a small clearing." He pointed toward the trees. "You can change there, and when you're ready take off, Balmeer will join you in the air."

Winston nodded and then gave my hand a quick squeeze before he hurried off into the trees. Before he'd gone more than ten feet he had disappeared, swallowed by the dark shade around him.

"Will he be all right?" I kept staring at where Winston had gone.

"He'll be fine," Rhys said. "Now, come help me find a stick. You said you can fence. Let's see how good you are."

"What?"

"Well, what else do you want to do while they're hunting? We might as well see if you can actually use a sword. When the Time of Waiting ends you may need it."

"But I thought that was the army's job? I can fence a little bit, but you're the one with the soldiers."

"And my soldiers and I will do everything in our power to keep you safe," Rhys said. "There may be a chance, though, no matter how hard I, or my soldiers, or your friend the dragon tries, that you'll need to protect yourself."

"Do you think it will really come to that?" Mercedes asked.

"We have no idea what's coming for us," Rhys said. "It's better that we be safe rather than sorry. And if I were you, tomorrow on your nature walk with Darinda, I'd ask to learn a weapon. You never know when you might need it to guard yourself and your tree."

"I will," she said quietly. "She's already offered to have me trained on the bow, so I'll start taking lessons."

"Good." He nodded. "Now, you find two somewhat-straight sticks while I send Balmeer up to hunt, and we'll work on your fencing, Princess. Just in case."

"Okay." I started searching the ground around the clearing for branches that we could use as practice swords. "Rhys?"

"Yes?" He didn't meet my eyes, just held his arm up and let Balmeer begin to inch down toward his hand.

"I'm really sorry about your dad. Once this is all over, I want you to know, I'm going to find each and every one of us a way home. Anyone the book stole will have a way home."

I found a branch near the tree line and grabbed it. A few feet away was another one, a bit twisted in the center, but it would work.

"Why?" Rhys asked. "I already told you—there's nothing for me there. For any of us. I've been gone for five years, Princess. *Five years*. My mother has forgotten me, and no matter what the Fate Maker says, there's no way I can go back and just slot into that life again. Not after everything I've seen.

"I wouldn't even know where to find my mum anyway. It's been five years. Where would I go, Princess? Where would any of us go?" Rhys asked, his voice bitter. "And how would we explain what we've seen? Done?"

"I don't know," I said, feeling defeated. "I'm sorry that you feel you can't go home."

"My place is here."

Rhys clicked his tongue against his teeth, and Balmeer launched himself upward with a shriek, soaring into the air.

"Will he come back?" Mercedes asked, distracted by the large bird's takeoff.

"He always has before," Rhys said. "He's not easy to lose, much like your erstwhile prince."

"Oh, no." Not Jesse, I really didn't want to deal with *him* along with everything else today.

"Perhaps we'll leave fencing practice for another day? I don't feel like teaching him not to stab himself if I can avoid it. Besides, I think the less your crown prince knows, the better off we'll all be. Especially when it comes to your fighting abilities."

"What? You mean Jesse?" Mercedes dropped onto the grass and stretched her legs out in front of her, crossing her ankles.

I remembered how he'd supported the Fate Maker last night, how willing he'd been to justify the wizard's behavior. I definitely didn't want to take the chance of him telling the Fate Maker that Rhys had been training me for war.

I sat beside Mercedes and tried to look innocent. "Oh yes, Prince Jesse the Valiant and Brave."

Rhys sat beside us and then laid back, his arms crossed behind his head, like we were all just hanging out instead of skirting around the edges of an outright rebellion.

"How did he know we'd be here?" I asked.

"He's been following us," Rhys said. "I thought we'd managed to lose him when we came into the forest, but he should be coming into the clearing in three, two, one…"

"Allie," Jesse said, breaking through the underbrush, his face flushed and his voice faint as he gasped for air.

"Jesse." I tried to smile. "Hi."

"I've been looking for you since breakfast," Jesse said. "The Fate Maker said you were taking a day off. Why didn't you wait for me? We could have hung out in the palace. Instead of out here in the...wilderness."

"I thought you might want to hang out with Heidi, since she is your *girlfriend* and all."

"That, and we don't like you," Mercedes added under her breath.

"I told you last night." Jesse sat beside me and wrapped his arm around my shoulders, rubbing his hand along the length of my arm like he was trying to warm me up, or something equally strange. "Heidi and I aren't really a thing."

"Since when?" Mercedes asked, her eyes wide at the sight of Jesse caressing my upper arm.

Rhys coughed, his eyes twinkling with suppressed laughter.

"Since..." Jesse froze. "Well, we've never really been a *thing*. She thinks we are, though, and I didn't want to hurt her feelings."

"Right." Rhys didn't bother to hide the scorn in his voice. "How very gallant of you. Princess Allie is lucky to have such a man willing to be her knight devoted. I don't know why she'd have chosen to spend time with a dragon changeling instead."

"You mean Winston?" Jesse asked.

There was a loud *crack* and then the harsh crackle of leaves, like we were trapped in a windstorm. Then a large black dragon appeared above the trees, its wings beating steadily until it reached the roc flying above.

I gasped. "Is that... There's no way that's..."

"The guy who's going to shish-kebab Prince Charming over here?" Mercedes asked.

"He's amazing," I said, my eyes fixed on him. "I can't believe it."

"He's all right, I guess," Jesse said from beside me. "If you like flying lizards."

"I think we can definitely say that some people are into that," Mercedes said. I would've smacked her if I hadn't been so awed.

Rhys chuckled. "He will be a magnificent warrior."

"He's not that great," Jesse said. "I mean, it's not like I wouldn't be just as great if the Fate Maker had turned me into a dragon."

"I wonder why he didn't, then?" Rhys asked dryly.

"Because…" Jesse lifted his chin and straightened his shoulders, almost like he were trying to appear kingly or something. "Because I'm better suited to ruling."

"Ruling?" Mercedes asked. "What makes you think you're going to rule anything?"

"Well, I'm Allie's crown prince. Once she's crowned queen they'll name me king."

"No, you'll still be a prince," Rhys said.

"What?" Jesse asked.

"The Golden Rose of Nerissette is a female monarchy. Only the women rule. Allie will become Golden Rose, and you'll still be Crown Prince Jesse."

"But I'll be her consort. That makes me king." Jesse looked between me and Rhys. "Doesn't it?"

"Wrong," Rhys said. "You're nothing but an accessory. Like a pair of earrings."

"Or a snack she keeps in her purse to feed her dragon,"

Mercedes said.

"No way." Jesse moved his mouth, but no sound came out. "But when I spoke with the Fate Maker this morning he said I was essential to the ruling of the kingdom. I'm not just some…"

"I'm still going with snack," Mercedes said. "A snack for a dragon who I bet is getting really hungry."

He glared at her, his eyes blazing, and his grip on my shoulder tightened. "When I'm king I'll show you who's the dragon snack."

"Like Rhys just told you," Mercedes snapped, "you're never going to be king of anything."

"You don't realize how wrong you are," he argued. "Once we've rededicated Nerissette to the will of Fate—"

"So." I pushed Jesse's arm off my shoulder and desperately tried to come up with some way to change the subject before the two of them started hitting each other. "Why didn't you hang out with Heidi today? Even if you aren't a thing, you two *are* still friends."

"Hardly," he spat. Jesse wrapped his arm back around my shoulders, and I scooted away from him again, this time putting more space between us. "She's a maid."

"But last night you said—"

A high-pitched wail interrupted as a flock of dark birds flew overhead. Balmeer stopped circling and dropped straight down, the wailing growing louder until he exploded into the middle of the pack of birds, scattering them around him.

Winston dodged after a few of the birds that had managed to escape Balmeer and began to chase after them like they were a ball that had gone out of play during a basketball game.

"What's he doing?" Mercedes asked, as Winston headed

farther away to play his little game of cat-and-mouse.

"Following his instincts," Rhys said. "He's a dragon now. He sees a bird and thinks food."

Balmeer shrieked once more, and I could see something clutched in each of his claws. The roc swooped low and dropped two carcasses onto the ground at Rhys's feet.

"Good boy," Rhys said when the bird landed. Balmeer chattered at him once and then took one dead bird across the clearing and began to eat.

I curled up my nose.

"Don't get fussy, Princess," Rhys said. "There's no difference between the meat Balmeer eats and what they serve you from the kitchens."

The roc perked his head up at the sound of his own name and flew over to look at me. When he reached Rhys's hip he landed and stalked toward me, his red eyes never breaking contact with mine.

I bowed my head before him, and the bird bowed low in return. He launched himself up in a short hop to grab the second bird he'd killed and brought it back to me. He laid it next to my hand and dropped his head down to rest next to my fingers.

Rhys looked as stunned as I felt—which wasn't any help. I lifted my hand and began to gently run my hand down the roc's silky, red feathers. Balmeer began to make a cooing sound and nested down beside me.

"It seems, Princess, that Balmeer is quite taken with you. He's even shared his kill."

"Is that a big deal?" I asked.

"A very big deal," he said. "It took three years for Balmeer to share a kill with me, and I raised him from the time he was very young, still a nestling in fact."

"You're kidding…"

"No. That may be why Fate turned your friend into a dragon. If you're good with animals, that ability could sway some of the other races to fight for the Golden Rose and not against it."

"What do you mean?" Jesse asked. "Are you saying that Winston might fight with the enemy if we go to war? He might be our competition?"

"Winston would never fight against us," Mercedes said. "I don't care if he is a gigantic black fire-breather, he's our friend first."

"The dragons have never sided with any faction," Rhys said. "They have always remained outside the wars of man. But now? With you all here? Maybe they'll change their mind and fight beside us when the time comes."

"There's no maybe about it," Mercedes said. "Winston would never do anything to hurt Allie."

"When the time comes he might not have a choice. The dragons will choose their side or choose to stay away. Either way he'll be forced to live with their choice."

"You don't know Winston then," Mercedes said, "because I'm telling you right now, there's no force in this world or any other that will keep him away from Allie if she's in danger."

Chapter Fifteen

I stepped out of the dining room that night, alone, and tried to ignore the sound of the bickering nobles behind me. Throughout the whole meal they'd fought over who had owned what and how I should settle land disputes for places I'd never even heard of. Now I had a migraine, and the half of my mind that wasn't throbbing was contemplating just giving their lands to other people. People who wouldn't spend all of dinner arguing.

"You know that I have a legitimate claim to the Leavenwald." Lady Arianne's voice echoed through the hall.

"The lands of the Leavenwald belong to the woodsmen. They are our forests," Sir John shot back.

"Allie!" Jesse was hurrying after me. "Wait up."

I tried to smile but couldn't manage it with the pounding in my head.

"I was thinking that maybe we could hang out."

How to get away from him without being mean was the

only thing on my mind. I didn't want to be that girl—the one who stomped on guys like it was nothing. Then again, I was seriously starting to not care, because really, how much more obvious did it have to be? "I really can't, Jesse. I've got this awful headache. Maybe you and Heidi could go explore instead?"

"That's okay." He stepped back. "Maybe we could ask the Fate Maker if he could help you. I'm sure he's got a magical equivalent of Tylenol or something."

"Thanks, but I think I'm just going to go to bed. Maybe I'll stop by the library and get something to try to read."

He stopped. "A book. Are you sure?"

"Yeah, I'm sure. But I'll see you tomorrow."

"I guess." He shrugged. "I hope your head feels better."

"Great. Thanks. So I'm going to go." I jerked my thumb over my shoulder toward where I'd been told the library was. "Get a book."

"Okay." He started toward the stairs.

I stepped back away from him and waited for him to start up the stairs.

"Your Majesty?"

I looked up to see Rhys standing in the doorway to the dining room, his arms crossed over his chest and an amused grin on his face.

"What?"

"You should tell him."

"Tell him what?"

"That you're not into him."

"I've been trying. I haven't come out and said it but, well, you'd think he'd get the hint. It's not like I'm being vague about it or anything."

"Guys like him"—Rhys jerked his head backward, toward the stairs Jesse had gone up—"they don't take hints. You're going to have to tell him, otherwise a certain dragon might set him on fire for messing with his girl."

"I'm not Winston's girl."

"Aren't you?"

"We're just friends."

"Does he know that?"

"Of course he knows that," I huffed. "He doesn't think of me even as a girl. I'm just his friend Allie, who happens to use a different locker room in gym class."

"Right." Rhys nodded. "You want to double-check that particular assumption?"

"You want me to go ask Winston if he likes me? What are we? Ten-year-olds playing kiss and chase on the playground?"

"Possibly. Do you think the dryad would let me chase her?"

"Mercedes?" I raised my eyebrow.

His smile grew. "Come on. Let's go find out."

"What?" I asked as he held a hand out to me. "If Mercedes will let you kiss her? I don't want to see that. If you want to kiss my best friend, you need to do that in private."

"I meant about the dragon you're leading on."

"I'm not leading him anywhere."

"Whatever. There's something I want to show you."

"Rhys, not tonight." I shook my head. "I wasn't lying when I told Jesse I had a headache."

"Too bad. Winston and Mercedes are waiting for us in the courtyard. So come on."

"Where are we going?"

"You'll see." He stepped farther into the hallway and looked around. "We'll need to hurry, though."

He pressed on one of the wall panels. It slid back to reveal a dark hallway beyond.

"What's that?" I asked.

"Servants' passage. Now, come on already before someone sees."

"Where are we going?" I asked again.

"To show you your kingdom." He led me into the dark passage, and I heard the click of the door sliding closed behind us. He ran his hand along the length of the wall, and there was a crackle as torches lit themselves, illuminating our way.

"But the Fate Maker has forbidden me to leave the palace grounds, remember?"

"That didn't stop you this morning. Besides, I didn't plan on telling him," Rhys said. "He's in his tower, and we're hitching a ride into your capital city with the soldiers going to the fort."

"How will we get back?"

"The grocer's wagon in the morning. We have to meet him an hour before dawn, and he'll sneak us back in with the vegetables for tomorrow's feast."

"This is insane." I shook my head. "If we get caught we'll all be in big trouble."

"You're the crown princess. The future queen of Nerissette. What are they going to do? Ground you?"

"That's—" He had a point. The Fate Maker could yell. And he could threaten me. But what could he really do? Besides torture and kill me himself?

I sighed. "Fine." I followed him to the door at the far end of the passage.

"You'll need to wear this." He handed me a rough, brown

woolen cloak when we reached the door. "We don't want people to see your dress and start to talk."

"I thought we didn't care if anyone found out."

"We don't. That doesn't mean I want to deal with a rioting crowd, desperate to get close to their future queen."

I slipped the cloak on and let him pull the hood up over my head.

"Good." He twisted the fabric closed over the front of my dress. "Just keep your head down, and no one will even notice you. You're just another girl out and about in the capital city at night."

"Right. Just a girl out for a walk in the city of Neris."

"Something like that."

"Allie." Winston hurried forward and then glanced behind me as the door to the servants' passage closed. "You ready?"

"Yeah." I smiled and hoped I didn't sound too nervous. "Let's go see my new kingdom."

"Come on," Rhys said, motioning toward a wagon full of men. "Someone will notice if the soldiers are late."

"All right, we're coming." I hurried over to the large wooden wagon. One of the soldiers held his hand out to Rhys and helped him up, then hoisted Mercedes up, as well. Winston took the man's hand next and let himself be pulled inside before turning to me.

"Allie?" He knelt and held both hands out toward me. Instead of taking my hands in his, he wrapped his arms around my waist and lifted as I jumped, helping me hop into the wagon.

"Your Majesty," various men mumbled as Winston stood and then helped me inside the wagon.

"Your Majesty." A man on the ground caught my eyes

with his own dark ones and then leaned closer. "Be careful tonight."

"I will," I said.

He stepped back and slammed the door of the wagon closed with a dull *thunk*.

Winston led me to a seat, and I watched the men in their long tunics, each of them wearing a chest plate of gleaming metal like a bulletproof vest.

"Hello." I smiled but none of them met my eyes.

Okay. This was awkward.

The carriage lurched and then began to roll down the hill. No one said anything, and I looked over to see that Mercedes and Rhys were holding hands. That was fast. An arm wrapped around my shoulders then, and I had to fight the urge to lean into Winston.

Five minutes later the silent carriage stopped with a sudden jerk, and I looked up at the men who were all so busy not meeting my eyes. "You'll want to stay to the shadows," a gruff-sounding man near the back said.

"Okay." My voice high and reedy from nerves. "Thank you."

"Let us get out first and then slip away. No one will notice you in the crowds," the man added. "You'll be fine."

"Crowds?" I asked.

"Aye, the crowds near the fort. It's a harvest night, so there's bound to be a crowd. Stay back. Don't make yourself known and you'll be safe."

The door creaked open, and I pressed myself against the wall of the wagon. The soldiers poured out of the door, and I felt Rhys's hand on my shoulder, helping me slide toward the back as they blocked the view from the entrance.

We huddled together in the shadows as the last man

descended, and then the door slammed closed behind him.

"Let me go first." Rhys stood and made his way to the door, ducking underneath the low ceiling. He opened the door a crack and peeked out before he pushed it open wider.

"Come on." He slipped out of the wagon and landed on the ground below. "Hurry. No one's watching."

Winston followed him out, his hand in mine, and then he let go of me as he jumped down.

"Ready?" Mercedes asked.

"Why not?" I stepped out of the door and froze. The night was burning. Bonfires climbed into the dark sky around the wooden walls of the fort we were in, and the sheer noise of what must've been a thousand people all crowded into one place was astounding.

"Allie." Winston held his hands out to me, and I took them, letting him help me out.

Rhys grabbed Mercedes, and we all scurried away from the wagon, making for the shadows near the fort walls.

"It's best if we get out of here," Rhys said. "Make our way into the city."

"What's going on?" I asked.

A woman stumbled past us, her eyes sunken in her head and breath reeking. "Hey, there." She smiled and bowed elaborately in front of us. "If it's not one of the wizard's pets. His boy general."

"We've got no money and nothing to offer you," Rhys said. "We don't want trouble."

"Then you're in the wrong city," she laughed. "Trouble made her home here a long time ago."

Rhys backed away from her. "Come on. Let's get into the city. You don't need to see this."

"What is it?" I asked.

"A harvesting."

"What's that?"

"The hordes," Rhys said. "They all come in from the mountains once a month. They come to take their tribute."

"What do they want?"

"Food. Money. Weapons." Rhys urged us toward a large, open drawbridge. "They take what they like, and we must give it to them."

"What happens if you don't?"

"Then we die."

"No one told me anything about a harvesting," I said.

"Tell you what? That the wizards and their allies are stripping the land dry? Why would the Fate Maker tell you that? Or Esmeralda? You would just try to stop them."

"Wait, what?" I shook my head. It couldn't be.

"He's a wizard, and she's his partner," Rhys explained. "They are in charge of the harvesting. *He's* the one who came up with it in the first place."

"But why would they do something like this?" I asked.

"The giants must be fed, and the trolls must have workers for their mines. If we don't comply then they will join forces with the Army of Bathune to attack us, and the Fate Maker has no stomach for a war that involves more than conjuring tricks. Better for the wizards to take the gold from the monsters and leave the common folk to suffer."

"Miss. Miss." A faint voice called out, and I looked down to see a small boy with dirt-smudged cheeks and ragged clothes tugging at the side of my cloak. "Food, miss? Drink? Grilled griffin on a stick?"

"I'm fine."

"Servants then? I'll take you to find a new maid. Come along, miss."

"The lady is fine." Rhys spoke, and the boy stepped back. "But you should be home."

"You must need a servant, miss. A boy to water the flowers? Wash your plates? I'm a hard worker. I'll carry boxes and follow behind you when you go into the plaza to shop for pretty things."

"The lady isn't interested," Rhys said firmly.

"Please, miss."

"You there." A man stood a few feet away from us, pointing. "Are you taking him or not? Seven gold pieces."

I looked between him and the boy. "I don't have any money."

"Right then. Back to the pen with you, boy."

"Please…" The boy grabbed my cloak, but the man had snatched him up by the scruff of his neck and pulled him away before he could get a decent grip on me.

"Where is that man taking him?" I asked.

"Back to the pens," Rhys said quietly, not meeting my eyes. "He'll be sold to the giants."

"But why would giants want a little boy?" Mercedes asked as Winston tightened his grip on my shoulders.

"Because they eat children," Rhys said. "They eat them raw."

I swallowed, fighting down the bile rising in my throat.

"Come on," Rhys said. "Let's get you out of here."

He pushed us through the crowd, past men in cages and blue-skinned creatures with long, wicked swords that guarded them. "Men for the trolls' diamond mines," Rhys said as we passed.

"Hurry up," Winston said as we walked through the crowd.

Before I could get a hold of myself, we were on the drawbridge and out of the fort.

"Welcome to your new home, Princess," Rhys said, his words dripping with cynicism. He didn't stop, though, and led us down a dark street, away from the fort and farther into the city.

In the darkness I could hear the scrape of scampering feet, and everywhere I looked were dirty people standing on the street, their hungry eyes staring at us.

"In case you were wondering," he said when we reached the square in front of the Hall of the Pleiades. I watched as people huddled before small fires, hawkers moving around them, and music playing as small groups of people danced or sang.

"In case I was wondering what?" I asked.

"These are the people you're meant to be saving. It's for them that the Time of Waiting must come to an end."

"What am I supposed to do?" I asked.

"Save them," Rhys said. "Save us all."

"But I don't know how."

"When the time comes, you will."

Chapter Sixteen

I could still hear the screaming. The trolls and the giants had breached the fort at the same time we'd come back from touring the city. The giants had filled the courtyard. Fifteen feet tall, they'd towered over the squat buildings, their knuckles scraping against the ground.

The children had seen them and screamed. Wails of fear like I'd never heard before. They'd known what was coming. Then the men and the women who'd been caged for the troll hordes had begun to weep and pounded against the bars of their own prisons, fighting to save themselves and the children, but no one had helped them. No one had even moved.

We'd all just kneeled, our heads bowed and our eyes fixed on the ground as both sets of cages had been loaded into enormous wagons and the creatures took them away.

It had been three days since Rhys had taken me into Neris, and every night I'd had nightmares about it. Every time I closed my eyes I could see the people, begging, and there I'd knelt, the girl who was supposed to save them all, staring at the dirt as they were taken away. I'd wanted to stop them, but I remembered Rhys's voice in my ear that night.

"There are four of us and hundreds of them. If you try to stop them now then you'll die, and they'll still be taken. It's better to wait. Wait until we have an army behind us, and then we can kill them all."

"Allie?" I heard Winston's soft voice and looked up from the book I hadn't been reading to see him standing in the doorway to the library. We hadn't seen each other since we'd gotten back to the castle that disturbing morning as he'd been swept away by Ardere for lessons.

I smiled in spite of myself. "What are you doing here? I thought you were supposed to be training."

"We're taking a break, and I thought I'd come check on you." Winston came into the room and sat down across from me. "You look tired."

"I haven't been sleeping well," I said.

"Neither have I," he admitted.

"I keep hearing them, but in my dream, when I look up, it isn't them in that cage, it's us. They're loading us into cages and putting us in wagons so they can take us away and eat us."

"Allie."

"I'm supposed to be here to save them. Esmeralda said when she brought us here that I was meant to save this world from Fate, so that must mean that's what I'm here for. I should have saved them."

"What were you supposed to do?" Winston asked. "What were you, with just me and Mercedes and Rhys, supposed to do?"

"I don't know," I said. "But I should have done something.

I can't let this continue."

"Then what are you going to do?" Winston asked.

"I want to use the mirror."

"Why?"

I held a book up. "I've been reading about it. The Mirror of Nerissette is meant to allow me to touch the dreams of the waking world. I can use it."

"For what? To see what someone else is dreaming?"

"I don't know!" I pushed my chair back and stood. "All I know is that I've got to do something, and that's the only idea there is. Maybe I could get inside the head of a general or something, and they could tell me how to defeat an army of trolls and giants."

"Or they could give you a banana nut muffin and tell you to sing 'Ten Little Indians.' Even if you can get into someone else's head, then all you'll be is a whacked-out dream they probably won't remember the next day. Besides, I can guarantee you that the army doesn't have a plan for giants and trolls."

"Then what do you think I should do?"

"Once the crown is on your head, you are the law in Nerissette. Whatever you say goes. So ban the harvest."

"If I ban the harvest then the trolls and the giants will march to war against the people. We'll be in the same place they were when they set the harvest up in the first place. We need some other solution that doesn't involve violence."

"But you have an army," Winston said. "Ban the harvest and then, if the trolls and giants come against you, we fight them."

"And what if we lose? What if you're killed? Or Mercedes? Or Rhys?"

"It's better than the alternative," he said. "It's better than going to bed every night hearing those screams. I'd rather die than watch that happen again, Allie."

"So you're willing to die for people you don't even know?"

"Aren't you? Allie, if we don't stop it when you become queen, then we're no better than the Fate Maker and the wizards who started this."

"I know. I don't want to die, okay? When we were kneeling in that dirt, do you know what I was thinking? I was thinking, 'Please don't see me. Don't realize I'm here because if you see me you might take me, and I don't want to die.'"

"I don't want to die, either," Winston said. "But this is bigger than we are. Look, I have to go. I told Ardere I'd only be a few minutes, and if I don't get out there they'll send someone to check on me."

"Okay." I knotted my hands in the fabric of my skirt and tried not to let him see that I was trembling.

He stood and wrapped his arms around me, and I could feel his hands shaking against my spine. "We'll figure something out, together. Me and you. We'll find some way to stop this."

"Win?" I dropped my head against his shoulder. "I want to go home."

"I know." He let go of me then and pressed a kiss against my forehead. "One day, when this is all over, we'll find a way home. I promise."

Before I could say anything, he turned and fled the room. I watched as he disappeared from sight, then bit my lower lip as I thought about the feel of his lips against my skin.

Maybe I wasn't the only one who thought about being more than friends. A small hope flared in my chest.

"Quit being stupid, Munroe," I said to the empty room.

"There are more important things to worry about right now than boys. You're about to become queen, and there are giants eating your future subjects."

I turned to the tall pedestal in the middle of the library and peered down at the map trapped underneath its glass. I ran my finger along the labels, trying to find one that might be related to trolls or warfare or something useful.

"Where would I find a book that will tell me how to defeat giants and trolls and other scary monsters?" I asked.

The map hummed, its edges glowing gold, and a bright white dot appeared on one of the sections. ROYAL BIOGRAPHIES, the label read.

"Anything else you can tell me?" I tried not to let it see that I was impressed by the fact that it was magic. After all, I was sort of getting used to the fact that everything here had some trick to it.

The map flickered again, and the light glowed brighter.

"How about a title? Or a call number?"

The spot just continued to glow. YOU ARE HERE appeared on the map in black cursive script.

A bright golden trail burned between the two spots, like the line on a GPS.

"Fine. Whatever. I'll go to Royal Biographies. But if there's nothing about trolls there I'm coming back here, and I'm going to rearrange all the books so that you don't know how to find a single thing. You hear me? I will completely disorganize you."

The map hummed in response.

I started along the path it had shown me, and before I reached the stacks, a faint golden light glowed from one of the shelves. When I reached Royal Biographies I saw that the light was coming from a small white leather book crammed between two larger books.

I read the title on the first book. *Dedasava, Fourth Great Rose—A Critical Evaluation of Her Rule.* The book on the other side of the glowing one was *Fesir and the Rose.* The one that was glowing didn't have a title on its spine.

"What are you about, then? Glinda the Great Goblin Slayer?" I picked the book up and started back to the table I'd been sitting at.

When I got there I set the book down and began to read the familiar, messy scrawl across its pages. I'd seen it before, but I wasn't sure where. But I knew I'd seen it.

We came home today from the Palace of Night. I always hate it there. Bathune is such a dreary place. The Land of Hopeless Dreams. I can never sleep when we go to stay there. I can hear them in the night. The monsters in the trees. The lizards they call dragons, slinking along the stones of the palace outside.

"Well, duh," I said under my breath. "Bathune is the Land of Nightmares. It's not supposed to be nice."

Bav likes it there, though. She told Mother that when she becomes Rose that's where she'll make her capital because the Crystal Palace is too boring. And if we moved the royal family to the Palace of Night then we could have fun watching the Court of the Silver Thorn try to adjust with all the monsters around. I don't know what I'll do if she forces us to live there once Mother dies.

"This Bav sounds like a real winner. Wonder if she's the new queen of Bathune's mother? Like mother like daughter." I turned to the next page.

There wasn't much there. The writer, whoever she was,

mainly rambled about balls and dresses and the gossip of the palace. Whoever she was she'd constantly complained about some boy named Piotr who was constantly following her around and asking her out while she was busy making eyes at someone named John.

"Okay," I said as I flipped past more dense writing about the loveliness that was John. "Let's get to the important stuff. What can you tell me about how to defeat an army of trolls?"

I turned a few more pages and felt something thick and smooth against my fingertips. It slid along the page, and I found myself holding a small, glossy piece of paper with a group of women staring out at me.

My breath caught. The youngest-looking of the women was my mom. I'd suspected it but to actually see her was something else. She looked so young. So alive. So different than the last time I'd seen her in her hospital bed. I flipped the card over and stared at the same scrawl from the diary.

Me, Mom, and Bav. Sixteenth birthday.

I dropped the card onto the desk and turned to the front of the book. Mom had always written her name in her books. I'd picked on her for it when I was a kid because she used to tell me not to write in my books or I'd ruin them.

Preethana.

The same script I'd seen in all of her old books, except they'd read "Ana Munroe." My mother had been the Golden Rose, and that meant Bav was Queen Bavasama, my aunt. The Empress of Bathune, the Land of Nightmares.

I picked up the book again and flipped to the last page with writing on it, halfway through the book. It was dated six months before I was born. Six months. That meant that whoever my father was…he'd been from here. From

Nerissette.

I don't know what to do. The war is coming, and there is no stopping it. Piotr rules in my place. The court ignores me, and when I try to speak against him…

There were several lines scratched out.

I cannot risk staying. I must hope that the prophecies are true, and the relics will work so I can pass through the mirror and that the World of Dreams can survive until I'm strong enough to return. If the trolls find me before I can escape, I'll be no better than those people that Bavasama has sent them to steal. If she could arrange for my capture she'd light the fires for her pet giants to cook me on herself. So much for sisterly love.

"Oh, Mom." I closed the book and stared at it.

"Your Majesty?" Esmeralda said.

I turned toward her, rage boiling up in the pit of my stomach. "You knew. You've always known. I suspected, but you *knew* and you didn't tell me."

"Yes." The cat didn't take her eyes from mine. "I knew. I'm the one who convinced her to go through the mirror."

"Why?"

"To save you. Now come with me. There's something I'd like to show you."

"No. Whatever it is doesn't change anything. You exiled my mother from her home, just like you stole me from mine."

"I want you to see her portrait. The one I tried to distract you from that first day. The one I've protected all these years."

"I don't want to see it."

"Your Majesty—"

"My mother was the Golden Rose when the harvesting began, wasn't she? She was in charge when you started selling our people to be eaten. She left them to die."

"What do you know about the harvesting?"

"Never mind what I know about it," I said through gritted teeth. "Tell me the truth."

"Your mother had just been crowned when the trolls came. Her mother, your grandmother, had died the month before. When she died, she split the kingdom."

"Why?"

"She had two daughters. So she gave your mother, her heir, the Rose Crown and the throne of Nerissette. She gave her other daughter, your aunt Bavasama, the tiny province of Bathune."

"Well, good for her. Now how did the trolls and the giants get involved?"

"The trolls came when the old queen died. They brought the giants with them and demanded men and children. If we didn't give in they'd have killed us and taken what they wanted anyway."

"So you just handed over your children? No, not your children. Other people's children. Poor children."

"Your mother didn't want a war. Now please, come with me. Let me show you her portrait, and her mother's, and all of the other Golden Roses'. I'll tell you stories about them, wonderful stories."

"I don't want to hear fairy tales. My entire life has been nothing but a fairy tale. All of it. Lies to keep me stupid, to keep me from paying attention and finding out the truth. I'm being crowned queen in a matter of days, and everything I know about the country I'm meant to rule is lies. Everything." I stalked past her, and when I reached the hallway, I broke into a run for the back garden. I needed to be somewhere, anywhere, that wasn't here.

Chapter Seventeen

I came down the stairs carefully the next night, trying my best not to trip over my heavy skirts as we made our way toward the ballroom where the first of the balls to start my coronation was about to begin.

A small party, they'd called it. A welcome home party/ball thing, for everyone to wish me well before the coronation ceremonies began. You'd think it would have been fifty people at most for that kind of gathering. But no, according to Timbago, they'd only invited the five hundred most important people in Nerissette. Obviously someone had a different idea than I did about what a small party was.

"Are you ready, Your Majesty?" the Fate Maker asked.

"I'll have to be, won't I?" I stepped down into the foyer and stared up at him. "There's no going back now."

"No. There's not."

"Then let's get this over with. Or is there something else I need to know before I go in?" I asked. "Something besides the absolute *nothing* you've taught me since I arrived?"

"Esmeralda told me that you've spent the past several days in the library, reading all about Nerissette. She even said that you could now name all the regions."

"I could do that when I was a child," I said. "What I need to know is how to be a queen, remember?"

"Like I told you that first morning," the Fate Maker said. "All you need to know is that the only things that should come out of your mouth are things I tell you to say."

"And what about my powers?" I asked. "When will I learn to use them?"

"What powers?"

"My powers. Everyone has powers. Winston can turn into a dragon, and Mercedes is a dryad. What about my magic? You promised to teach me how to use it, and we haven't even started."

"I only said that to make Esmeralda happy." The Fate Maker narrowed his eyes at me. "You don't need powers."

"Why not?"

"Does Rhys have powers? Is he magical? No. Fate blessed him with a strong arm to hold a sword. And Prince Jesse? Does he have a power? No. He's nothing more than a pretty head to put a crown on."

"I'm not Rhys or Jesse."

"No, you're a doll that Fate and I have sat upon the throne. There's no reason to teach you magic. You're just a child. Besides, why would you even need to use the relics?"

"The relics?"

"Never mind. All you need to know is that your fate is to sit on a throne and do what people smarter than you say. As long as you never forget that, there's nothing else you ever need to learn. Now, come along."

He wrapped my arm around his biceps and marched me toward the ballroom. "And remember, Your Majesty, step one foot out of line and the maid becomes a practice dummy. I might change your crown prince along with her, so the army's got a matching set."

"Where is Jesse?" I asked. "You've had him bring me to dinner every night since we got here. Why not tonight?"

"He escorts you because he's your crown prince. That's his role."

"So why isn't he doing it tonight?"

"I thought I would take you myself for a change," the Fate Maker said. "But if I'd known you and the crown prince had grown so close I would have asked him to meet us."

"We're not."

"You're not what?"

"Close. He's just a guy. I don't want to date him."

"Don't you?" The Fate Maker raised an eyebrow at me. "Would your maid agree with that?"

I bit my lower lip and thought about the way Jesse had avoided Heidi all week long, not even trying to be subtle about running in the opposite direction of his ex-girlfriend as he chased me around the palace. "Probably not."

"Even if he's not someone you wish to date, he does serve his purpose."

"What's that?"

"He's an excellent hostage."

"You don't need a hostage." I raised my chin as I glared at him. "I'm not going anywhere."

"Then let's say he's here to ensure your good behavior."

I gritted my teeth and didn't say anything.

The Fate Maker gave me a bright smile, and my stomach burned at the sight of his self-satisfied glee. He was like every one of those bullies who thought they had gotten one over on someone by knocking their books out of their hands or making fun of the fact that they'd done well in school.

"Come along," the Fate Maker said, unconcerned about the rage boiling through me, and turned back to the door. "Chin up, big smile on your face, and let's both pretend that this is exactly what we want to be doing with our evening."

I plastered on a smile and knew it looked more like a grimace when he glanced over at me and his own smile dimmed a bit. "Well, I guess we'll have to make do with what we've got."

I stayed silent as he led me toward the ballroom and nodded toward Timbago, who was waiting to open the doors and announce my grand entrance. The goblin nodded in return and then caught my eye, giving me a shy smile. I smiled back, more naturally this time, as the goblin waved his fingers at the heavy, carved doors, and they began to slowly creak open.

"There's no backing out now," the Fate Maker said as the doors parted, and I could see a crowd of hundreds all stopped, mid-movement, staring at us.

"This is something," I said quietly. "I'll give you that."

Timbago stepped through the doors in front of us and clapped his hands together. "Lords and ladies, graces, peoples of Nerissette." The goblin's voice echoed as people hurried to either side of the room, leaving me with a wide aisle between them, a long, empty corridor between me and the throne.

The room fell silent as everyone turned their attention to me. I lifted my head and tried not to look like I was about to cry. I saw Winston near the throne with a group of large, muscle-bound men, and my heart beat harder as his dark eyes met mine, that fluttery feeling starting in my stomach like it always did when he was around.

"Her Gloriousness, the Crown Princess Alicia Wilhelmina Munroe, first of her gracious name and future Golden Rose of Nerissette. Kneel, all of ye in attendance, and show honor at her presence."

The words hung in silence for a second, and then everyone began to kneel, slowly. Women spread their skirts out across the floor in giant puddles around their bodies and curtsied low. The men littered around the room tucked their swords behind their backs as they put their hands on the floor and knelt forward, their heads touching the white marble they'd been walking across just a moment before.

Breathless, I spotted my best friend among a group of women. Their heads touched the floor, too, and their hands were held up in front of them, filled with flowers.

I looked back to Winston and found him kneeling, his head bowed but his back straight, one knee up like a medieval warrior. His hands were crossed in front of him, and he lifted his head slightly to wink at me.

"Men!" Rhys said, his voice a barking command. "To arms!"

Several guardsmen in brilliant red coats and black pants came forward from the sides of the room and made a barrier between the people and me. Once they had lined the man-made aisle, each of them pulled out a sword and lifted it high in the air. The sword points touched above my head, making an archway for me to walk under.

"Come along," the Fate Maker whispered in my ear. He led me forward, his head held high as we walked along a path of swords toward the ornate silver chair in the center of the dais. Beside it was a smaller, less ornate wooden throne, with a plain black high-backed chair next to that one.

"What's with all the chairs?" I asked.

"You can't sit on the throne until you actually have the crown on your head," the Fate Maker said quietly.

"So where am I suppose to sit, then?"

"On the Bower of the Dryads until you've been crowned, and then it will be passed along to your consort, until such a time as the next crown princess is chosen to take that place."

"So I'm taking your spot, is what you're saying?" I couldn't help the way my smile grew.

"Just because the people demand a Rose on the throne," he said as he led me up the stairs to where Rhys was standing, his sword drawn, "doesn't mean you have any power or that you ever will. No matter what you and your toy general might think."

The Fate Maker stepped away from the group of thrones, his eyes locked on mine, and I swallowed. Whatever he had planned, he seemed sure that there was no way that I could use the army to stop him. I couldn't help but wonder if he was right. Could we really take on the giants and trolls?

Rhys stepped forward, his eyes fixed on mine, and I could see my fear reflected in his gaze. If we weren't very careful—and very lucky—there was a good chance that soon most of the people in this room would die—fighting for either me or the Fate Maker.

"Your Majesty." Rhys dropped to one knee in front of me and held his sword up for me to take. "I pledge my loyalty and that of my men to defend you and your throne until the last breath leaves my body."

"Thank you." I clenched my hands in my skirt and tried not to let the Fate Maker see how much they were shaking. I didn't care how powerful he was, Winston was right. I couldn't be a queen who let things like the harvesting continue.

"You will be a truly amazing queen." Rhys looked up at me again and smiled, all the fear I'd seen a moment before hidden again. "And the evil amongst us will tremble in the face of your judgment, for we will be swift and ruthless in your name."

The Fate Maker sucked in a breath beside me, and I felt him stiffen as Rhys stood, still smiling.

Rhys sheathed his sword and bowed his head. "My future queen."

He stepped to the side then, so that I was facing the rest of the ballroom, and I glanced over to see Winston staring at me, his eyes dark. He inclined his head toward me, and I nodded back, stiffly, trying to keep my nerve.

"Soldiers, nobles, peoples of all the realms and corners of this land," Timbago began again. "I give you the crown princess. Long may she reign."

Everyone stood and the soldiers all dropped their swords back into their sheaths and turned to face us, their hands resting on the hilts, mirroring Rhys's stance.

The people roared back so loudly that the windows rattled.

Once I took my seat and Rhys moved to the side of the dais, the Fate Maker sat beside me in an even more uncomfortable-looking chair. He shifted irritably, smoothing the folds of his coal-black robe around him.

"Yes. Yes, let them all cheer and dance at the idea of a hundred years under a Golden Rose," he mumbled. "Nothing will ever really change. No matter who sits on the throne. And everyone here knows it."

"Says who? The Time of Waiting will be over soon. Maybe once the new age has come, we'll all have a brighter future. One where people can choose their own fate."

"Don't flatter yourself," he said with a sneer. "You can't beat Fate."

"Really? I wonder how many of these men would choose to fight for me if we asked? How many would go to war against you if they thought it would give them the chance to decide their own future?"

"Not nearly enough to make a difference."

"We may have to see about that." I turned back to my people and made a show of ignoring him.

Timbago walked slowly up the aisle, a large box floating behind him, and stepped onto the dais beside me. "Your Majesty."

"Timbago."

He didn't say anything, simply waved his hands over the box, and the lid opened slowly. "The crown jewels of Nerissette. The first of many gifts from the people of your realms."

"I don't have anything for them," I said quietly.

"You are queen, and that is gift enough for your subjects."

"That seems like a really crappy gift."

"I think you may be surprised. Now, are you ready?" Timbago asked.

"I doubt it."

"Well"—he leaned closer so that his pointy nose was almost pressed against my ear—"prepare to be amazed."

Timbago turned back to the crowd and clapped his hands together, the doors at the far end of the room flying open. "The delegation from the Leavenwald!"

A group of men came through the door, each of them carrying a bow. Jugglers threw balls and pins in the air, and acrobats flipped about in front of them as the musicians in the back played a fast, jangly song. The acrobats began to dance as a group of warriors came forward to kneel in front of my throne. The one in the center placed an ornate wooden bow in front of me.

"May your hunts always be bountiful," the young woodsman said.

"And yours," I said.

He stepped back, and the men dispersed to the side.

"The warriors of the Veldt!" Timbago said.

Another group came through the doors and bowed low before me, Lady Arianne leading the way. She made a motion with her hands, and three men lugged a chest forward and set it next to the bow, throwing the lid open to show that it was loaded down with gold coins and expensive-looking jewels.

Timbago waved a hand at them, and Lady Arianne narrowed her eyes at him before she motioned her delegation to the other side of the hall, away from of the men of the Leavenwald. The hunters sneered at her, and I couldn't help glancing between the two groups, curious why they disliked each other so much.

"The mayor of Neris," Timbago announced.

A skinny man in blue brought me a golden key and a large wooden trunk filled with more gold.

"The Free Peoples of the Sorcastian Plain," the goblin cried out.

This time a group of big men in tattered work clothes came forward, women in long cotton dresses tucked in between them, each of them carrying a bag full of flowers or big baskets of vegetables that they sat in front of me.

"The Dragos Council," Timbago said.

My heart began to pound even harder as Winston came up the center aisle, at the very center of a group of men who all knelt and lowered their heads again. Then he stepped forward and knelt on the stair in front of me, holding up a large, clear crystal shaped like a dragon's claw.

"For you," he said, his voice quiet, as I stood and let him slip it over my neck. "May your rule always be just, and may you hold everyone you protect close to your heart, no matter how unworthy they may be."

"Thank you," I whispered.

My breath caught as he ran his hands along my arm. The rest of the room could have disappeared for all I cared.

"Your Majesty."

I moved away from Winston, my cheeks flaming, as the wizard raised an eyebrow at me.

"My queen." Winston bowed toward me again and backed down the stairs to the rest of his delegation. They made their way over to stand next to John of Leavenwald, and Timbago grinned at me.

"You're going to enjoy this," he said quietly before returning to using his surprisingly powerful voice. "The Wizard Council!"

The sky above us went dark as thunder began to roll, and fireballs lit up the room. Between the booms of thunder, there was a piercing wail as a brilliant green dragon flew through the air. Purple smoke billowed from its mouth, and it came straight toward me, eyes blazing, before it disappeared.

"What was that?"

There was another fireball, and then the floor around us

turned to a green carpet of grass that began to move and I, along with everyone else in the room, was taken on a flyby tour of the lands of Nerissette as it spread out among us.

People exclaimed as they saw the villages full of imaginary dragons and the encampments of people who lived in the desert. The scene changed to a long green plain, and creatures that looked like deer stampeded through the ballroom to disappear just as they looked about to charge me.

The scene changed to a deep-green wood, water dripping in the background as birds sang. Then there was a loud clap as men filled the scene, all of them wearing army camo and battling with one another. A red-faced man beheaded another, and the blood seeped onto the floor in front of my throne. I fought my instinct to lift my feet, and I let the phantom blood puddle around my delicate gold slippers.

Another clap, louder than the last, and the scene disappeared. The smoke cleared, and I looked out at a ballroom crowded with cowering nobles. I scowled down at the Fate Maker, standing at the front of a delegation of wizards with a defiant gleam in his eyes.

Instead of bowing or kneeling in front of me like the delegations, he simply nodded once, then he and the rest of the wizards marched out of the ballroom, their heads held high.

We all watched as the wizards stalked out of the room, and then everyone turned their eyes to me, waiting for me to do something. Except, the problem was, I wasn't sure what I was supposed to do about a group of wizards who obviously felt like they didn't have to bow their heads to me as their queen.

When the Fate Maker came back in a few moments later, alone this time, he didn't even bother to hide his self-satisfied smirk.

Chapter Eighteen

"Dragon's blood, my queen?" Lady Arianne asked two hours later.

I sat on my sort-of throne and watched as the nobles in front of me danced and flirted among themselves, all of them occasionally glancing at me watching them.

"No, thanks." I waved her away as I watched Winston talking to a blonde girl in bright-pink silk who seemed extremely interested in getting as close to him as possible. She kept motioning to the dryad band in the corner, playing a sweet melody on wooden instruments, and then back at the dance floor, obviously trying to persuade him to dance.

Not that I cared. Really. There was no reason for me to want to go over there and rip the girl's hair out of her head. There really wasn't. Even if he had been snuggling me more than was normal for people who were strictly friends since we'd arrived in Nerissette.

I curled my fingers around the glass and bit my lower lip.

"Are you quite sure, Your Majesty?" Lady Arianne tried again. "It's from my own vineyards. Our own private species of ember fruit."

"I'm not thirsty, thanks." I tried to ignore her prattling, scanning the crowd for the rest of my friends.

Heidi was near one of the banquet tables, taking away dirty goblets that had been abandoned, a sullen look on her face, as Jesse picked through the various cakes and sweets on display, blatantly ignoring her as he got us both something to munch on. Not that I was particularly hungry.

"Well, I was hoping we could discuss some issues with my current territory in the Veldt," Arianne said.

"Uh-huh," I hummed noncommittally. There was Mercedes, arguing with Rhys in a corner as he tried to drag her onto the dance floor with him.

"Your Majesty?" the lady asked.

"Yes? The Veldt. What about it?" I raised my eyebrows at her and she used that as an excuse to kneel beside my seat so that we were almost eye-to-eye.

"You may not know this, Your Majesty," Arianne said, "but the Veldt is by far the largest area of your kingdom. Much larger than the Borderlands to the north."

"So?"

"So, I have a son of my own, a native child of Nerissette, close in age to yourself. A wise boy. Clever as well. A native of this land, as I said."

"And?" I asked impatiently. She wasn't going to push for him to take over the army again, was she?

"Yet he is only a soldier." Yep. She was. "A commander of a small legion of catapult artillery, while that Rhys Sullivan is lord general. A man who fell through a book from another world, who controls only a small portion of land, outranks a child of our own blood."

"Yeah? I came through the book, too. What's your point?" I narrowed my eyes at her.

"That's different. You were always meant to take this role."

"Enough," the Fate Maker said loudly. He was glaring at the steward of the Veldt from his spot beside my throne. "Your son is a shallow fool who seeks only his own glory, and Fate has decreed that Rhys Sullivan is meant to lead our armies."

"My son—"

"Is a fool," the Fate Maker finished for her. "A fool who let ten men die as he attempted to hunt a kidnapped Hound for sport."

"That was the playing of boys," Arianne protested.

"Play that left ten dead—none of them your son or the Hound."

"I don't understand. They were hunting a dog? Why?" I asked.

"Not a dog, Your Majesty," the Fate Maker said sharply. "The half human children of the dragon clans. They're trained as scouts. They've a strong nose on them and are said to be able to hunt better than any animal, even their parents. Those children are known as the Hounds."

"So, your son kidnapped a person, and then hunted him? Why?"

"They were making sport, Your Majesty," Arianne tried to explain.

"Where I come from that's not a sport. That's murder."

"Then maybe we should discuss something else," Arianne said.

"What, like the time he decided to bomb your palace?"

the Fate Maker asked.

"We could talk about how the woodsmen keep us from our traditional hunting grounds in the Leavenwald. If we had those lands back my son wouldn't need to kidnap his prey from outside our borders. He'd have more than enough game to satisfy him."

"Maybe we shouldn't." I knew moms like her. Nothing was their perfect children's fault. Their kids could be the worst bullies in town, and those mothers would find some way to make it your fault that their kid was kicking the crap out of you.

"Your Majesty, please. My Gunter is a good boy."

"Come dance with me?" a dark, smooth voice rumbled, and I turned away from the Lady Arianne to smile at Winston.

"I'd love to." I took his hand and didn't bother to look back at the Fate Maker or the scheming noblewoman on my other side.

"You looked like you were about to lose your temper like you did last year in American History when Tommy Blankenship kept insisting that California was one of the original thirteen colonies."

"Only an idiot would think that." A surge of irrational anger flooded through me at the mention of the whole Tommy Blankenship scenario.

"So what did *that* idiot do?" He pulled me into the middle of the dance floor, and all the other couples moved away from us so that we had a circle of empty space to dance. I wrapped my arms around his neck, and we started to sway back and forth to the sweet-sounding dryad music.

"She wants me to fire Rhys and make her son the head of the army."

"Are you going to?"

"He kidnapped a dragon halfling and hunted it—for fun." I saw Winston grimace. "Obviously I'm not putting someone like that in charge of anything."

"At least she didn't ask you to make him ambassador to the Dragos Council."

"The Dragos Council? Is that who's in charge of the dragons?"

"Yep." He pulled me closer, and I tried to ignore the way my heart was starting to pound. "As it stands, I've been named their assistant ambassador to you under the tutorship of Ardere—unless you want to put the other guy in my place, that is."

My eyes followed Winston's as I looked over my shoulder at Lady Arianne, talking angrily with a chubby, messy-haired boy with blond hair and a sullen expression.

"Who are we looking at?" Rhys asked as he danced Mercedes over next to us.

"The boy standing next to Lady Arianne," I said.

"You don't want him as an ambassador to anyone. Not only will he get himself killed, but he'll have an army at your door before his first week as ambassador is out."

"Wow, is he really that bad?" I asked.

Rhys smiled. "He once threw a boulder at his own castle. What do you think?"

"Ouch." Mercedes giggled.

"He wants to be head of the army," I said.

"We'll lose the country in two days if you give it to him. Not to mention he'll probably destroy your palace," Rhys said. "I'd tell him no and then blame Fate for it."

"For all our sakes, it sounds like," Mercedes said.

"You've got that right." Rhys turned to me. "But we didn't come over here to talk about Gunter's inability to aim a catapult. I was hoping you would like to dance, Your Majesty."

"I *am* dancing."

"With me." Rhys raised an eyebrow. "I would consider it a great honor."

Winston let go of me, and Mercedes and I switched places. "Besides," Rhys continued, "it would be a mercy for my toes. The dryad has two left feet."

"I do not!" Mercedes yelped as Winston pulled her a little farther away, making sure that her swinging arms couldn't reach the grinning general.

"She's not that bad of a dancer, is she?" I asked as we both turned to Mercedes, swaying back and forth, bickering with Winston.

"Nah, but I think getting her mad might be my new favorite way to spend my free time. I never knew that a blushing dryad could be that pretty."

"Sooo…" I drew the syllable out. "You think Mercedes is pretty?"

"Extremely," Rhys said as the tops of his ears began to flame.

"Hmmm."

"Hmmm nothing."

"As a future queen, should I be worried about the fact that the head of my army is trying to date my best friend? Do I need to warn you about what happens if you hurt her? 'Cause trust me, I'll make sure whatever I decide to do to you—it will be painful. Bloody and painful."

"No worries, then. Just keep your big, royal nose out of it, and we'll all be fine." He brought a finger up to tap my nose and then froze. "Crap."

"What?"

"Prince consort, three o'clock. I think he's going to want to dance. Want me to kidnap you instead?"

"No, I can manage him." I smiled and tried to hide my dread at spending more time explaining to Jesse that no matter what he thought was going to happen, he really wasn't going to get to become king. Meanwhile, I could see the blonde from before working her way toward Winston, and my grip on Rhys's shoulders tightened.

"Ow." Rhys turned to the girl I was staring at. "Oh."

"I don't like her."

"May I cut in?" Jesse asked. "Rhys? Mind letting me dance with my girlfriend?"

"Your girlfriend?" Rhys asked. "I didn't know you'd gotten that serious yet."

"Neither did I," I said.

Jesse held his hand out to me. "I *am* the prince consort."

"That doesn't mean anything," I said.

"It's okay, Your Majesty." Rhys bowed low. "I should go save Winston's toes."

"Okay." I nodded and moved over to Jesse, who slotted me into his arms. I watched Rhys head over to intercept Winston and the girl who was about to cut in on Winston and Mercedes.

"I'm so glad we finally get a minute alone," Jesse said as we started to sway. "The past few days it's been like you're avoiding me, always hanging out in the library like we're back in school."

"Well, I'm trying to learn about the country I'm supposed to rule. Being a queen is kind of an important job."

"Then tonight you've been so busy talking to people we haven't gotten any time together. I came back from getting us food, and you were gone."

"It's my job to get out there and meet people. I'm their queen. Or I'm going to be soon. I need to be out, mingling, with the people, hearing how I can make their lives better."

I watched as Rhys cut in to dance with both Winston and Mercedes for a few seconds. Soon the blonde was pulled into their circle, and the next thing I knew, through a flurry of limbs, Winston and Rhys had ended up dancing together while Mercedes led the stunned blonde away.

I giggled, and Jesse turned his head to take in the two bulky, muscle-bound boys in formal wear pretending to prance together through a fancy sort of waltz, both of them on tiptoe, their noses high in the air.

"So juvenile," Jesse said coldly. "They shouldn't be trying to embarrass you."

"Winston could never embarrass me," I said softly as Rhys lowered Winston into an elaborate dip.

"One of them is supposed to be in charge of the army, and the other is meant to be a dragon warrior. If they're acting like this, how are you going to trust them to run a war when the time comes?"

"I'd trust them with my life," I said with a smile.

"Thankfully, with the Fate Maker's help, it won't come to that," Jesse said.

"Who said it's not the Fate Maker I'm worried about?" I glanced over at the wizard, who was still sitting on the dais, glaring at me.

"Why would you worry about the Fate Maker?" Jesse asked, his eyes glazed. "He's only here to help you."

"You keep telling yourself that," I said and tried to ignore the man sitting on the throne, staring daggers into my back.

Chapter Nineteen

I was poking at the slices of a pink fruit on my plate the next morning. It sort of looked like an orange but tasted more like a kiwi, I considered, trying to decide if it was really a breakfast food. Then again, it was a fruit, and Gran Mosely always nagged that I needed more of those.

Jesse sprinted into the dining room and slid to a stop. He straightened up and smoothed his jacket before sauntering toward the rest of us like it was no big deal. "Hey, Allie."

"Hey." I poked at the fruit again and then popped a slice of it into my mouth.

"Hey," Mercedes said from her spot two places down from me.

Instead of answering, Jesse ignored her and sat at my other side. I narrowed my eyes at him and then saw Rhys, who sat next to Mercedes, clench his hands into fists beside his plate, and Winston—sitting next to me—tensed his shoulders.

"I just got done meeting with the Fate Maker," Jesse said,

his attention focused on me.

"You two sure are spending a lot of time together."

"It is my duty."

"Your duty?" Winston asked. "Why is it your duty to meet with Allie's royal adviser and the general high lord of creepiness for Nerissette?"

"Because I'm the crown prince, and there were things we needed to discuss. Things only I can handle."

"Such as?" I asked.

"About the coronation."

"Wait, shouldn't he have had that conversation with Allie?" Mercedes asked.

"She doesn't need to worry about it," Jesse said. "There are other things that are more important that should be occupying her mind, and that's why I'm here. To make the decisions that she doesn't have time for."

"What are you talking about?" I asked. "I'm not doing anything but eating breakfast. If the Fate Maker wants to talk about the coronation I'm sitting right here."

"Darling." Jesse put his hand on top of mine, and Winston lunged across the table. Rhys threw one beefy arm out and smacked Winston in the chest, pushing him back into his seat.

Jesse raised one eyebrow at them and then turned back to me. "Darling, this isn't something for you to worry yourself about. It's simply a few small details that need ironed out."

"What details?" I asked. "And don't call me *darling*."

"Oh, like the guest list, the music, the order of events, the date."

"Sounds like you're basically planning everything."

"The Fate Maker and I just want this to go well. We need to make the effort to show the people that nothing has changed with the new monarchy in place."

"But everything's going to change," I said. "That's sort of the point. Fate brought us here to change things."

"Allie, I think you should let the Fate Maker handle it. He knows more about this than you do."

"The Fate Maker—" Winston started.

"Is the wisest person in this place," Jesse said. "He's going to help us unify this world and then spread out among the stars. He said it's the will of Fate that we come to rule not just this realm but all of the Realms of Possibility."

"He's going to *what*?" I asked. "Are you reading from a script or something? A textbook?"

"Because megalomania is always such an attractive quality to cultivate. That's why Dictatorship 101 is such an in-demand elective—right after Marching Band and Introduction to Button Collecting," Mercedes said.

Jesse looked at her, confused.

"Forget it." Mercedes elbowed me. "Just go back to planning your party."

"This is a big deal," Jesse said, turning to look at me. "The Fate Maker says that this coronation will set the president."

"You mean a precedent?" Rhys asked.

"Yeah, whatever," Jesse said. "It's going to go down in history. King Jesse and Queen Alicia crowned the rulers of Nerissette in front of a crowd of thousands."

"You mean Allie will be crowned," Winston said. "She's the queen."

"Then she'll crown me king, and we'll be a team. Ruling Nerissette together. That's what the Fate Maker promised me. Plus, he said we're throwing another party like the one last night but throughout the entire city. Five days of nonstop partying, and when it's over, we're royalty."

"Fabulous," I said, trying to ignore Jesse's whole *I'm gonna be a king* bit because that was just ridiculous. "That's just what we need, another party."

Then again, once I was *officially* crowned as Golden Rose, then I would be in complete control of Nerissette, at least in public. And my coronation ball would be a good opportunity to announce my plans for everyone to hear. Well, after I figured out what my plans were exactly.

"Allie, it will be great," Jesse said.

"Oh yeah," Mercedes said. "More time with the nobles. Just what we all really want. Maybe Carolina of the Veldt will show up again and throw herself at every guy in the palace."

"It'll be fine." I bit my lower lip to hide my smile. "We'll stick together and keep the guys safe."

"What do you mean you'll stick together?" Jesse asked. "You won't be there."

"Excuse me?" I asked. "It's my coronation, so I kind of have to be there."

"Not you." Jesse waved his hand toward the others. "*Them.* The coronation is meant for the nobles at court only. Not the peasants."

"Were you referring to me or your former girlfriend with that peasant comment?" Mercedes said, her voice snapping like a broken twig. She stood and pushed her chair back before stalking toward Jesse and looming over him.

He swallowed loudly.

"Because you better not have meant me, otherwise I'll give you a whole new version of flowery speech."

"You're not even human anymore," Jesse said, his voice filled with scorn.

"And Heidi?" Mercedes asked. "Is she coming?"

"Of course Heidi won't be coming. She's a maid. She cleans up after other people."

My jaw dropped open, and I didn't try to hide it.

"What? She's a maid, not royalty like we are."

"We *all* fell through the book together. I don't care what people became once they got here, but we came together, and that means we are in this mess *together*—whether you like it or not."

"Allie." He wrapped his fingers through mine and tugged my hand toward him.

I tried to jerk my hand back and glared daggers at him when he didn't release his grip on my fingers. Seriously, enough with the touching and the dating and all of it already. If he didn't dial it down I was going to banish him to a dungeon—in someone else's kingdom.

Winston growled, and I watched as Rhys tightened his grip on Win's shoulder. "Get your hands off Allie," Winston said.

"Fine." He let go of me. "Whatever. I'm just saying, the coronation isn't meant for your type of people."

"Their type?" I challenged, my eyes narrowing at him.

"Allie, let's go somewhere and talk about this."

"Talk about what? The fact that you're suddenly trying to run a kingdom that isn't even mine yet, or the fact that you just told my friends they aren't welcome at *my* coronation. My coronation, Jesse, not yours. *Mine*."

"But, sweetheart, I'm just trying to make things easier for you."

"Sweet—" I started, but Winston lunged for real this time, and Rhys couldn't hold him back. He grabbed Jesse's shirt and started to drag him over the tabletop.

"Win!" I pushed on both boys' shoulders, hoping to break them apart, but Jesse was struggling and I couldn't get a good grip on either of them.

Jesse swatted at Winston, fighting to break his hold, and I tried to get between them. "Both of you, stop it! For Christ's sake, knock it off."

"I'm going to kill him." Winston jerked Jesse off his feet, pulling him closer.

Jesse's flailing hand smacked into my nose, and I felt a sharp crack. I sat down heavily, my hands cradling my face.

"Allie," Mercedes yelled.

My eyes started to water while piercing pain radiated through my entire head, and my vision went speckly white as I saw stars. I pressed my fingers carefully against my nose and winced, the pain lancing upward into my brain.

All three boys stopped, frozen, and then turned to look at me.

"Oh my God," Winston said.

"See what you made me do?" Jesse jerked away from Winston's hold and straightened his shirt.

"Come on." Rhys grabbed Winston's arm and marched him from the room. "Come on, Winston."

"I'm going to destroy you," Winston said, his eyes fixed on Jesse. "I'm going to rip you to pieces for that, and then I'm going to roast your bones."

"Winston." Mercedes hurried over to grab Win's other arm and helped Rhys drag him from the hall.

I stood up, still cradling my nose. Thankfully it wasn't bleeding, and the pain was starting to ebb, so most likely it wasn't broken.

"You stay here," Mercedes said, "and deal with…*him.*"

"Jeez, Allie," Jesse said as Mercedes and Rhys managed to drag Winston away. "Are you okay? I can't believe he did that."

"He didn't do that, Jesse." I let go of my nose and glared at him through watering eyes. "You're the one who hit me."

"Yeah, but it was only because he was trying to kick the crap out of me. I would have never done it otherwise. Are you okay?"

"I'm fine." I shook my head. "But I can't believe you. You just tried to uninvite Winston and Mercedes from my coronation ball. Which FYI? Totally isn't going to fly. I get to decide who's coming to my own coronation."

"But look at how he behaved. He was an animal. He flipped out for no reason. You're my girlfriend, and he just blew a gasket when I got near you."

"I'm *not* your girlfriend."

"But you are," Jesse said. "It's fate."

"How is it fate? You didn't even know I existed until we were trapped here."

"Because you weren't a princess then. Duh. Plus, you can't hide how you feel about me. You did save my life after all."

"What?"

"When we first arrived, you saved my life. I don't know any better indication that a girl is into you than that."

"I saved you because it was the right thing to do, not because I was into you."

"That's great, but it doesn't change anything. You're the princess, and I'm the prince, and so that means we're meant to be."

"So, it's not me that you're fated to be with, it's the princess?

Whoever she might be?"

"But it's you, so it's the same thing."

"And what if I'm not fated to be with you?"

"Of course you are. You're the most popular girl in Nerissette."

"And that gets me you? What's the consolation prize?"

"I know you don't really understand how things work, but there are two types of people in the world."

"Yeah, I'm starting to see that," I said.

"Good. There's us, and then there's them. People like us, we have to stick together."

"Like us?" I crossed my arms in front of my chest.

"The better people. Royalty, like we are. Think about how awkward your life would be for your friend Mary if she was constantly in the palace."

"Mercedes," I said. "Her name is Mercedes, and I know that this is weird for her. It would be weird for anyone to find out they're now part tree, no matter where they lived."

"It's not just that," Jesse said. "You're the Golden Rose, a queen, and she's a *thing*."

"*She* is my best friend."

"Eventually she'll accept the idea that you can't be friends anymore, and everyone will be happier because of it."

"How can you think either one of us would be happier not being friends?"

Jesse reached for my hand, and I pulled it away from him. "You're royalty, and she lives in the forest. Did you see her that day in the woods? She was covered in dirt."

"She'd spent the morning learning how to nurture a tree. Besides, I don't care if she was dirty. She's my best friend, and dirt is nothing that water and a little soap can't wash away."

"It's not just that," Jesse said, his voice low and steady, like he was trying to explain some basic idea to a small child. "She's a dryad now. They aren't like us."

"Where did you get that stupid idea? Mercedes is still the same person she always was, the only difference is that she's now green and can heal trees. That's no reason to act like she's got some sort of disease."

"Look, Allie, I know you think Mercedes is your best friend, but I've been talking to the Fate Maker. He's told me about them. They're like animals. They hate being around people. They think we've destroyed the land, and if they had their way they'd kill us all and return this land to forests."

"That's not true." I stood and pushed my chair back. "They're a group of women who take care of trees. They're just tree sprites. No one said anything about hating us or wanting to turn the land back into forests."

"Well, they aren't going to tell you to your face." Jesse followed me out of the dining room. "No one tells you they're jealous of you to your face. They wait till your back is turned, and that's when they start to whisper."

He led me into the main foyer of the palace. "I know that you don't want to accept it but she's not like you. You are going to be queen."

"Only because that's what my mother was. It has nothing to do with me personally. I'm not better than anyone else just because I happened to be born into my family and not Mercedes's."

"That's what Fate does. She makes some of us better than others. She makes some of us more important. Its our destiny."

"Destiny is nothing more than luck. I don't care what any goddess says otherwise." I jabbed my finger into his chest. "It was luck that you were there when we fell through the book, and besides, you didn't even want to be a prince. You wanted to be some sort of shape-shifting bird thing."

"I'm not a bird, though," Jesse said. "Fate knows what we're supposed to be and makes it happen."

"There's no such thing." I glared at him. "Fate doesn't exist. It was luck. Good luck, bad luck, I don't know which, but it was nothing but luck. It was good luck *for you* that the Fate Maker decided I was to be the crown princess and you were to be my prince."

"That's not how I remember it. Fate decreed that we were to be together. That we're meant for each other."

"Oh, please. We were brought here—against our will—by a magic cat."

"A magic cat who does the bidding of the goddess Fate. It's the same thing."

"No, it's kidnapping." I narrowed my eyes at him and tried to mentally remind myself about how my mother always said violence never solved anything. Even if she was wrong I was still going to try to do her proud.

"You're not thinking straight. If you were, you'd see the cat did it for your own good. For our own good."

"No, she kidnapped us because she wanted to. And Fate is just the excuse they used to get away with it." I threw my hands up in the air and shook them for emphasis like I was some scared peasant in one of those old horror movies. "Oh, I had to do it, Fate made me. She forced me," I said, my voice pitched unnaturally high.

"Fate didn't make them do anything. She doesn't exist. They read a stupid book of prophecy and decided to use it as an excuse to kidnap people," I said in my normal voice.

"You don't think Fate brought us all here for a reason? You don't think that book chose us, chose *you*, for a reason?"

"I don't know," I said. "I thought I did, but I don't. I only know one thing anymore."

"What's that?"

"It doesn't matter what Fate decided we were meant to be. We're all the same people we've always been. Titles don't change that."

Instead of waiting for him to answer I turned and stormed off. If he didn't get what I was trying to say, there was no point in bothering to explain it to him. I rushed up the stairs and through the halls, trying to make my way back to the portrait gallery. After a few wrong turns I recognized where I was and found my way to the hallway full of paintings.

There, in the middle, on the largest canvas, was the painting that Esmeralda had distracted me from the first day. I stopped in front of it and stared at a younger version of my mother, an elaborate gold crown on her forehead and an older woman standing behind her, the woman's hands on my mother's shoulders, squeezing them tightly.

"Princess Allie?" Esmeralda purred as she sauntered into the corridor, her tail pointed toward the ceiling.

"Why?" I asked her. "Why did you try to hide the truth from me for so long? The harvestings? My mother fleeing Nerissette? Why did you try to keep it secret?"

"You can't fight him and win just because you think that's what she'd want you to do. You have to do it for yourself. You have to choose to stand up to the whim of Fate. Your mother couldn't do it, but you can't do it simply to fight her battles for her."

"I'm not my mother."

"No." Esmeralda shook her head. "You are so much stronger than she ever could have been. That's why, when you face him, we will win. But you must choose it. Not for her. Or because it's what you think you're expected to do. You have to choose to save us because it's what you want to do."

"Us?"

"I serve you, Princess Allie. I always have."

"Why should I believe you?" I swallowed and looked back at my mother's portrait, staring into the painting's eyes.

"Because I'm the one who defied the Fate Maker's original order and brought you here. That's why he wasn't waiting for you like he was everyone else I've pulled through."

"So, you thought you'd what? Surprise him?"

"Take him off guard, yes."

"Why?"

"Because he forbade your return. Because he knew, as do I, that when you become queen, our time, his and mine, is at an end."

"And that means I should believe you?"

"You should believe me because even though I knew you'd hate me when you found out what I did, I still brought you back to save these people. I brought you here knowing that I might die because of it. I brought you here to end the darkness."

"You want me to end it?"

"More than anything," she said, her green eyes gleaming.

"Good. Then it looks like we've got a war to plan."

Chapter Twenty

Instead of waiting for her to say anything, I started toward the back of the palace, intent on finding Rhys and Winston.

"Your Majesty?" the goblin cleaner I'd met my first morning asked as I came through the main foyer.

"Hello." I tried my best to smile at her. "Have you seen Lord Sullivan and Winston come through here?"

"They're in the library," she said. "With the dryad."

"Can you do me a favor?"

"Anything, Your Majesty."

"If anyone asks where we are…"

"I haven't seen you at all today."

"Thank you."

I hurried away from her and toward the library. Once there, I pushed the door open and slipped inside before closing it behind me, flicking the lock on the door after it shut.

"Allie?" Winston jerked his head up from the heavy leather-bound book that he, Mercedes, and Rhys were huddled around. "I thought you were with Jesse planning the coronation."

"He doesn't need me to plan a party," I said. "I thought I'd be more useful here. With you. Figuring out how to depose the Fate Maker, and if need be, to start a war."

Winston stood and began to pace around the room, opening the curtains and making sure each of the windows was locked. He came back to where our chairs were and sat across from me. "War?"

"I won't let the giants and the trolls take any more children. And I refuse to be a puppet sitting on that throne while the Fate Maker rules through me. So I'm going to let them put that crown on my head, and then my first act as queen will be to overthrow Fate."

"You're going to make war against a goddess?"

"A goddess that no one has ever seen," I said. "As far as I know."

"You have a point," Mercedes said. "The only people who even claim to speak with her are the Fate Maker and Esmeralda."

"And Esmeralda just told me that she brought me here to end this, to end the rule of Fate. And that's what we're going to do."

"We're going to what?" Rhys asked. "Start a war because the magic cat said so?"

"No, we're going to start a war because I said so. Me, the future queen. If we don't fight back then the Fate Maker will just keep doing what he's doing. I've seen my mother's diary. She tried to stand up to him, and they just ignored her. I won't let that happen again."

"Wait, what?" Mercedes asked.

"My mother is the Lost Rose," I said. "I found her diary. Someone named Piotr had taken the throne from her, done to her what the Fate Maker is trying to do to me. She was still queen but only in name. Even the nobles wouldn't listen to her. She was a prisoner. That's why she ran into our world."

"She abandoned her people," Rhys said. "She left all of them, all of us who ended up here later, she left this world and all its people to suffer."

"They were going to hand her over to the trolls. He was going to kill her—while she was pregnant with me. And what do you want to bet that Piotr *is* the Fate Maker?"

"That would make sense," Rhys said. "He has been the power behind the throne for a long time. And he has always been ruthless."

"Ruthless might not be a strong enough word for it," I said. "He used the threat of Fate to take my mother's kingdom from her, and this is what happened."

"The Fate Maker will not just give up his power," Rhys warned me.

"I know that."

"What will you do when the fighting starts?" he asked. "Will you run like she did? Will you find some way to go home so you don't have to watch the carnage?"

"No." I bit my lower lip and tried to keep from trembling. If we started a war, people would die. Me, my friends, any of us could die.

"You haven't seen battle, Allie. None of you have," Rhys said, his voice low and hoarse.

"And you have?" Mercedes asked, her voice nothing more than a croak. I watched as she leaned back against the table, staring at him, her eyes wide and her green face pale.

"I've fought bands of trolls when they've come across the White Mountains and into Nerissette. I've seen men die, and I know what battle sounds like. And I know that all you want to do when you're faced with that is run. As far and as fast as you can."

I took a deep breath in through my nose and let it out before I straightened my shoulders and met his gaze. "I'm not going to run."

"No?" he asked.

"No. I'm not my mother. I will stay and see the war through. I'll rid this world of the Fate Maker's rule and the harvesting, all of it. No matter what it takes."

"And you two?" He turned his attention to Winston and Mercedes. "Will you fight?"

"If it comes to it," Winston said, "I'll fight."

"It will come to it," Rhys said. "And people will die."

"People will die no matter what we do," I said. "At least this way they're dying for a reason."

"So be it," Rhys said. "We fight."

"We fight," I agreed.

He dropped down on one knee in front of me and took out the dagger he kept strapped to his hip. "I pledge my loyalty to you, Queen Alicia, Golden Rose of Nerissette. I will give my life to protect you and the crown. If I should die in your service I only ask that you remember my sacrifice."

"Uh—"

"You're supposed to say 'I accept your oath,'" Rhys prompted.

"I accept your oath," I answered. "And if we lose then we lose together, and let Fate do her worst."

"Allie," Winston said, and I turned away from Rhys to

look at him.

"We should go," Rhys said, and then motioned to Mercedes. "Come on, Mer, we should go."

"What?" Mercedes asked. "Why? We're in the middle of planning a war."

He looked at me and then at Winston. "We can plan later. We should go now."

"Oh." Her eyes widened. "Right, we should go. You two should stay here, and we'll go."

He tugged at Mercedes's hand again. She still wasn't budging. "Come on or I'll be forced to kiss you again."

"Wait." I turned to him as he quickly ushered Mercedes out the door. "Mercedes is right. Shouldn't we be planning a war?"

Rhys just rolled his eyes at me and then glanced at Winston. "Later."

"But—" I turned back to Winston.

Before I knew it, he pressed his lips against mine, and I forgot everything I'd been planning on saying as I kissed him back. He wrapped his arms around my waist and then lifted his head, breaking our lips apart.

My knees started to knock together as my mind started swimming a million miles per minute. Winston had just... His lips and mine had been... I swallowed. Oh crap, I hadn't had a chance to brush my teeth after lunch, and I'd had a really garlicky sandwich.

Was I supposed to say something now? Kiss him back? "What was that for?" I finally managed to ask.

"I want more from you," he said. "From us."

"What?"

"I want us to be together, as more than just friends. I

thought you should know that before the war starts. Just in case."

He let go of me and then stalked off, not meeting my eyes as he opened the door and slipped outside.

"Okay," I said and gave him a brief nod, not sure what else I was supposed to say. He bowed his head and then shut the door between us with a decisive *click*.

I brought my trembling fingers up and pressed them against my lips. I was in the middle of declaring a war and Winston Carruthers had just kissed me. And it had been even more amazing than I'd always fantasized it would be.

Chapter Twenty-One

"Queen Talia?" I pushed open the doorway between the labyrinth and the mermaids' pool. "Are you here?"

"Where else would I be, Your Majesty?" The mermaid queen slipped out of the water and moved beside the pond, keeping the bottom of her tail in the water, flipping it back and forth.

I kicked off my shoes and sat next to her, hiking my skirt up above my knees so I could put my feet in the shimmering liquid. I was surprised to find that it was warm like bathwater, not cold like a swimming pool.

"I never got a chance to come out here and swim with you. I wasn't here long enough to come back." I felt tears building up in my eyes. "Tomorrow we might all be…"

"We all might be what?" she asked.

"It's just that my coronation is tomorrow night, and then there's this thing. I can't really say what's going to happen, but I've been thinking about what you said when we met last time, and we never got a chance to have that swim."

"Shhh." Talia wrapped an arm around my shoulders and pulled my head down to rest against her collarbone. "We have plenty of time to swim together. Years and years to swim together."

"But what if we don't?"

"We have many years together still. I'm not so old that you have to cry for me yet."

"It's not you," I said with a sniffle. "It's just the coronation and everything. I mean, I went out into the city the other night, and there was a harvesting. The children were going to be sold to the giants, and they were begging and crying, and there was nothing I could do."

"I know what a harvesting is, Allie." She tightened her grip on me. "And I'm so sorry you were forced to see it."

"No." I shook my head. "I needed to see it. I needed to know the truth. Then I found my mother's diary in the library, and the things inside it were just horrible. Really, really horrible."

"Did you know I met your mother once?" she asked.

"What?" I shook my head, distracted at the change in subject. Talia had met my mother? Why hadn't she told me that before? More important—why was meeting a mermaid another one of those things that my mother kept from me?

"Your grandmother brought her to the Sea of Gallindor for a holiday. She was…"

"She was what?"

"So beautiful," Talia said. "She was the prettiest human I'd ever seen. She had these violet ribbons in her hair and when she laughed it was like the sea sang. When I heard she was lost I cried for her. I cried for the girl who'd come to our sea in her pretty violet ribbons."

"She used to tell me stories about you," I said quietly. "The mermaids of Nerissette. Great guardians of the Sea of Gallindor. She made them seem like fairy tales, but I believed them. I wanted them to be real. That's why I became a swimmer."

"Is it?" Talia asked.

"Yeah. Mom always wanted me to do things like fence and take judo, but I wanted to be a mermaid. One day we were at the pool, and one of the swim coaches was there. She told me about the swim team, and I just nagged and nagged until Mom let me join."

"It sounds like you were very persistent."

"I was such a brat. I didn't realize that there was a reason she wanted me to learn to fight. Wasn't there?"

"Yes."

"So what am I supposed to do? Tomorrow I'm going to be crowned queen, and I have to stand up to the Fate Maker. But I'm so afraid." The admission fell from my lips freely. I knew I was safe here with Talia.

"Afraid?"

"There are so many things I didn't do. I didn't go visit her one last time before we were pulled here. I didn't hug Gran Mosely good-bye before I left for the library. I didn't even make it out here to swim with you."

"So you're afraid of all the things you haven't done because you think that if war comes the Fate Maker will win?" Talia asked. "That you will not survive?"

"Is that bad?" I sniffled and wiped my nose against the sleeve of my gown.

"To fear losing a battle?" Talia asked. "Or to be afraid

of death? Only fools are not afraid to die, Allie, and you are many things, but a fool is not one of them. I have a question for you, though."

"Yes?"

"Is being afraid to die going to stop you from going into battle tomorrow?"

"No." I shook my head and then wiped my nose again. "I want it to. I want to say no, I'm the queen and you should go fight in my place, but *I can't.* I can't take the chance of losing Mercedes and Winston. If we never go home again they're all I have."

"So even though you might die you'll still fight for the people of Nerissette?"

"I don't have a choice. I won't let him destroy this world in my name. Does the fact that I don't have a choice in whether or not I go to battle determine if I'm a coward or not? Is it part of the equation?"

"It's the only part of the equation." She patted my shoulder again.

"That seems like a very screwed-up math problem," I said with another sniffle.

"Now, I cannot tell you what the next setting of the sun will bring, but you said that you worried about never having the chance to swim in my pool, and *that* I can do something about. Turn around and let me see your laces."

"Why?" I turned my body so that my back was facing her.

"Because we are going swimming."

"I don't have a suit."

"So?"

The dress sagged around me, and she pushed at the material so it slid off my shoulders. I turned to look at her over my shoulder and smiled shyly. She smiled back, and I tried to ignore how pointy her teeth looked close up.

I stood and pushed the rest of the material down, stepped out of the dress, and then pulled off my slip. Once I was down to nothing but my underwear and bra I sat beside her again and put my feet back in the water, kicking them.

"You can't swim there." Talia slipped into the water, grabbing my hand as she went. I waded in beside her and sighed at the warmth surrounding me.

I let myself float on my back for a second and laughed before kicking off the dirt side of the pool, twisting into a backstroke. I covered the width of her pool in less than ten strokes and did a quick flip turn before swimming back toward the mermaid.

"That's a rather unique way to swim," Talia said. "You sort of remind me of a confused otter."

"You think that looks funny?" I rolled over so I was on my stomach. "You should see the breaststroke or the butterfly."

"What are those?" she asked. I began to do a quick breaststroke across the pool. I let my head dip down and took in a mouthful of water, spitting it out at her as she shrieked with laughter, splashing at me.

"I don't know why you called that a butterfly. You look more like a frog."

"That's the breaststroke. The butterfly is even messier."

"Show me," Talia insisted, still giggling. "Show me how mortals swim in your world, Allie."

I grabbed on to the edge of the pool and pushed myself forward, moving into an awkward butterfly stroke, pulling up as much water as I could to splash with each stroke. "Now you look like a young merchild trying to learn to swim without her mother."

"Definitely not mermaid material, then?"

"I wouldn't say that," Talia said and swam toward me in a loose-limbed freestyle. "Just different."

"Is that a good thing?"

"It's not a bad thing," she said. We both twisted to float on our backs.

"Tomorrow," I said, watching the stars come out above us in the sky, "if something happens—"

"You will come tell me everything tomorrow night," she cut me off. "Whatever it is that you think I need to know, tomorrow night you will come and tell me what it is."

I didn't say anything, staring up at the stars and trying to keep from crying like a little girl. Whatever my life had become since coming here, I no longer had any space in it for tears.

"When the Sea of Gallindor was dying," Talia began, her voice catching. "When the sea was dying, the Fate Maker came to tell us that it couldn't be saved. I remember that my mother didn't cry. She didn't weep for what was to come. She never once fought against it."

"What did she do?"

"She just hugged me, kissed my cheek, and watched while we disappeared. Even though we would never see each other again, I remember that she didn't cry. She saw us safe, and then she returned to help the Sea of Gallindor die."

"She must have been very brave."

"She was a queen," Talia said. "Even though I wore her crown, she was a queen, so she didn't swim away and pretend it wasn't coming. She faced the future head-on, with no tears and no regrets."

"She must have been terrified."

"I think she was, yes. But whatever happens with the setting of the sun tomorrow, remember this. You are a queen, and you will not falter because of your fears."

We floated in silence for a while, and I watched as the sun set behind the trees. "Talia?"

"Yes?"

"Thank you."

Chapter Twenty-Two

"Why are you pacing?" Heidi asked the next day.

She spread out the dress I was supposed to wear to my coronation on my bed and smoothed the wrinkles in the skirt with her hands. "All you've done is pace around this room, muttering to yourself, since yesterday. What's up?"

"I'm nervous." I brought my right thumb up and started to chew on the nail, still pacing. "They're getting ready to crown me queen. What if I suck at it?"

I didn't tell her that it came down to more than my ability to wear a tiara, though. What if I announced my independence from Fate and the Fate Maker, and then we lost? What if he beat the crap out of us in no time? What if no one rallied to my side and they all fought for him instead? I was the queen, sure, but I was asking them to defy one of their *gods*.

"It doesn't matter." Heidi smacked at my hand as I passed, pushing it away from my mouth. "No one really cares what a queen does anyway. You show up, let them put the crown on your head, and then you wave in the parade."

"I think it's a bit more complicated than that." Especially when you were about to wage a war—not that I was going to get into that with her.

"Trust me, it's not. I've been on the homecoming court. Before that I was Miss Baby Bethel Park, Little Miss Bethel Park, Young Miss Bethel Park, and Miss Teen Greater Pittsburgh Area. "

"So?"

"So, I've got tons of experience wearing a tiara, and let me tell you, no one cares what you say or do as long as you give them a big, bright smile and manage to keep looking interested."

"Those are beauty pageants. This is an actual ruling monarchy."

"And that's so very different?"

"Yes! I'm the absolute head of an entire kingdom; half of a world. More than half of a world really, since Bathune is only a small strip of land at the edge of this world."

"So?"

"So, there are more important things here than my appearance."

I stopped at the window and watched as the goblins who maintained the palace grounds launched large, floating balls of light into the air and decorated the back garden. I couldn't see him but I could hear Timbago below directing the others in the proper placement of things.

"Nothing is more important than your appearance," Heidi said. "Really, Allie, no one cares about anything besides that. So go take a bath, and try to get your head in the game already. Think pretty thoughts. Lots and lots of pretty thoughts."

I nodded and wandered into the bathroom. The instant I stepped into the bathroom, steaming water poured into the lake-size tub in the middle of the room. The smell of rose petals enveloped me, and when I stepped into the water my skin immediately turned the pink of a freshly cooked shrimp.

I was about to officially be crowned the Golden Rose of Nerissette—the ruler of an entire country. I was going to let them put a crown on my head, and I was going to have to take a stand. I was going to be forced to face down a wizard and possibly start a war.

"I hope you've been thinking lots—and I do mean lots— of pretty thoughts." Heidi pushed the door to my bathroom open. "Oh crap, you're in here sniveling again. What did I expect? Come on, get it together."

"Sorry." I looked over at her, my eyes wide. She put her hands on her hips and shook her head at me in disgust. "The water was scorching hot."

"Oh, boo hoo, hot water will give you a rosy complexion," Heidi said. "Now, get to work. You've got to do more than think pretty thoughts."

"But that's what you said to do." I didn't want to have to make decisions right then, and I looked up at Heidi, pleading for her to just tell me what to do.

"Clean yourself up. We've only got an hour before the start of the festivities, and I'm going to need every single second of it to make you look presentable, much less turn you out to look like a real queen."

Instead of answering, I slipped beneath the water to wash my hair.

• • •

Forty-five minutes later, I stood in front of the mirror, staring at myself while Heidi laced up the back of my dress. "You owe me so much for this when we get home," she said. "I can't believe I'm actually dressing you."

"Sorry. If there was anything in my closet with a zipper I would have worn that." I plucked my fingers against the skirt and wrinkled my nose.

The dress I was wearing was a heavy white silk with golden roses embroidered over all the full skirt. The bodice was tight, off the shoulder, and covered in heavy golden embroidery and jewels around the neckline. It had to weigh at least ten pounds.

"Is all this really necessary?" I hefted the skirt up slightly. Yep, it was as heavy as it looked.

"The pixie in charge of your wardrobe told me that this was the coronation dress for the Golden Rose of Nerissette. I told her that you didn't have the personality to pull it off, but she insisted."

"You're kidding?"

"The pixie said that every queen of Nerissette has worn this dress to accept the crown. It's sort of gross that they make you wear a secondhand dress, but at the same time they seem to think it's tradition."

"Every queen? Even the last one?" I asked.

"The pixie said every queen," Heidi repeated. "It would be pretty stupid to make you wear it if the last queen didn't, anyway. This dress is so not you."

I looked at the dress in the mirror and swallowed. My mother had worn this dress and the same crown they were going to put on my head tonight. She had been the queen of Nerissette who had let it down. Now it was my turn to save it.

"She must have been a lot smaller than you, though," Heidi said, tugging at the laces at my shoulders.

"Who?" I asked absently.

"The last queen. She had to be smaller than you because I've barely got enough ribbon left to tie you closed up top. Everywhere else fits though. Has anyone ever told you that you've got enormously wide shoulders?"

"She was tiny," I said, ignoring the jab about my size.

"How do you know? Have you seen her picture or something? Is she in the book you had your nose stuck in last night when we should have been getting our beauty sleep?"

"She was my mother."

For the first time, Heidi was stunned into silence. I waited a beat before continuing. "My mother was the former queen of Nerissette. She was—*is*—the Lost Queen." I ran my fingers over the skirt again, wondering if she had touched it the same way the night she'd worn it.

"Wait, you're saying that you've been a princess the whole time and didn't tell anyone? You've always been royalty?"

"I didn't know until we got here. And even if I did know, would you have believed me anyway? Seriously, if I'd have come to you and said I'm the princess of a fairy-tale land, would you have believed me?"

"If you'd have used some of the money they've got around here and lived like a princess, then maybe. I mean, come on, how cool would that be? I could have been best friends with a princess."

"We're not best friends." I gave her reflection my best death glare.

"We would have been if I'd have known you were a royal." Heidi snorted. "Duh. Imagine how that would have looked at the Miss Teen Pennsylvania pageant. Me with a royal princess in my entourage."

"Right, well, sorry I couldn't be more help with your attempt at beauty pageant domination. If we ever get home I'll come up with some way to make it up to you."

"You better." She gave the dress an extra-hard pull.

I sucked in a breath and then wheezed. "Can't breathe."

"Doesn't matter," Heidi said. "If you can't breathe then you can't eat. No temptations there."

"But what if I want to eat?"

"Don't. No one wants to watch a queen stuff her face. So don't eat, don't breathe. Just sit there and try to look pretty. Besides, knowing you, if you try to eat you'll just spill something on that dress. It is white, after all."

"Unfortunately," I sighed, "you may have a point there."

I took a deep breath and ran my hands over my mother's skirts one last time, trying to dig up whatever residual courage some former Golden Rose—a braver Rose than me—might have left in the dress in case I needed it for later.

There was a knock at the door, and Heidi and I stared at each other in the mirror. "Time for you to go," she said quietly.

"Yeah."

"Allie?"

"What?"

"Good luck." She rolled her eyes. "You know, just in case you need it."

Before I could say anything she stalked over to the door and jerked it open. She sighed and glared at Jesse standing in the doorway, dressed to match me with a white jacket covered in golden roses over the top of his black pants.

"Are you going to let me in or just stand in the door?" he asked.

"Stand in the door," Heidi said. "What do you care?"

"I've come to pick up my date."

"Obviously," she said.

"So, are you going to let me pick her up or not? We can't keep the Fate Maker, and our people, waiting."

"Or not."

I shook my head. The last thing I needed tonight was to deal with their drama on top of everything else.

"Heidi." I stepped around her.

She slunk back then, her hands shaking with anger and her eyes blazing.

I reached out to grab her hand and gave it a squeeze, trying to comfort her. "Come down for the party later. It'll be fun."

"Or you could go help in the kitchens," Jesse said, gloating. He took my hand in his and laced our fingers together. "I'm sure they'll need another pair of hands to do the dishes."

"Jesse!" I gaped at him. Sure, I'd always known he was a bit of a tool, but this was way harsher than I'd ever heard him talk to anyone before—even the Computer Club people, and he was normally brutal with them.

"What?" He turned to stare at me. "She's a maid. That's what her fate is, isn't it? Washing up after other people. That's what the Fate Maker says, at least."

"Yeah, well, he also thought that the two of you should have died that day in the tower. And it was me, not Fate, who saved you from that. So apologize."

"I'm sorry Fate made you ugly." He grabbed my elbow and started ushering me out the door.

"That's not what I—"

"Oh, go trip down the stairs and die." Heidi snarled at him and slammed the door in both of our faces.

"Sorry about that." Jesse shook his head at me and started leading me down the stairs from my tower to the corridor below. "She's such a pain. Up until we got together, Allie, I thought all girls were like Heidi."

"We're *not* together. How many times do I have to tell you that? And how you treated her was horrible."

"Allie, come on. I'm a prince, and you're a princess who's about to officially become queen, and that's as together as you can get without being married or something," he said, completely ignoring how he treated Heidi.

"No, it's really not."

"Yeah, it is," Jesse said. "Anyway, like I was saying, before we got together I really did think that girlfriends were just one of those headaches that you had to put up with. Like Geometry homework."

"You thought having a girlfriend was like Geometry homework?" I asked when we reached the bottom step.

"That was when I was dating Heidi." He stopped once we'd reached the crossway between the two corridors and pulled me close. "Once we got the chance to be together I realized that girlfriends aren't like Geometry at all."

I tried to follow his logic but it wasn't going to happen since I didn't speak moron.

He leaned closer. "You're more like winning the state soccer championships every single day."

"Wow." I tried not to roll my eyes at the comparison.

"And once you've crowned me as Nerissette's first official king, then it will be even better."

Like that was going to happen.

"And then we'll be the most powerful couple in all of Nerissette." He brought his face closer, and I realized he was going to try to kiss me.

"Hey, did I ever tell you about the really cool trick that Esmeralda taught me to get around the palace?" I asked quickly, trying to distract him from both his attempted coup and the kissing.

"What?" Jesse pulled back.

I slipped out of his arms, then grabbed his hand and dragged him over to the carving. "See this?"

"Yeah?"

"Watch." I rubbed my fingers over the carving and closed my eyes. "The main entrance."

There was a puff of smoke—this one with glitter, because the corridor outside my tower liked to make things more festive than the rest of them—and we were standing in the main entrance of the palace. I coughed and waved my hands in front of my face before Jesse could say anything.

"That was—"

"Princess," Timbago cut Jesse off and bowed low in front of me. "You are exactly on time."

The goblin took my hand in his gnarled one and pulled me forward. Once we reached the doorway he stopped and looked up at me with a big grin. "You look as beautiful as your mother did."

"Really?"

"Really." He motioned to the goblin on the other side of the doorway. They both wiggled their fingers, and the double doors opened slowly, leaving me standing between them, staring at a crowded courtyard full of people who'd come to see me off to the Hall of the Pleiades to be crowned queen. And quite possibly commit suicide. All in the same night.

Chapter Twenty-Three

"Come with me, Your Majesty." Timbago tightened his grip on my hand and gave me a small smile. "Watch your step."

"Thank you." I walked forward carefully down the main stairs as we followed Jesse toward a large glass, wheelless carriage that rested on a big marble block.

I kept smiling as he nodded to the men at the carriage door, and I swallowed when I realized that, instead of horses, there were large golden birds tethered to the front. Their heads tossed back and forth, the feathers on their wings ruffling as they shifted from taloned foot to taloned foot.

Which was why the carriage didn't have wheels. We weren't going to drive into Neris—we were going to fly.

"Almost there." The goblin's voice was steady as the door to the carriage opened and a small set of jeweled steps unfolded.

Jesse climbed into the carriage and then waved to the people watching us. I slowed down, but Timbago urged me forward, toward the carriage that would take me into the unknown.

When we reached the jeweled staircase he let go of my hands, and I turned to look down at him. "Come now." He motioned me up the stairs. "Time to go out and meet your fate. You're leaving here a princess and will soon be back a queen."

"Then as my last act as a princess…" I knelt down beside him and grabbed his face between my hands, pressing a kiss into his forehead. "Thank you. For everything."

The crowd began to cheer wildly, and one of the birds at the front of the carriage gave a loud squawk, trumpeting his agitation at the crowd.

"It has been my distinct pleasure, Princess," Timbago said as the people around us continued to cheer. "I'll see you after the official ceremonies when you return to the palace for the ball."

I stood up and climbed into the carriage. The steps folded up behind me as I straightened my skirts, and the door slammed closed before I could really catch my breath.

I leaned my head out the tiny window and smiled at Timbago. "You'll save me a dance, right?"

"Any dance you like, Your Majesty."

"Yaw!" a man called from the front of the carriage. I heard the sharp crack of a whip before the birds let out a loud cry, and we began to rise into the air.

I turned hurriedly and stared out the glass behind me at the crowd waiting in the courtyard of the palace and waved at the goblin standing in the middle, his own hand raised to me. Soon though, Timbago and the others faded from sight as the carriage flew toward the small capital city of Neris. I turned back to stare at my kingdom as it appeared beneath me.

The carriage dropped down to fly through the streets, and people stood below us, cheering up at me, their voices one loud roar. They were standing on the roofs of the tall, skinny houses, waving signs and throwing flowers. "Princess! Princess!"

I pressed my face to the glass and waved, trying my best to smile as I drank in the sights around me. There were so many people. Men in dark velvet suits and women in bright dresses, all of them waving. I saw children dancing in the streets below as they sang songs I'd never heard before.

There were so many things that I'd never suspected even existed from inside the palace walls. So many people whose lives I could make better.

The carriage swooped toward a large square, packed with more people than were at the palace. The crowd parted, and the birds landed gently in the center of the square on another stage, this one surrounded by wizards who all had their arms raised, casting spells that kept me from crashing to the ground, I imagined.

Jesse reached for my hand, but I pulled away. Instead, I hung on to the window, watching as we landed on the spot they'd laid out for me in the midst of the cheering throngs.

The carriage door opened, and I tried to collect my nerves before the footman held a hand out to me. I caught his gaze, and the young man nodded, his green eyes sparkling.

"Almost done, Your Majesty," he said. He took my hand, and I let him help me down, Jesse right behind me.

"Present arms!" Rhys called out as I stepped out of the carriage.

The crowd fell silent, and I heard the sharp snap of a

hundred boots clicking together, then the loud snick of their swords being pulled free and lifted.

I took a deep breath and looked out at the people in the square, kneeling in front of me, and decided then and there that the very first law I was going to enact was one that forbade all this bowing when I was around.

I lifted my chin and let go of the footman, preparing to step down and make my way to the Hall of the Pleiades. My eyes drifted upward, taking in the building that was shaped like a crowned woman with her arms raised, a brilliant glass dome cupped between her hands. *A crystal ball the size of a billion wishes and unanswered prayers.*

Taking in one more breath, I planted a smile on my face and started forward between the swords. Roses started to fall in my path, the people who threw them silent as I made my way up the aisle, my path carpeted in flowers.

When I reached the hall, the Fate Maker, along with a dozen other nobles, stood at the door waiting for me. The nobles all dropped to their knees, their heads bowed, and the Fate Maker stepped forward, his hand out to escort me up the stairs.

"Princess." He bowed his head slightly.

I tilted mine forward in return, my eyes narrowed. "Fate Maker."

"It seems that it's time for you to become a queen."

"Long live the queen, then."

"And the king," Jesse supplied *helpfully*, and I had to fight the urge to smack him upside the head.

"For the last time, Jesse," I said, my eyes never leaving the Fate Maker. "You'll *never* be king."

"So decrees the queen," the Fate Maker chuckled. He held

his hand out, palm down, and I took it reluctantly, letting him lead me up the stairs.

When we reached the doors, I turned to look over my shoulder one last time, gazing out over the people of Neris. The people my mother had condemned to suffer. The people who might die from my attempt to save them.

I tried not to stare at them as the Fate Maker urged me forward. My mom had left these people behind. A woman who made me scoop up bugs in the house with paper and release them outside. And she'd left these people to die. The mom I'd always tried to live up to. A woman I couldn't even stand to face while she was lying in a coma because it hurt so much to see all her light gone, and it was all a lie. She wasn't good or kind. She wasn't noble. She'd been a coward. And a liar. She'd let me live a life that wasn't mine for years, and as much as I loved her, I wanted to hate her so much for it. I wanted to hate her for the war she left for me to fight.

"Are you ready?" the Fate Maker asked, pulling me from my thoughts of my lost mother, as the elaborate, gold doors slowly creaked open.

"As I'll ever be." *I'll be more prepared to fight you than she was, at least.*

"Just remember what I told you," he whispered. "You serve at my will."

I didn't answer him but turned back to the hall instead, ready to meet the fate I'd chosen for myself. Time to be brave.

He escorted me inside, his hand clenched into a fist under mine, and the hall fell silent as the nobles inside turned en masse to stare at me. There was a brief shuffling, and then the men bowed as the women dipped into low curtsies, all of them keeping their eyes fixed on the ground.

Darinda stood at the end of another long aisle, on the dais, one of her hands resting on the box I'd first seen my crown inside that day inside the Fate Maker's room, her face an expressionless mask.

I lifted my skirts slightly and started forward. I walked slowly across the room—Jesse trailing four steps behind me—trying to keep my knees from wobbling, and looked over at Mercedes when I passed her. She gave me a tight smile before dropping her head again.

I kept moving forward, my hands shaking now, and pinned my eyes to the ground in front of me so I didn't trip. A pair of glossy black boots came into view, and I found myself face-to-face with Winston, dressed entirely in black from the tips of his shoes to the high collar of his inky-black velvet jacket.

He extended a hand, covered in a tight-fitting black glove, to me, and I took it. He brought it to his lips and kissed my knuckles. He dropped to one knee and lowered his head in front of me.

It was time.

"Your Highness?" Darinda asked from the dais. "Are you ready to begin?"

"Yes." I took a deep breath, like I was getting ready to dive into the pool, and tried to steady myself. "Yes, I'm ready."

The head of the Dryad Order nodded and then opened the box the crown was kept in.

"Kneel," she said loudly, her voice commanding.

I knelt in front of her, my head bowed. *Ready or not, Allie. Here goes nothing.*

"Do you, Alicia Wilhemina Munroe, pledge yourself to the people of Nerissette?" Darinda continued. "Do you swear as their queen to protect them, love them, and nurture them as your own?"

"I do."

"Will you lay down your life to protect the people of this realm?"

"Without a second thought."

"Then, in the name of the Pleiades, and in accordance with the Declaration of the Sight given to us by the Great Oracle of Devim, I name you the Golden Rose of Nerissette, Queen Alicia Wilhemina Munroe the First. Long live the queen."

"Long live the queen," the crowd of nobles roared, making the stained-glass windows shake in their frames.

Darinda placed the gold-and-silver crown down over my forehead, and I felt it tighten against my scalp. It wasn't uncomfortable, but I knew that there was no way it was accidentally coming off, either. The silver thorns twined around my head, elongating and twisting through my hair until it all tangled together.

I glanced over at the Fate Maker and saw that his face was flat and expressionless, but his eyes were blazing. I raised my chin, keeping my eyes fixed on his. I wasn't going to let him hurt anyone else. I was going to stop him. Or I was going to die trying.

"Rise, Queen Alicia, and meet your subjects." Darinda took my hands in hers and helped me stand. Once I was upright she dropped to her knees before me and bowed her head.

"I, Darinda, head of the Dryad Order, protector of the great maples, defender of the Tree Folk, guardian of the eastern lands, swear my fealty to you and to the throne of Nerissette. The Dryad Order shall follow the rule of yourself and your offspring until the day the next story ends and the Time of Waiting begins again." She stepped back, her eyes still locked on mine.

"Thank you." I met her eyes and saw a brief flash of terror there before she tightened her grip on her staff.

Darinda's jaw clenched and she gave me a curt nod. She must have suspected what I had planned, and I could only hope that her head bob was a sign that she was on my side. Winston stepped forward and dropped to his knees in front of me, taking my hand in his. "Your Majesty."

"Win."

"I, Winston Carruthers, ambassador of the Dragos, warrior of the black dragon clan, swear my fealty to you, Alicia Wilhemina Munroe, Queen of Nerissette. We are always your obedient servants and will fly wherever you and winds request of us. Against all enemies. You need only say the word."

He'd spoken to the dragons and convinced them to our side. We wouldn't be alone in this war against the wizards and their allies. The dragon forces wouldn't be much, but they might be enough to tip the war in our favor.

And I would have Winston. No matter what happened next we'd be together, and it would be better to die fighting, together, than to give in and live, knowing that others would die. I knew that now.

I turned to Jesse. His eyes were fixed on the plain brown box next to the one my crown had been in, staring into the open lid at the crown inside that was meant for him. He licked his lips. Already imagining what it would be like to rule. And if I crowned him prince consort that's what he'd do. He and the Fate Maker. They'd strip me of my powers, and I'd do nothing but sit on the throne, a doll for them to bring out and show off.

I'd be my mother. I would be weak. *Worthless.* And the people in front of me would powerless again. And I couldn't let that happen.

I slipped my hand into the box that Jesse was staring at and my fingers wrapped around the cool metal of the prince consort's crown. I wasn't sure if my plan would work. With the way items seemed to be violently attached to their rightful owners, I wasn't sure what would happen, if Winston would be hurt.

No one had tested Jesse against his crown to see if he was fit to wear it, though. It was assumed that if Fate had declared him the crown prince then obviously he must be a prince. But I wasn't interested in listening to what Fate thought was best right now. I lifted the heavy crown, and I looked up to see Rhys staring at me, his eyes wide.

"Winston Carruthers, Ambassador of the Dragos," I said loudly, lifting the crown up higher as the people watching all seemed to suck in their breath at the same time.

"Allie?" Winston asked, confusion painted on his handsome face.

"Do you pledge yourself to me and the people of Nerissette? Do you swear to protect them, love them, and nurture them as your own? To defend me and the crown of Roses, even unto the death?"

Like Coach had always told us at swim meets—go big or go home. If I was going to risk my life and everyone else's then I was going big, and I was going to make sure I had a crown prince I knew would support me—and not the Fate Maker—when the war came.

"What do you think you're doing?" Winston whispered.

"I'm making my own fate. And if the goddess Fate herself

wants to rain down revenge upon me from her palace in the stars above, then so be it. I am the Golden Rose of Nerissette, and we're not going to be hostages to a goddess no one has ever seen ever again."

"No!" the Fate Maker cried out, stepping out of line from behind Rhys and throwing his hands out. "You can't go against Fate."

"Really?" I raised my eyebrows in challenge. "Watch me."

People gasped, and I turned back to Winston, intent on finishing what I started. "Now, do you, Winston—"

"No!" The Fate Maker rushed forward. Two strong hands enveloped mine and jerked as Winston pushed the crown onto his own head.

"I accept your offer." Winston stood and turned so that we were standing shoulder to shoulder, staring down the Fate Maker.

"Good. I, Queen Alicia the First, Golden Rose of Nerissette, name you crown prince of Nerissette."

"You can't do this," the Fate Maker screamed. A huge black ball of sparked light grew between his hands. "*I* am the Fate Maker. *I* declare the roles of the people of Nerissette. *I* choose who will rule and who will *be* ruled."

"Not anymore," I said.

Rhys and Darinda hurried to the dais, their people flooding in behind them to form a solid block of warriors behind me. I lifted my chin and glared at the Fate Maker. "I, Alicia Wilhemina Munroe, Golden Rose of Nerissette, hereby banish—"

The ball of pulsing black light came hurtling at me, and strong arms grabbed me from behind, pulling me backward while Winston and Rhys both ducked. I looked back and saw it was Darinda who held me.

"I think it's time to stop talking now, Majesty." She lifted me off the stage. "You can talk more later. Right now, we're going to shut up and flee to safety."

"But I'm supposed to be fighting. Warrior princess, remember?"

"Do you have a sword?" she screamed in my ear.

"No."

"That's why we're fleeing. Unless you want to die in the first few minutes of your war."

The hall had erupted into chaos around us. People were screaming, and men had drawn swords. A large creature that I thought might be the ambassador from the giants had turned to attack someone from the Dragos Council. Members of the nobility had also pulled weapons, facing off with one another as they chose sides in an instant.

The Fate Maker lobbed another black sphere at me and I felt myself pushed back as it exploded in between us, a bright light that forced me to bring my hands up to cover my eyes or risk blindness. "I'm going to make you watch as I rip apart everything you love. They'll die screaming your name."

"Soldiers of Nerissette." Rhys held up his sword, now standing between me and the Fate Maker. "Defend your queen."

More swords were pulled, and men spilled off the platform behind Rhys and Winston, battling against the trolls and the giants who had sided with the wizard.

"Flee now, Queen Alicia." Darinda ushered me toward the back of the hall, underneath the dome.

"But if I could just get my hands on a sword, I could—"

"Leave that to us," Lady Arianne said as she and a mass

of armored men swarmed around Darinda and me. Mixed in with the gleaming metal of the knights' armor were the softer dark-green clothes of the woodsmen.

"You?" I looked from her to Sir John. "And you?"

"The chance at freedom will cause stranger alliances than this," Sir John said, his eyes fixed on mine. "Now, run."

"But I can't lead my people if I'm running."

He turned to Darinda and put a hand on her shoulder. "Keep her safe. She's worth more—"

A glowing orb flew at us, and the knights raised their shields to block it.

"Come, Your Majesty. We must go." Darinda pushed me into the hall, steering me toward a set of doors leading to an escape.

There was a *crack* and then the sizzling sound of black magic coming toward us, and I spun around, staring like an idiot at the malevolent black sphere coming toward me. I froze unwillingly as I watched it coming closer, arcing above the heads of the warriors, and I knew it was going to hit me. I couldn't move. I couldn't think. I was going to die, standing there with my mouth hanging open.

Darinda threw up her hands, a mass of brilliant, intertwining vines popping up between us and the hurtling mass. The ball of magic rammed into the shield, and I felt the entire room shake from the force of the explosion as light surrounded us.

"What should I do?" I yelled.

"Make for the doors," she said, her entire body trembling with the magic she was using to protect me. "There are woodsmen waiting for you. Find them and go."

"But—"

"Go!"

Another orb of magic crashed into the barricade she'd built, but this time instead of blinding light, flames licked along the lengths of the vines.

"Sapling. A little help would be very much appreciated." Darinda screamed the words, and Mercedes turned from her place on the dais and sprinted toward us. Mercedes slipped behind the shield with us. She reached up to touch the wall, and I could see her own vines beginning to interlace with Darinda's, strengthening the protection.

"Well," my best friend said, panting. "I think it's fair to say he isn't going to accept your rule without a fight."

"Nope," I said. Another ball hit the wall, and this time I could see it buckling.

"What's up with making Winston crown prince?" she asked, her face steeled as she used her magic.

"Last-minute decision." I pushed myself back up. "Why? Too much?"

"No." I could see sweat collecting on her forehead. "I'm happy you two figured out that you're perfect together, but a little advance warning next time would be helpful."

"Will you two quit talking so the Rose can run?" Darinda hissed.

"No," I said. "I'm not leaving. This is my war, and I'm going to stay and fight."

There was another explosion, and we shifted backward as the force of the explosions shook Darinda and Mercedes, straining against their vine barricade.

"Sword Slayer, Breather of Fire," Darinda screamed. "We cannot hold."

Rhys and Winston were covered in grime, and my crown

prince had a rapidly swelling eye.

"Oh bloody—" Rhys snarled and turned back quickly, swinging his sword into an enemy in front of him. He grabbed Winston's jacket and pushed him toward me. "Take the queen and go."

"But you need warriors here."

"Go!" Rhys yelled.

The two men clasped hands briefly before Winston turned and sprinted toward me. He jerked me away from the two dryads and moved directly underneath the dome.

"What are you doing?" I shouted over the melee.

"Keeping you alive."

"But I'm supposed to stay and fight. I'm a warrior queen, remember?"

"Yeah, we'll try that tomorrow. Today let me keep you alive. Please."

"Where are we going?" I asked.

"Dramera, to raise the dragon forces." He pushed his sword into my hands. "And just so you know, I really liked this jacket."

Black flames erupted around him, and he howled, his head thrown back, as the flames flickered higher, engulfing him. His whole form seemed to waver. The scream deepened, changing from the anguished cry of a boy into the full-fledged roar of an angry dragon. He opened his mouth, roaring again, making the entire world seem to vibrate from the sound, and then sucked the fire back into his mouth, swallowing it.

He dropped onto all fours and lifted his head, letting flames pour out over the top of the hall.

Winston bellowed again, and I cowered back, bringing my hands up in front of my face as he let loose another blaze, the heat causing the windows overhead to shatter in their frames. When he'd cleared a circle around us he lowered his head, and I could see the impatience in his eyes as I dropped my arms and stared at him.

"You have got to be kidding me." I scrambled up onto his neck, hiking the full skirts of my gown up over my knees, and let my shoes drop off onto the floor. I lay flat and wrapped my arms around his neck, clinging to him when he let out another loud roar before launching himself upward, straight toward the dome.

Chapter Twenty-Four

Winston exploded upward toward the glass, and I instinctively nuzzled my head into his neck, pressing the length of his sword between us as I clung to him. He kept flying higher, and I squeezed my eyes closed tight, bracing for impact.

There was a great, shattering explosion as he hit the dome, and I shrank into him, trying to cover my face from the falling glass. He let out an angry roar and another cracking sound echoed through the air as his wings cleared the dome and the cold wind swept against the back of my neck.

I lifted my head and gazed over my shoulder, watching as the remains of the great crystal dome buckled and began to collapse inward. "Oh my God," I breathed as the glass fell into the hall, onto the people fighting below.

I heard an enraged howl and turned to see giants rampaging in the square, their clubs swinging, as people screamed and began to pelt the monsters with anything they could find. Dark magic exploded in the sky around us, and I couldn't do anything but turn and stare as the battle spilled out of the hall and into the square.

"Oh, crap," I said. We flew above the city streets and watched as the battle followed behind us, the world below soaked in blood as the people of Neris began to fight back against the giants and the trolls who had terrified them for so long.

We dipped lower, and I saw that a group of men had surrounded two wizards and managed to tie them up, gagging them so they couldn't perform any spells. One man raised his sword, and I buried my face in Winston's leathery skin, unable to watch what came next.

Winston leveled out and extended his wings, soaring higher. Once I was sure he wasn't going into another rapid climb, I loosened my hold on his neck and sat up, watching as we flew toward the Crystal Palace. The crowds that had been waiting for me when I'd left were now working together, attacking the giants and the trolls, and I could see flames licking at the sides of the palace itself.

"We need to land." I nudged my heels against Winston's sides.

Instead, he turned us away from the palace and began to beat his wings faster, flying so quickly we did nothing more than blitz past the warring people below. He turned south and began to race toward the very farthest reaches of my kingdom.

I watched as the fighting below faded away and the city turned to countryside, then forest, as we soared across the lands of the kingdom I now ruled. It was dark below us, but I could make out lights in the distance from what looked like tiny villages.

Winston snorted, and I felt him shift his weight slightly,

tipping downward. I tightened my grip on his neck and squeezed my knees around his wide shoulders, trying to keep from slipping forward and tumbling over his head to the ground below. This flying thing had definite possibilities, but he had to figure out some way to do the takeoffs and landings so that I wasn't clinging for dear life. He circled once and dipped lower.

We broke over the treetops, and I saw that we were at a large lake. He skimmed over the top of it, his talons dragging along the surface, and I saw myself reflected in the water, eyes wide and crown gleaming.

We reached the shore and he landed silently in a tiny village square with a large fountain in the center. There was a yell from one of the houses, and before I could catch my breath enough to ask where we were, the square was flooded with people, most of them holding lanterns in front of their faces, surrounding me with a sea of bobbing lights.

I slipped down off Winston's back and pushed my skirts down before I ran a hand up to straighten my hair. I wasn't normally vain, but the idea of meeting people for the very first time as their queen sort of made me want to make a good impression.

"The Rose," someone from the crowd said. They all dropped in front of me, pressing their heads to the ground.

Winston puffed a warm breath against my neck and then lumbered off into a large, barnlike building on the other end of the square where I assumed he was going to change shape.

"The junior ambassador has brought the Rose."

"Where is Ardere? Where is the Drakos himself?" another voice called out.

"Hi." I lifted my hand to wave. "It's nice to meet you. Uh,

Ardere was…" What was I supposed to say? He was delayed by the war I set off before I ran away?

"Queen Alicia." A raven-haired man from the back of the crowd pushed his way through to me.

I stepped forward and held out my hand for him to shake. Instead he bowed his head, his eyes meeting mine.

"Welcome. I am Tevin, Keeper of the Flame for the holdings of Dramera. What brings you to visit on the night of your coronation?" He took my hands and bowed his head slightly in front of me.

"Well, there's been a bit of trouble."

"Trouble?" He lifted an eyebrow at me in response.

"I may have started a small war."

His head jerked up, and both of his eyebrows were almost at his hairline, but in the next second his face was a mask of complete indifference again. "That sounds very ambitious for your first day as queen. I understood that most of the others were simply content to hold a ball to celebrate."

"If you have somewhere that we can go and wait for Winston, I'll explain everything once he gets back."

"I can't wait to hear about what happened to you." Tevin picked up a piece of glass that had fallen out of the folds of my dress when we'd landed and held it up to show me. "Or why you're shedding feathers of glass."

"We left in a bit of a hurry."

"Because of the war you started?"

"I wanted to stay and fight," I said. "But my advisers thought it best if I left before the Fate Maker took the chance to kill me."

"That was most likely the best course," Tevin agreed. "Queens are not meant to fight wars. The risk of you being captured is too high."

"It's a risk I would have been willing to take."

"Then why didn't you?"

Why hadn't I? Because I was afraid? Because all I'd really wanted to do when the killing started was run away, just like Rhys said I would?

"Because I didn't have a weapon, and I was in this dress, and there were people dying, and I just...froze... Winston and Darinda said to run, and I just did it. I didn't think, I just did it."

My heart sank. I had been afraid, and I'd just done what I was told. *Just like my mother had.* And now other people were dying in my place. I was no better than she was with the harvesting.

My hands started to tremble and I could feel tears burning in my eyes.

"Ahh." Tevin met my eyes. "This was your first battle?"

"Yes."

"Then I can see why you panicked. After all, it is natural that if someone is trying to kill you your first thought is to run away. That is what sane people do."

"I'm not supposed to be sane. I'm supposed to be queen."

"And I am the war leader of the dragon clans of Nerissette. But every time I see battle all I want to do is run as far away as I can. Although, I must admit, I've never done it by breaking through the three-thousand-year-old dome of the most sacred building in Nerissette."

"How did you know?" I asked.

"The glass. It is unique."

"Oh."

"It seemed like the quickest way out," Winston said from

the darkness. He was wearing nothing but a pair of brown trousers and his crown, and I couldn't help wondering how it had stayed in one piece while his clothing was destroyed.

"Your crown." I pointed at it. "It should have been torn apart when you went from normal to dragon-sized."

"Magic," Tevin said. "Both crowns have spells woven around them so they always fit snugly on their wearer's brow. No matter how thin or fat the head wearing them might be. Even if one of the wearers happens to be a big-headed dragon."

"Yeah, well, it could have stretched a bit more." Winston scratched underneath the crown, and when it shifted I could see deep red creases where the metal had dug into his skin.

"Yes, well," Tevin said, "being the prince consort isn't all balls and dancing. Sometimes there are downsides. Now, if we could return to explaining why you decided to destroy the Hall of the Pleiades?"

"It wasn't like I was going to fit through the doorway." Winston took the dingy white shirt in his hands and slipped it on over his head.

I looked down and noticed that his feet were bare. He had long, almost elegant toes, and for some reason it made my heart start to beat harder. The stars protect me, now was not the time to get all stupidly in, like...*love* with Winston and start mooning over his freaking toes.

"You could have shifted outside," Tevin said dryly, bringing my attention back to him and away from Winston's weirdly attractive feet.

"I could," Winston said, "but I thought smashing through the ceiling might have a bit more impact."

"I would agree." Tevin led us into a small hut. "Usually.

Now, though, I'm curious about how you've managed to come home to Dramera with not just the queen, but a new accessory as well…"

"That might be why the war started," I said, glancing at Winston. "Well, it's not really the reason, it was just sort of that last straw that flipped the Fate Maker from slightly crazy to full-on psycho."

Winston reached out and wrapped one of his muscled arms around my shoulders, pulling me into his side. He smelled like brimstone and sweaty boy but not in a gross gym-class sort of way. More like a "hanging out together on a hot summer day" sort of way.

"Queen Alicia has named me her crown prince," Winston said. "The Fate Maker obviously took issue with it."

"He went nuts and tried to kill me with black magic," I added.

"Ah, well, congratulations on your marriage, Queen Alicia and Prince Winston." The man sat down in one of the chairs and motioned to the other one across from him. "And may I say I'm glad the Fate Maker's assassination attempt didn't work."

"Marriage? What do you mean marriage? We're not married. Winston's my co-ruler, not my husband," I said, completely ignoring the whole assassination thing because hello? *Marriage?*

"He's your crown prince," Tevin corrected. "The Golden Rose doesn't share power with anyone. You rule, and we are ruled by you, and by law the crown prince is your partner and mate."

"Wait, what? The Fate Maker didn't tell me that I had to marry my crown prince. I thought it was some sort of ceremonial thing, like all the bowing and scraping."

"It is a ceremonial *thing*, as you call it," Tevin said. "You've just performed a ceremony marrying you to the crown prince."

"But if I'd have known it involved getting married, I would have never done it." My voice was small and squeaky. "I'm way too young to get married. I haven't even gone to college yet. Forget that—I haven't even managed to pass chemistry. I can't be married."

"I don't think the Pleiades are concerned about the things you may not have done yet. You've performed the ceremony, and now you are married."

"We're not married." I pulled my hand away from Winston's. "No one told me that the coronation was also a wedding. People our age don't just go out and get married in one night."

"How many of them become queen?" Tevin stood up.

"What?" I narrowed my eyes at him.

"How many of these other people become the absolute ruler of Nerissette? How many of them become not just ruler of a country, but of nearly an entire world? How many of them even know the World of Dreams exists, much less agree to actively rule it?"

"Uh…" I turned to Winston for support, but he just shook his head at me, his eyes wide.

"Exactly," Tevin said. "Things are run a bit differently here. Besides, my queen, it is merely a formality. After all, I believe your mother had nothing to do with her crown prince once she'd decided to return to the World That Is."

"Wait, what? My mother was married?"

"Of course." Tevin started toward the door. "Who else would the goddess Fate have made regent? The Fates declared her queen, and the Fate Maker himself was to be her crown prince. When she was trapped on the other side it became his duty to guard her throne until her return. Or, in this case, yours."

"Excuse me? The Fate Maker was my mother's what? That means he could be my…" I swallowed and then shook my head, trying my best to ignore that thought and focus on the more important stuff first.

"Wait a second…but he's the Fate Maker," Winston said. "He's supposed to interpret the will of Fate, right? So, what? He told you he was supposed to be the crown prince, and no one thought to question it?"

"It was the will of Fate," Tevin said. "Who were we to argue?"

"People with your own minds," I said.

"Yes, well," Tevin said. "Perhaps we could focus less on the past and more on the war you've started?"

"Right, okay." I jerked my head up and down once. "War now. Marriage mix-ups later."

"I can have scouts sent out within the hour," Tevin said. "And the rest of the clans will be waiting for your orders at dawn. I suggest you decide where it is that we're going to attack first and then get some sleep. You're going to need it."

I watched the older man walk out the door and turned to stare at Winston. "This is so messed up."

"Yeah, you're telling me." He sat down in the chair Tevin had abandoned and then wrapped his fingers around mine.

I stared at the floor, then looked up into his eyes. "The Fate Maker could be my dad."

"No." He shook his head. "There's no way you're related to that guy."

"How do you know? I could be."

"Allie, you heard Tevin. Your mother had nothing to do with the Fate Maker once she was crowned. And besides, you said yourself that he and the Court of the Silver Thorn basically deposed her. That's why she ran. Do you think she'd have a baby with someone like that?"

"No, but..." I swallowed. "What if he is? My father, I mean."

"It doesn't change anything," Winston said. "It really doesn't, and not to be a jerk but it's not something you can really freak out about now. Once the war is over we can find out who your dad is, and you can lose it if you want, but right now we've got to focus. There are lives at stake."

I let the conversation drop. He was right—but it still niggled in the back of my head. Mom had never talked about my dad. What if this was why? What if he was some evil sorcerer who tried to steal her crown?

"So what do we do now? I mean about us?" I asked. Sure, he was right we had a war to deal with and everything, but hello? We had just gotten married. It was probably something we should talk about.

"What about us?"

"No one told me that naming a crown prince meant that we had to get married. I wouldn't have gotten you into it if I'd have known."

"You heard Tevin," Winston said. "It's a formality. Everyone will call us married, and that will be it. It's like my little cousin Teresa making Daniel Bailey down the street marry her all the time. It's no big deal. Not compared to the war."

"Yes, it is."

"Why?"

"Because we're not six, and there's a lot more at stake here than whether or not I'll share my bubble gum with you."

"That was at stake no matter what," Winston said. "We were going to war anyway, so the risk hasn't changed. To be fair, though, I think I'd have preferred the bubble gum."

"Win!"

"What? Look, I know this is all sort of freaking you out right now, but we're not really married. It's all part of the craziness of Nerissette. We'll get rid of the Fate Maker, and then we'll figure something out, okay? You being queen, me being your prince consort, how you want to go about doing us, all of it."

"Us?" I asked. "You want there to be an us?"

"Yeah." He squirmed in his seat and didn't look at me. "I wouldn't have kissed you if I didn't want an us, but right now we have more important stuff to worry about. Like finding out what happened after we left. Then we can decide what we're going to do."

"I'd like there to be an us," I said quietly.

"Me, too. But first, we have a war to win."

"Right. I hope Mercedes and Rhys are okay." I looked down at our hands and then back up at him. "We just left them there, and now we're here and they're there, and what if something happened to them?"

"They'll be okay." Winston gave me a tight smile. "Rhys won't let anything happen to her. Besides, you probably couldn't see from behind Darinda, but the battle was going our way."

"So why did we run?"

"Because the Fate Maker wasn't going to just give up,"

Winston said. "And we couldn't risk him getting to you. If he captured you, or even worse, managed to kill you, the entire rebellion would have died with you. The people would have been too afraid to fight."

"We have to go back. Even if he does capture me. We can't hide here, waiting for someone else to fight our battles."

"Scouts will be sent to let us know where the dragon forces are needed. Then I'll take the warriors, and we'll finish this."

"Good. If someone can find me some clothes to change into and a sword, then I'll be ready to go. But I can't fight in this dress."

"No." Winston shook his head. "The dragon warriors will go. As soon as the battle is finished I'll send a messenger back to get you."

"So, you want me to do what? Wait? There are people out there dying, and you want me to just wait here while you go fight my battles for me?"

"There's nothing you can do tonight."

"Because you brought us here."

"I needed to keep you safe."

"I'm not going to just sit here and let everyone else fight a war I started."

"Allie—"

"No! I'm their queen, and I need to be the one leading them. No matter what might happen."

"Fine, you're right. You're the queen, and I have to let you do your job. So when the messenger comes back and says that it's safe, we'll go. We won't wait. But for tonight, until we know what's happened, please let me keep you safe. Okay? Just for tonight."

"Win…"

"Please."

I sighed. "Okay, but just until the scouts come back and tell us where we'll be most useful."

He let go of my hands and brought his fingers up to trace along my cheek, leaning closer. I licked my lips and leaned forward to meet him. "Thank you."

He let go of me and stood. Before I could say anything, he had made his way to the door and slipped out.

Chapter Twenty-Five

"Queen Alicia," a soft voice called out a few hours later. I stopped staring at my hands to look up at the front door.

"Queen Alicia?" the voice broached again. "Are you awake?"

"Yes," I croaked, my throat feeling grimy and raw. I sat up and tried to smooth down my rumpled dress. "I'm awake."

"Good." A girl about my age with flaming red hair smiled at me as she slipped into the front room of the cottage, lugging a large bucket of water in front of her.

"The scouts are expected back soon, and I thought you might want to wash before they arrived. Things will become hectic once they've returned, and there won't be much time for a bath. Or food for that matter."

"A bath?" I instantly felt every single speck of dirt that was embedded into my skin. "You have some way for me to take a bath?"

"Not a real bath, unfortunately." She wrinkled her nose,

and I noticed that her face was covered in freckles, as were the exposed parts of her arms. She hoisted the bucket up and poured the water into a kettle over the fire. Then she put some more wood in the fireplace and blew a low stream of blue flames onto them.

"You're a dragon?" I asked, stunned because she was so short and dragons were—well, *huge*.

"Sort of," she said with a quiet laugh. "If we're being specific about it, I'm a wryen. My name is Kitsuna."

"Hi, Kitsuna." I stuck my hand out for her to shake before looking down and realizing that it was still covered in filth. I brushed my hand off on my skirt and grimaced at her before offering it again. "I'm Allie."

"Yes, my queen." She curtsied and gave me a wide smile, a deep dimple coming out in each of her cheeks. "I know who you are. Now, why don't you peel yourself out of that heavy gown? I've brought clothes that might be more appropriate for battle."

She held up a bundle of clothes, and my eyes widened. She had pants—real pants. They weren't jeans or sweatpants, but they were pants, with two legs and a way to move without tripping. Whatever a wryen might be, Kitsuna was now officially on my very short list of favorite people. There was only one problem.

"I can't get out of the dress on my own," I said. "I tried to undo the laces after Winston left, but I couldn't get the knot undone. I think my maid trapped me inside of it just to be spiteful. It's so uncomfortable."

"Your maid trapped you inside your own dress?"

"She doesn't really like me," I said.

Kitsuna motioned for me to turn around, and when I

did she began to tug at the laces. She uttered a few strange-sounding words that I thought might be curses underneath her breath, then stepped away from me and walked into the tiny kitchen area. The next thing I knew there was something pointy running up my spine and the dress sagged.

I pushed my arms out of the sleeves and sighed at the feel of being free from its weight. I climbed out of the puddle the dress made, and she pulled it away from me, tossing the heavy silk into a corner.

I felt the edge of the knife run up my back again, and my corset fell free as well. My ribs rejoiced at being able to expand again, and I wanted to get on my knees and kiss Kitsuna's feet.

"You should be able to strip the rest of it off now and get clean while I make you something to eat," she said. She picked a rag up off the table and a small bit of soap. "The water should be warm enough for you to bathe. There's no way to clean your hair, but at least you'll have the dirt and the smoke off you."

"Thank you." I took the rag and the soap from her and smiled.

Instead of responding, she walked into the kitchen area, purposely turning her back to give me privacy, it seemed.

I stripped off my slip and underwear before dipping the rag into the water and starting to scrub at the dirt on my arms. The smell of roses from the soap mingled with the smells of frying meat. I dipped the rag back into the water and lathered more soap before scrubbing at the rest of the dirt. "Kitsuna?"

"Yes, Queen Alicia?"

"You said you were a wryen? I don't want to be rude but—"

"What is a wryen?" She laughed, and the throaty chuckle coming from such a tiny young woman was a surprise.

"Yes," I said as I finished scrubbing my toes and then reached for the towel. "I mean, you can breathe fire and you live at Dramera, so that means you must be some type of dragon. Right?"

I finished drying myself off and started pulling on the clean clothes she'd brought for me. Once I had the green cotton shirt on I started tugging on the brown trousers, wiggling to get the narrow fabric over my hips.

"Not exactly." Kitsuna picked up a plate and a mug and brought them over to the table. "A wryen is a child whose parents are two different types of dragons. In my case, my mother was a red dragon and my father was a dragon from the east, a landwalker from Bathune."

"Oh. Okay." I shifted my eyes away from her, uncomfortable about digging into her personal life, and saw a pair of soft brown boots underneath the table. I pulled them on over the heavy woolen socks she'd given me.

"Aren't you going to eat?" I asked, trying to change the subject.

"I've already had dinner, my queen," she answered.

"Call me Allie."

"Allie." She smiled at me again. "Now, you should eat so you have your strength. While you do I'll brush out your hair and explain about the dragons here in Nerissette."

"You don't have to." I felt her start pulling the pins from my hair, letting it fall free down my back. "I didn't mean to pry."

"You should know these things, and it's not prying. Really."

"Okay, then, I'd really like that, thank you."

"Eat." She pointed to my plate. I picked up the wooden fork and started shoveling bits of sautéed meat and limp green vegetables into my mouth while she untangled the complicated twists Heidi had wrapped my hair into.

"There are many types of dragons in the world. Not just different clans, like the black dragons and the golden dragons. Clans are just different families of the same type of dragon. It is like humans."

"Like humans?" I asked.

"You are all humans, even though you might have long brown hair and someone else may be a blonde with green eyes. True?"

"Sure." I shoveled more meat into my mouth and reached for the hunk of bread sitting at the edge of the plate. I hadn't eaten in a while, and I hadn't realized how hungry I was until there was food in front of me.

"And all the members of a family look the same or similar? It's what they call a resemblance?"

"Right," I said, my mouth full.

"It is the same with dragons. Some may have golden skin, or some may be blue, and another might have a multicolored pattern because their father belonged to one clan and their mother to a different clan. They are all dragons of the same type—but there are other types of dragons. Giant lizards that never fly but stalk across the ground, slithering into tiny crevasses and breathing fire. Similar but different."

"So a wryen is one of these lizardy dragons?"

"No." She began pulling a brush through my hair, firmly but gently working the knots out of my hair before starting a simple braid. "Wryens are the children of two different types of dragons. Halflings, if you will."

"Okay, I'm not following. So, you're only half dragon?"

"No, I am a dragon. It's just that I was born to two different sorts of dragons and that makes things complicated because my body doesn't know which form to shift into, so I'm stuck in human form."

"Two different sorts of dragons? What do you mean?"

"My father was a lizard dragon. The ambassador to Dramera. He fell in love with my mother, who's a red dragon, but when she found out she was going to have me, he left. He went back home, and we've never heard from him again."

"What? Why?"

"The Lizard People believe that wryens are demons in disguise. Bad omens. They believe it's unnatural for a dragon to spend its life trapped in human form."

"That's horrible."

She finished the braid, tying it with a piece of twine. "It's the only life I've ever known. Perhaps it would be better if he were here, but then again maybe it wouldn't."

"Yeah." I picked up the cup of tea she'd put on the table for me and thought about my own absent dad. "I know what you mean."

"Your Majesty?" she asked.

I pushed the thoughts of just who my dad might be further back in my head and tried to focus.

"What will you do in the war that comes?" I asked, trying to change the subject. "You're not one of the warriors, are you?"

"We will all fight. Anyone who doesn't have a nestling to care for will follow you."

"But you can't fly. You said yourself that you're trapped in human form."

"So are you, but yet you intend to go back to your palace. How will you go to war without wings? Without sorcery? How will you fight magical creatures with nothing but a crown on your head?"

"I'm not sure." I lifted my crown gently off the table and slid it over my forehead, feeling it tighten against my skin. "I guess I'll think of something."

"Then you shall think of something for both of us." She picked up a mirror from the bundle of things she'd brought with her and held it up to me.

I stared at my reflection in the mirror and tried to recognize the girl staring back at me. Who was this person? She wasn't me. She wasn't Allie from Bethel Park or even the Princess Alicia who had flown off to be crowned queen earlier.

The girl in the mirror looked wild, like some sort of woodland princess you'd find in one of the paintings at the Carnegie Museum or the Warhol. She was a girl out of a fairy tale.

"What do you think?" Kitsuna asked.

"I think I don't look like myself," I said.

"No, you don't look like who you *were.* Now, you look like who you have been forced to become. Never forget that. A mirror is nothing more than a reflection of what it sees in front of it. An illusion."

"I think you look beautiful," a voice said from the doorway. I turned to look at Winston, dressed all in black. "The scouts have returned," he said. "They have news."

Chapter Twenty-Six

"What do we know?" I asked when he stepped into the room.

"The Fate Maker is gone. So are the giants. And the trolls. Some of the noble families have fled as well, but most are still in Neris. The fighting has stopped."

"But?"

"The palace was damaged and so were parts of the city. The Hall of the Pleiades was completely destroyed."

I felt like I'd been punched in the stomach. The Hall of the Pleiades was gone? It had stood for three thousand years. It couldn't just be gone, could it? And if it had been destroyed, what else had we lost?

"And the people? The citizens of Neris? The soldiers?"

"There were losses," Winston said quietly. "We don't know exactly how many yet, but we don't think it was too many."

"Even one person is too many," I said.

"The fighting has stopped though," Winston reminded me. "And it's time for you to go back. If you're ready, we can leave in an hour."

"Right." I nodded. "Good."

"Come on." Winston held a hand out to me. "The other dragons are in the square."

We walked outside and through the narrow, winding streets of Dramera. Once we'd reached the entrance to the square I staggered to a stop, stunned at what I saw.

Hundreds of dragons were milling around an area the size of an NFL football stadium. As one, they turned to face us and lowered their very large heads to the ground. Tevin, still in his human form, stepped out from a clutch of golden dragons, their scales glowing like a thousand small suns. He bowed low to me, his hands clasped in front of his forehead.

"Your Majesty. We are honored to ride to war with you. With the blessing of the stars we will destroy your enemies, and then peace will reign for a thousand years."

"Thank you," I said, still staring at the mass of dragons bowing to me. "Thank you all. And good luck."

I turned back to Winston. "So, what do we do now?"

"We go win you a kingdom back." He wrapped his arms around my waist and pulled me close, pressing his lips against mine.

"Enough kissing now." Tevin laughed and pulled us apart. "Shift already and let us ride."

The other dragons began to roar in approval, and I stepped back, my eyes wide as blue-black flames flared up around Winston. The others stood up on their back legs, beating their wings when he shifted silently from boy to dragon. Once the change was complete, he balanced on his back legs, too, his nose pointed toward the sky, and let out a long plume of fire.

"Hey." I pointed my finger at him. He dropped back down onto all fours and put his snout close to my face.

"Don't you remember anything they taught us about preventing forest fires? If you burn down Dramera I'll make you come back and rebuild it on your own."

Winston snorted and smoke curled out of his left nostril. He rolled his eyes, and I poked him once at the tip of his nose, giving him my best imitation of Gran Mosely's evil glare.

"Don't you give me any attitude. Otherwise, if we ever get home again, the first thing I'll do is tell your mom you set an entire village on fire, and I don't care if you are a dragon, she can still kick your butt."

"Did you just threaten to get his mother if he didn't behave?" Kitsuna asked as she came up behind me in clothes identical to mine. "You'll fit in with the dragons better than I thought."

"You haven't met Winston's mom. She's fierce."

"What do you think they are?" She nodded her head toward the assembled mass of dragons.

"Point taken," I said.

She hurried off toward a pack of red dragons with black stripes down their sides. I turned back to Winston and could see that he was trying his best not to laugh—even in dragon form he could still manage to smirk.

"Don't even start." I poked his nose again.

He shook his head back and forth before craning his neck down enough for me to scramble onto his back. Instead of clinging to his neck this time, I maneuvered myself backward so that I was wedged between two of his upraised back ridges and could hook my feet over his shoulders. I grabbed on to another spiky protrusion and held on tight. Hopefully, he'd fly more like a jet plane this time and less like a rocket ship.

"Wait!" Kitsuna's lilting voice yelled. She slid off the back of a large red dragon with gold markings along its neck and ran back over to us, a large bundle cradled in her arms. She shoved it at me. "Mom says you should be careful."

"That was your mom? Wow."

"What? Yours doesn't look like that?" She pulled the brown blanket that was wrapped around the bundle free and nodded toward a long, curved sword strapped to a leather belt that had been swaddled inside.

"Nope."

"Oh well, put your sword on anyway. Let's hope your army is good enough that you never actually need it, but either way it doesn't hurt to be prepared."

"Now that sounds like something my mom would have said." I laughed and buckled the sword low around my hips like Kitsuna's was, trying not to think about the fact that if I had to use it, then it wouldn't be like fencing practice. There was no buzzer, and the person I stabbed wouldn't get up again when it was over. My hands started to tremble, and I pressed them against the sides of my legs so that no one could see.

She snickered. "Oh, and Mom also said to tell you the pointy end goes in the other guy."

Winston snorted, and I turned around to glare at him. He turned his head over his shoulder and tried to fake-cough.

"That one I knew already."

"Great. So, now that we've got that settled," Kitsuna said, "let's go back to your castle and take our place at the head of an army full of angry villagers intent on overthrowing the wizard who's been tormenting them for the past seventeen years. What do you say?"

"Let's do it," I said, my hands still shaking.

She nodded and then ran back to her mother. She scrambled onto the red dragon's back and smiled at me.

"Okay." I leaned forward and kissed the top of Winston's scaly head. "I'm ready. Just don't launch yourself upward like you did—"

He reared up on his hind legs with a loud roar and shot into the sky, completely ignoring me. I threw myself flat on my stomach and clung to his neck, squeezing my eyes shut and trying not to wet myself.

Once we were airborne, I turned, watching the other dragons flap their wings and take off in a smooth, horizontal glide. Why couldn't Winston do that? I was starting to think the only reason he shot into the air like he did was because he liked tormenting me. Stupid boys. Stupid, insufferably cute boys who could make your brain go mushy.

Winston dipped lower, skimming the lake of silver water, before climbing higher and taking me up over the trees. We leveled out, and I turned again, this time to find the sky behind me filled with dragons, all of them soaring through the clouds in a V-shaped formation against the pink of the dawn sky. Ahead in the distance I could see east tower of the palace on top of its hill.

I leaned forward, resting my chin against Winston's back as he flew toward our new home and all that was waiting for us there.

. . .

An hour later the sun was fully up, and we were close enough to Neris that I could see smoke billowing up from the city and the now-scorched white bricks that had been used to build the palace.

I scanned the trees, looking for enemies who might be waiting to ambush us, but there was nothing. No magic hurtling through the air trying to take us down. No giants. No trolls. No one. Just smoke and ruins, as if everyone in the world had disappeared.

Once we were closer I nudged at Winston's neck and pointed toward the mermaids' labyrinth. He nodded and turned toward it, dipping low enough that we grazed over the top. Talia waved from her rock, and I breathed a sigh of relief that they had been kept safe. Once we were clear he rose again, and I saw the extent of damage the battle had done to the palace.

The kitchen was covered in black streaks of smoke and part of the roof was missing. Where the household staff's quarters had been was now nothing but a muddy field with huge chunks of dirt missing. But there was no one outside.

I could see where the battle had been fought, but where were they all? Winston had mentioned losses but surely not everyone. He would have told me if we'd lost everyone…

He circled again and dropped lower, his claws scraping the marble courtyard as he landed. Birds sang in the distance, but I couldn't hear a thing from anywhere else. The entire world was silent. The other dragons landed behind us, waiting quietly while I slid off Winston's back and began to look around. The place looked completely abandoned.

I heard a creak and turned toward the palace just as the front door flew open, and Mercedes rushed down the steps, launching herself into my arms. "Oh, thank the trees you're safe. I was so worried about you."

"I was worried about you, too." I hugged her tight and tried to keep from crying my relief. "Where is everyone else?"

"We're okay. We're all okay—mostly. All those who can move are in the lower levels of the castle. They saw the dragons, and until we were sure it was you and not an attack, Rhys had everyone take shelter."

I tried to contain a sob. "I was so scared that you were all dead. We flew over, and there was no one in Neris, and then we got here and it was empty."

"Most of them are here. The people who couldn't come have taken refuge in the caves at the other side of Neris, in case the Fate Maker comes back."

"What happened?" I asked.

"It all fell apart once you disappeared. For the other side, I mean." She squeezed my neck harder. "You and Winston went hurtling into the air like you had rocket engines strapped to your back, and when the Fate Maker's forces realized they couldn't capture you they sort of fell apart and ran."

"What do you mean they ran?" I asked. "The Fate Maker retreated?"

"They destroyed the Hall of the Pleiades but once they realized they weren't going to be able to capture you, they just bolted."

"They'll be back," Rhys said, coming up to wrap his arm around Mercedes's waist. Even though she was green she could still blush the color of a cherry tomato.

"It is good to see you again, Your Majesty." Rhys bowed low in front of me. "I hope your trip was pleasant?"

"Cut the crap, Rhys. Is everyone safe?"

"I see you've brought me a present." He nodded toward

the mass of dragons staring at us. "Your Majesty, you really shouldn't have. I'd have been happy with a T-shirt. An army of dragons is far too generous of you."

"What happened, Rhys?" I asked, trying to make my tone stern. "Who was hurt?"

"Jesse and Heidi are missing," Mercedes whispered. "We think the Fate Maker kidnapped them."

"Or they turned traitor and joined forces with him," Rhys said.

"He kidnapped them," I insisted, even though I had my own doubts. "They're not traitors. And we'll get them back."

"Allie," Mercedes said. "Think about how Jesse was constantly siding with the Fate Maker, rambling on about how he was going to be king, how he was better than us."

"No." I shook my head. "He wouldn't have betrayed us. He wouldn't have. I refuse to believe it. He's a jerk, but he wouldn't do that."

"Your Majesty, why would they take him hostage, though? It's much more likely that he went with the Fate Maker willingly."

I glared at Rhys. "Until we know differently, he and Heidi were taken prisoner, as hostages."

"Jesse could have taken Heidi with him to draw you out," Rhys said, as if reading my mind. "He had to know that you'd try to rescue them both. He might have seen her and just grabbed her on impulse, hoping to use her to trap you."

"They weren't together, though. She was here, and he was in Neris. They were taken to trap us, but it wasn't Jesse kidnapping Heidi. It was the Fate Maker taking them both."

"Allie," Mercedes said, her voice tired.

"I just can't believe that someone who came through the

mirror with us would join forces with a man who wants to kill us. Not willingly. Jesse is a lot of things, but a murderer?"

"I know you don't want to believe it, but he might be," Mercedes said.

"We'll find a way to get them back," I said. "No matter why they're with him, they're both in danger, and we'll get them back."

I sighed and ran a hand up my face, trying to concentrate. I'd never believed my own friends could end up the Fate Maker's victims—or Heidi and Jesse for that matter. Either way, we were at war, and I was supposed to be in charge. That meant it was time to start *being* in charge. Even if I had no idea what I was supposed to do.

Chapter Twenty-Seven

"Winston, you and Tevin please shift back into human form and meet us inside. Bring along the head of each of the dragon clans," I said, taking control of this situation.

I started up the steps toward my palace and motioned for Rhys to follow me. "Bring your generals and all the nobles. Also, is Darinda still here, or did she go back to the forest?"

"She went back to the forest to check on the rest of the Order," Mercedes said. "Why?"

"How long would it take for you to get her here?"

"No time at all. I can send a message through the trees. But why? What do you want all these people for?"

"We need a council of war. A formal one, not just us deciding to stop the Fate Maker. I want the nobles and the army and everyone else." I stepped into the main foyer, turning toward the ballroom. The throne was still on the dais there. I strode across the room and tried to channel my inner Heidi. She had been right: I wore the crown, and the people here needed me to start acting like it, even if that meant more than smiling and waving. I climbed the steps and shifted the clunky sword I was wearing forward before plopping down on a seat that didn't move. The throne didn't seem like it was going to throw me off.

"But—" Mercedes started.

"Go send a message to Darinda that the Golden Rose wants to see her," Rhys said, gently shushing her.

"But where are we going to put everyone?" she asked.

"It doesn't matter. They can all stand. Now go." He gave her a nudge toward the door. "I need to speak with the queen."

"Fine. I'll just go run errands while you and my best friend plan a war without me." She gave him a dirty look and stalked away. She threw her hand forward and the door flew open in response, smacking against the walls and causing the chandelier crystals to shake.

"She's been worried about you," Rhys said.

Mercedes slammed the doors behind her so hard that the glass shook in the windows. My best friend was ticked off, but she was still alive—and right now that was all that mattered to me.

"She's been going nuts worrying, actually. If the dragon scouts hadn't come this morning to tell us you were safe, she'd have insisted on mounting a search party," Rhys said.

"I know." I ran a shaky hand through my hair. "Can Darinda find a way to get her home? Winston and I have to stay, but once we get Jesse and Heidi back can Darinda find some way to send them home again?"

"I don't think that's possible," Rhys said.

"What about Timbago?" I asked. "He went through once.

To get me breakfast. He could take them back."

"He used the Bleak, the space between worlds," Rhys said. "He's a goblin. They're creatures of shadow, and he can travel there without drawing the wrath of Kuolema and his brothers, the monsters who guard the passages between this world and the next. If he were to take someone else they might not survive."

"What about the book? The *Chronicles*? It brought us here; it can take them back."

"The book only works one way," Esmeralda announced. I looked up to see her perching on the high, pointy back of my throne. "You can bring people to Nerissette through the book, but you can't send them back."

"Then how did my mother escape?"

"She used the mirror."

"Good, then that's what we'll do. Once we have Jesse and Heidi back, I'll send them, and Mercedes, through the mirror where they can be safe."

"And what happens when the Fate Maker follows them through?" Rhys asked.

"He can do that?"

"If we can go from this world to another using a portal, so can the Fate Maker."

"No. I control the portal, and I won't let him through," I said. I turned to Esmeralda. "Isn't that the whole thing you were proving when you testing the mirror the day we came through? That's how you knew I was queen. I could control the mirror. That means I can use it to send them back and stay here in Nerissette myself and protect the mirror so the Fate Maker can't use it."

"You can't use the mirror without the other relics, and I

don't know where they are," Esmeralda said.

"What do you mean I can't use the mirror? I used the mirror that first day. Remember? We saw my mother."

"You used it to *look* between worlds. Not to travel between them. To travel you need the other relics to keep you safe."

"Now you tell me it's more complicated." I sighed. "And these relics that you don't know where they are…what happened to them?"

"I misplaced them," Esmeralda said.

"You mean you lost them?" I clenched my teeth before speaking again. "How do you lose relics that let you travel between worlds?"

"I needed to lock the portal between worlds so no one else could ever use it. I trapped your mother there, and then I locked the mirror, so that she could never return."

"Why?" I stared at her, stunned. "Why would you do such a thing?"

"I had to do what was best for Nerissette," Esmeralda said. "But I'm just a sorceress. If I get access to the relics again, I can't promise that I won't use them. Their power is so beautiful that I don't know if I could resist."

"And if she opens it then the Fate Maker could go through," Rhys said. "He would wreak havoc in the World That Is, Allie."

"That's why the Dragon's Tear and the First Leaf must remain lost," Esmeralda said. "Without them, it's just a mirror. A way to look between worlds but not a gateway."

"This gateway…how does it work?"

"When the mirror is used along with the other relics, it will open a portal between worlds."

"And then?" I asked.

"You must use the Tear to guide you through the Bleak. Without it, you'll become lost in the space between worlds. Trapped in a place where neither the living nor the dead can truly see. And you have to use the Leaf to keep your heart beating in each realm. It's what keeps you alive as you move between worlds. It's the Key to Perpetual Life."

"So, my mom had these relics with her and used them to get to the World That Is, and once you shut the portal behind her, what happened? Did she take them the rest of the way or did she leave them in between?"

"She left them," Esmeralda said, "and I cast a spell that made the relics hide themselves away, in a place that even I don't know."

"So what can we do?" I asked. "If we can't send people to safety, what do we do?"

Winston stepped into the ballroom then, with the nobles and the leaders of each of the dragon clans following behind him. "We stay here. And we fight."

"But Mercedes…and Heidi, and even Jesse. They're all at risk."

"You've brought the kingdom into war already, Allie," Winston said. "We have to protect the people first. They need us now. All of us."

I took a deep breath. He was right. We had to stick to the plan.

I heard the doors fly open and looked up to see Mercedes running full speed toward us. She skidded to a stop next to Rhys and stood panting in front of me, her eyes wide.

"I used the trees to send a message to Darinda, and she sent one back."

"And?"

"She's coming back to the palace. Right now."

"Good." I nodded. "When she gets here we'll convene a council of war and figure out the best way to end this. We'll capture the Fate Maker and put him in jail somewhere, where he can't hurt anyone else."

"Imprison him?" an angry voice said from the back of the ballroom.

I looked up to see a knot of dragons, all in human form, standing in the doorway watching us. The others stayed silent, as the man—a member of the red dragon clan if his hair color was anything to go by—stepped forward.

"You're going to imprison him? He would destroy us all, but we'll simply lock him away somewhere?" the man asked.

"I won't deliberately cause someone's death." I could hear mutters coming from the rest of the dragons. "I won't kill him unless there is no other choice. He may be willing to kill anyone who gets in his way, but we are better than that."

I looked at Winston, who nodded, and then at Rhys, who just shook his head. Obviously he wasn't on board with the whole "not killing people unless we had to" idea.

"Can we get back to my news?" Mercedes asked. "Darinda is coming for a council of war with you, but she's not coming alone."

"She's not?" I asked.

"When she went back to the forest to check on the Order, and she sent word to the rest of the Nymphiad. They've met." Mercedes licked her lips. "The Nymphiad have sided with the Golden Rose of Nerissette. They're bringing their warriors to march with us against the Fate Maker."

"The Nymphiad?" I asked, confused.

"The council of leaders for the nymphs, my queen," Kitsuna supplied from the back of the room.

I nodded, still confused. "That's good, right?"

"Very good," Kitsuna said.

"Excuse me," Mercedes said. "But who are you?"

"That's Kitsuna." I gave my best friend a weak shrug. "She's a wryen."

"Oh, okay…what's that?"

"A dragon that can't change between forms," Winston said.

"So, she's a dragon who isn't really a dragon?" Mercedes asked.

"It's—" Winston stopped and I could see him struggling with how to explain it. "Complicated."

"Right," Mercedes said with a quick shake of her head. "Not the strangest thing I'll see today, I'm sure."

"Anyway," Rhys said. "If we're done playing guess the species, perhaps we should see to quartering your army before the ten thousand soldiers of the Nymphiad forces arrive?"

"Right." I looked out the window onto the front lawn and saw the army stretching out into the distance. "Esmeralda, you and Timbago find everyone a place to sleep."

"Me?" she asked.

"If anyone knows where all the hidey-holes in this place are it's the two of you. Now, go. You've got a lot of beds to find. And I do mean *a lot*."

Chapter Twenty-Eight

I paced the length of my suite two hours later, trying to figure out what we were going to do. What was I supposed to say to a council of war? They were adults, trained fighters, and I was… I stopped at the window, watching the men wandering around the back lawn. I was an eleventh-grader who didn't even stand up to the mean girls who bullied her in the hall.

Blue dragons circled over the top of the palace, making larger loops with each pass. In the distance, other dragons flew near the aerie. The dragon ambassador, Ardere, had told me that they would continue training their younger warriors for the battle they expected to come soon while they kept watch. Nearly half of their force had never seen battle, including Winston.

"Your Majesty?" I heard Esmeralda and turned to see her sitting in the doorway.

"Yeah?"

"I'm sorry this has happened," Esmeralda said. "I'm sorry

I didn't protect you better."

"It's not your fault." I looked back out the window toward the dragons. "This was meant to happen, I guess. It's the end of the Time of Waiting. It's all been foretold."

"You don't understand." The cat came into the room and hopped up on my bed.

I sat beside her and began scratching the top of her head. "Then explain it to me."

"I made the choice to bring you to Nerissette. It wasn't Fate, Your Majesty. It was me. I needed you, not them. Me."

"But—"

She looked up at me and interrupted. "Can you keep a secret, Your Majesty?"

"Yes…"

"There's no such thing as Fate," Esmeralda whispered.

"Excuse me?"

"There is nothing to decide the future for us. We make our own choices, and we live with them. I chose to bring you here to fight our war, just like I chose your mother's family out of all the nobles to lead us all those centuries ago. That's not Fate, that's me."

"I don't understand. Are you saying that you're the goddess Fate?"

"Of course not. Back when I was still in a human body, I was the sorceress Devim, and I claimed to know the will of Fate. I lied."

I sat, blank faced, completely gobsmacked. "You're saying that all of this, the *Chronicles*, Fate, it's all what? Some prank you decided to play on everyone?"

"I'd thought…" Esmeralda fell silent.

"You thought what?"

"We were in chaos. The last line of kings had fought themselves into extinction. The world was burning. Villages fought with one another. Giants had come in from the mountains. The harvestings that we have now? They were nothing compared to what was happening then. It was anarchy."

"And you made up a story to gain control of Nerissette? As a power grab?"

"No. My father had been court wizard, and I had the sight, so one day I announced that I'd been visited by Fate. I claimed to have been given a vision of a world at peace under your family's rule. And people believed me."

"But the *Chronicles*?"

"Your great-great-many-times-great-grandmother had me make things up and put them into a book of fables. We called them prophecies, and because she was queen no one opposed her. They *became* prophecies, though, and eventually everyone forgot that they hadn't always existed."

"So it's all a lie?"

"Yes…and once it was done, your ancestors had me imprisoned in this form by another sorceress. She trapped me like this, immortal, to watch over the line of the Golden Rose."

"For how long?" I asked.

"Until I've been forgiven, and the curse is broken."

"And how's that supposed to happen?"

"I don't know, but when the curse is broken I'll be able to escape this form and leave the mortal realm behind to take my place among the Pleiades."

"So why did you help my mother leave Nerissette?"

"Because she was pregnant with you, and I knew how special you were."

"*She* was special," I said, my heart pounding in my chest.

"Not as special as you," Esmeralda said.

"I doubt many people in the real world would agree with you about that. I'm just a girl and my mom…" I shook my head before wiping away the tears at the corners of my eyes. "She was amazing."

"All the people *out there* would." Esmeralda inclined her head toward the window. "Are they any less real because they're here and not there?"

"I don't know," I answered. "That world is all I've ever known, and this? This was nothing but a fairy tale to me. And now I find out it's not even that—it's all just a lie."

"It was meant to save people."

"But it didn't. It didn't save anyone. There are harvestings and people dying and no one was saved."

"No. I made a mistake, and I am so very sorry."

"That's not good enough."

"I know. Now come with me." Esmeralda hopped off the bed and started toward the door. "Please."

My anger simmered at what she'd done, but the look of regret on the cat's face was genuine. I followed her out into the hallway and felt the door swing closed behind me. She batted at my pants leg, and I leaned down to pick her up, cuddling her underneath my chin. I knew she would normally hate this much affection, but today she seemed like she needed it as much as I did.

"Where are we going?"

"The Fate Maker's apartments," Esmeralda said.

I felt us disappear, then, without a cloud of smoke this time. I don't know how she did it, but we reappeared in the middle of the room we'd first landed in when sucked though the book. I looked around appraisingly. The flowers Mercedes had made back then were dead, withered on their vines, and the mantelpiece now sported a skull and several large, dark-green candles. On the wooden table was the crystal ball from the drawing inside the *Chronicles*.

"The Orb of Fate," Esmeralda said when I peered into the ball. It was filled with blue smoke, and inside the mist I could see myself sitting on the Rose Throne, Winston beside me, crowds of happy people surrounding us. Instinctively I knew that, in the scene, we had defeated the Fate Maker and Nerissette was at peace.

"Does this show us what will come to pass?" I asked.

"No," she said, her voice shaky. "It's a ball of glass with smoke inside it."

"It can't be. I mean, I can see myself sitting on the throne."

"Another bit of magic to make it seem like Fate was influencing the lives of the people here. The orb shows you what you most desire. Nothing more. It doesn't show you what will happen in your life. It won't give you the secrets to the future. It's a trick. A spell."

"So what I see means nothing?"

"Of course not," she said. "It means you want the people of Nerissette to be free of the Fate Maker. It means you want to be a good queen. That's not 'nothing.' It's why I chose you."

"You chose me because my mother was the lost Rose."

I turned to look at the rest of the room. On one of the walls was a map of Nerissette, and I could see small flags, declaring what species lived in each area.

"I chose you because you're kind and loyal. When I looked at you I saw a younger version of your mother staring back at me. A better version. One that still had all the possibilities that she'd lost."

"Is being kind reason enough to give me a world to rule?"

"It's the only reason. Now, come here." Esmeralda stepped toward the mirror and brushed her paw over the glass.

"Open, my old friend," she whispered.

The mirror went dark.

"Come now." Esmeralda ran her paw over the glass again. "Open."

The mirror began to lighten again, and I peered into it. At first, all I could see was the room around me reflected back by the glass, but soon that image began to grow dim, fading out while something more vibrant sprouted up behind it.

There was Gran Mosely, in her kitchen, making herself some toast and humming along to the radio. I watched as an older man, Mr. Wapperly from down the street, walked into the kitchen and wrapped his arms around Gran, kissing her on the cheek. I looked closer and saw a gold band on her finger.

Mr. Wapperly had been Gran Mosely's boyfriend when she first took me in. We'd gotten along well, but it had strained their relationship. He hadn't been happy about the idea of her being anything more permanent than a short-term home for me, and she thought I needed a more stable environment to grow up in. Since neither of them was willing to compromise, their relationship had ended quickly.

"They got married without me around," I whispered. "She married Mr. Wapperly."

"They're very happy together in this version of reality," Esmeralda said. "But she was very happy with you, too. You have to know that."

I sat cross-legged in front of the mirror and watched them sit together at the table reading the paper. He said something, and she answered before he picked up a pen and began scribbling on the paper. She must be telling him the answers to the crossword. She rocked at crossword puzzles.

"What about everyone else?"

"What about them?"

"Do they exist there? Is it just me that's been wiped off the face of that version of reality?"

"All of you are gone," Esmeralda said. "Not lost, not stolen, not dead. Just gone. Right now, in their world you have never existed."

"What if one of us goes home? What about the rest of us? What happens then?"

"If anyone besides you goes through the mirror, it becomes locked to them once they reach the other side. They'll forget about Nerissette—and you—just like everyone else has."

"So, if Mercedes goes through she'll forget we were ever friends? I mean, if I found all the relics and opened the mirror and all of that. Would she forget me?"

"That's why I'm not going through without you," Mercedes said from behind me.

I turned around, surprised to see her and Kitsuna standing in the doorway.

"Even if you do find some stupid relics, I'm not leaving you here alone. We got into this together we're getting out of it together. Me, you, and Winston. The Three Musketeers. One for all and all for France, or however that saying went."

"It's going to be dangerous here," I said.

"It's dangerous there, too, if you haven't noticed. The difference is that there I'd be alone, and here we're all together. Besides, you're my best friend and I wouldn't go and leave you in the middle of a war zone just because I'm afraid."

"Are you?" I asked.

"What? Afraid? Of course I'm afraid." She sat down beside me. Kitsuna sat on the other side and leaned close.

"Who wouldn't be?" she continued. "We're getting ready to go to war with a guy who has giants under his command. So yeah, I'm scared, but I look at it this way—we made it through mono and algebra with Mr. Denilovsky together. What's one wizard and a couple of giants?"

"Yeah." I laughed and wrapped my arm around her waist. "What's a few fairy-tale creatures intent on killing us and using our bones as toothpicks after dealing with Mr. Do Not Fold, Spindle, or Otherwise Mutilate These Papers?"

I let a smile creep onto my face. "What about you, Kitsuna?" I wrapped an arm around her waist, too, trying to draw strength from the fiery, clever girl who naturally fit in our little group. She let her head drop onto my shoulder.

"I am afraid, too, but the future I fear cannot be worse than the past I'm leaving behind. So I am not troubled by it. Whatever comes must be better than the harvesting and the tributes and the fear of what new, unknown evil might come."

I brushed my fingers across the mirror again and let the image flicker away from Gran and Mr. Wapperly, instead settling on Mercedes's family, all sitting around the table, laughing.

"They look happy," she said quietly. "They don't even seem like they miss me."

"According to Esmeralda, the people on that side of the mirror don't know we ever existed." I looked around the room and noticed for the first time that the cat was gone.

"That's good," Mercedes whispered, her voice catching. "It'll make things easier now knowing they're happy."

"What things?"

"The things of war, Your Majesty," Kitsuna answered. "We came to find you because the Nymphiad have arrived. And trolls have been spotted to the north, driving an army of slaves toward the castle."

Chapter Twenty-Nine

Terror filled my heart.

"Herding an army of slaves in front of them, yes," Kitsuna said.

I stood and looked at the other two young women. "Then I guess we need to prepare for war."

"I guess we do," Mercedes said with a nod. We both tried to ignore the way our hands were trembling.

"Hold on to me." As soon as I said it, they both grabbed on to the sword belt I had slung around my waist. I ran my hand across the carving and felt it warm to my touch. "The main foyer."

The world around us split apart, and everything began to shake. Then, an instant later, there was a puff of black smoke, and I lurched forward, still holding on to my friends, and tried to keep from falling to the floor in the main entryway.

"We"—Mercedes said and then gagged on the smoke—"are never doing that again."

"I must agree with the dryad." Kitsuna leaned over so that her head was close to her knees. "That is quite unnerving."

"I think I'm going to be sick," Mercedes said.

"It's fine. I promise you'll get used to it." Timbago smiled from his place next to the door, and I couldn't help smiling back. The goblin stood with his shoulders thrown back and his head held high, a nasty bruise around his right eye. I could see that his knuckles were scraped up and bruised, too.

"Your Majesty." He bowed low to me, and I felt my heart start to thump. "Usually it's better to warn someone before you transport them for the first time."

Instinctively I knelt down to wrap my arms around him. "Oh, forget about that. I'm just glad you're safe."

"Yes, Your Majesty," he said, his own gruff voice choking, and then I heard him sniffle. "You do me great honor, Your Majesty."

"Timbago? It's still just Allie, and for the record, if anyone honored anybody it was you and the rest of the staff who honored me by keeping the palace safe."

"We were all happy to do our part, Queen Allie." Timbago shifted slightly, and I let go of him, standing back up.

"Now." He gave me a stern glare. "It's time to go meet with the nobles. Head held high, shoulders back. Remember, you are the queen. They will do as you say, or I shall know the reason why."

I gave him my most confident look, then nodded to let him know I was ready. He gave me a slight smile and then waved his fingers, letting the doors open with a slow groan.

I stepped forward and stared at the people standing in the ballroom. Everyone turned to look at me and then pressed together tightly, leaving a narrow walkway to get me to my throne.

I passed through the crowd of nobles, smiling at the ones I recognized and nodding to others. I walked up the steps to my throne and turned to sit.

"Her Majesty, the Golden Rose of Nerissette, Queen Alicia the First," Rhys said loudly from his place beside my throne.

"Long live the queen," some of the nobles muttered, but for the most part the hall was silent.

"Your Majesty," Rhys said, trying to act unconcerned about the chilly reception I'd just received. "The Grand Council of the Nymphiad: Darinda, Aquella, and Boreas."

"Your Majesty, I am Boreas, Most Mighty of the Aurae. It is my pleasure to serve however you may see fit. My army is now your army," said a tall, pale silver man who stood next to a dark-blue woman.

He stepped forward and bowed his head before me, pressing his fingers to his lips and kissing them before extending his hands toward me. "May your reign last as long as the winds blow."

"I am Aquella, Great Wave of the Naiads," the blue nymph said, her voice tinkling like water over a stream.

"It is a pleasure to meet you both." I swallowed and tried to keep my voice steady. "I'm honored that you've come to join us."

"We will fight as your allies until the Pleiades shine no more," Aquella agreed.

"Thank you." I nodded. "And our armies will fight with you whenever you need them."

"Now, hold on," someone in the back shouted. "Did you just make an alliance with the nymphs?"

"That is the queen you're talking to," Rhys said, stepping in front of the throne and drawing his sword. "Who are you, Gunter of the Veldt, to question her rule?"

"I swore no allegiance to that girl," Gunter said. "My mother and I gave our allegiance and that of the Veldt to the throne because the Fate Maker said it was the will of the Pleiades."

"You gave your allegiance to the crown because otherwise I will cut off your head," Rhys said darkly.

"The Fate Maker declared that girl queen and placed her upon the throne, then she declared war on him. How is that the will of Fate?"

Winston looked at me and raised an eyebrow. *What are you going to do?* his face clearly asked.

It was like when we played Risk and he purposely went after Russia, daring me to fight him for it. I'd never stood up to him, and even though everyone knew you couldn't defend Russia in that game he always managed to do it anyway, because I just let him keep it. Well, I wasn't about to lose over Russia again.

"Then leave," I called out, deciding to test Gunter's bluff. "If you don't want me to be your queen, if you want the Fate Maker to come back, that's fine, you can leave."

"What?" someone cried out.

I stood, pointing at the door. "Go join his army. From what the scouts have told us, they are marching here now. You'll be able to recognize them by the group of slaves that the trolls are using as a shield. Go on, join the Fate Maker. See how he treats you."

Everyone fell silent, looking first at me and then at the man in the back of the room. Rhys stayed stock-still, his sword out, his shoulders tense, and I knew without looking at him that he was silently daring one of the nobles to challenge him.

"Go on," I persisted. "Leave. Become a slave to the Fate Maker again. No one here will stop you. It's your choice. "

"Your Majesty." Rhys narrowed his eyes at me questioningly.

"But trust me, if there's one thing I know, it's bullies," I said. "If you leave us now you'll leave yourself exposed. Once he's done with us, he'll come after the next weakest link. Look around. Which of you will he attack next?"

"My clan fights with you," a grizzled man near the side of the room yelled.

"The woodsmen of Leavenwald are here to fight as well," Sir John said loudly. "We'll live or die beside you."

Soon, all the nobles who had shown up for the council were calling out their support. Together we might have a fighting chance against the Fate Maker, but alone we were all dead.

"The warriors of the Veldt will stay and fight," Gunter said once everyone else had spoken. "I warn you, though, girl, if we lose it's the executioner for us all, and I won't hold your hand while we wait for death."

"Then I won't hold yours, either." I tried to sound brave even though all I wanted to do was squirm at the mention of someone cutting off my head.

"Now, if we're all done posturing like peacocks..." Rhys slid his sword back into his scabbard. "The Fate Maker has been spotted on the Tannery Road. That's not far from here, even if you are marching a large army in front of you."

"How long do we have?" I asked.

"Unless some betrayal happens on the road, he will be

here before the sun sets. It is the time to prepare for war, Your Majesty."

"The red and the black dragon clans will harass the army from the air," Winston said. Ardere and Tevin had stepped forward to stand beside him. "Maybe if they are faced with dragons before they even reach the palace some of the men will scatter."

"The naiads will fly with you," Aquella said. "We are not normally ones for the air, my queen, but this time we will make an exception. Between dragon attacks and storms, the army should weaken considerably before they arrive."

"Good," Rhys said, his voice grim. "Any woodsmen present should join forces with the dryads. Together you can build as much fortification as you can for the palace. We want to meet the Fate Maker's forces outside the palace walls so we can protect the queen."

"I'm going into battle with you," I announced. "We need the fortifications to protect the palace but not me. I'm fighting with you. I'm not staying here while the rest of you risk your lives again."

Rhys gaped at me, his eyes wide and his jaw hanging open. "You're not serious?"

"I'm fighting with you," I said again.

"Fine, but if you get skewered and die I am going to personally take a wizard prisoner so that they bring you back to life. Just so that I can say I told you so and kill you all over again."

"And I'll help him," Winston said.

"Whatever." I rolled my eyes at them. "Can we get back to preparing for war please? The dragons are going to attack their army from the air. What should the rest of us be doing?"

"We arm ourselves," Rhys said. "And then we wait."

"Wait?" I asked.

"For the war," Winston added. "We wait for the Fate Maker to bring the war to us."

I turned my attention to everyone else and clapped my hands. "You heard the lord general. Let's move."

"To war!" one of the men near the door yelled.

"To war," everyone else shouted in reply. Instead of joining in, I swallowed, trying to keep my composure.

"Your Majesty?" Rhys turned toward me when the hall fell silent.

"To war," I said, my voice trembling, and I tried not to think about exactly what I'd gotten myself into.

Chapter Thirty

I stood on the rooftop of the palace, the wind whistling around me, and watched my army form for battle as the sun dropped slowly toward the horizon behind us. Outside the barricades, the Fate Maker's army was being pushed across the field, the trolls driving the slaves forward while the giants roared and pounded their chests in the background.

There was a group of men hidden near the trees too, and I knew they were the remaining wizards, hanging back and trying to avoid the fight. Somewhere, hiding with the rest of them, was the Fate Maker, letting other people fight his battles for him.

"Do you think there's any chance they'll just turn around and go?" Mercedes asked, coming up to stand beside me at the ledge. "Wait until morning to fight?"

"I doubt it."

I watched as Rhys sorted his men into groups: foot soldiers, archers to ride on the backs of the dragons, nymphs stationed around the barricades to work their magic and protect our troops to the best of their ability. We were a castle under siege, with ten thousand men ready to fight the minute the first attack came.

"These are our fellow people," Rhys yelled at the soldiers. I watched him, Balmeer perched on his shoulder, as he addressed his warriors.

"These are not men who have chosen to fight. They were forced, just as all of you have been forced by the Fate Maker at one time or another," Rhys continued.

The men shifted back and forth, their weapons clanking, and I could feel the fear radiating off of them. Rhys was right. Any one of them could have ended up on that side of the wall. It was possible that some of their neighbors were out there, and now they were going to have to kill each other.

"Try your best not to harm them," Rhys said, still striding up and down the front line of soldiers. "If they choose to switch sides, do not fight against them, but let them join us. Your objective is not to hurt your fellow men. Save your hate for the creatures that drive them toward us. Turn your anger on the monsters that would make your own people fight you when all of you long for nothing more than to be free," Rhys yelled.

"I know that some of us will fall. Today, some of you will make your peace and find a place among the Pleiades, but know this. From this day onward, the people of Nerissette will sing of the battle that took place here today. All of us shall be heroes of legend, and when our descendants sing of us many centuries from now, your names shall live on."

"Wow," Mercedes said as the mood below us shifted, and soldiers began to cheer as the dragons roared their approval.

"That was impressive. You're going to have a tough time topping that speech. Even with that fancy crown on your head."

"Would that speech make you fight for him?" I smiled at her and couldn't resist taking what could be my one last chance to tease her. "Or would you do it just because you think he's cute?"

"Shut up." She pushed my shoulder. "Just because he can kiss like nobody's business doesn't mean he's anything special."

I raised an eyebrow at her, and her skin turned a sort of mottled purple color. "Forget we even had this conversation. We've got an army at the gates to worry about, after all."

"Trust you to use a horde of invading giants as an excuse to get out of giving me the details about what kind of kisser Rhys Sullivan is."

"You found me out." Mercedes snorted. "I cooked this all up with the Fate Maker just to deprive you of gossip."

"I wouldn't put it past you some days," I teased.

A large boulder of dark magic flew through the air, directly toward where we were standing, and we all dropped flat against the roof, our arms over our heads as it exploded in the air above us.

"We'll talk later," I said.

I heard a thunderous roar and saw Winston launch himself into the air, the other dragons circling behind him. He landed heavily on the roof and gave me his usual annoyed glare—even as a dragon the look hadn't changed much.

I scrambled up onto his back, thankful for the hunting clothes that Kitsuna had given me, and shifted the sword so that I could help pull Mercedes up behind me. Winston launched himself off the roof—flat-backed this time so we didn't fall—and circled the castle walls once so our army could see that I wasn't harmed. We dropped lower, close enough to the west barricade that Mercedes could join the rest of the dryads protecting our flank.

"Good luck," she said before sliding off Winston's wing and onto the top of the wall. "Be careful."

"You, too." I grabbed her hand and gave it a squeeze before letting go and straightening up. I put my hand back on Winston's neck, and he began to drop lower, taking me to the front of my army. Another burst of black magic roared through the sky toward us. Winston pulled back up, dodging the attack, and climbed higher.

"We've got to get down there," I yelled as he circled back around for another pass.

A third shot hit the walls, and the nymphs hurriedly worked their magic to protect the castle.

"To war!" Rhys bellowed below as another volley of evil magic came rushing toward us. The doors of the barricades were thrown open, foot soldiers pouring out of the castle while dragons launched streams of bright-red fire down on the enemy.

Men screamed, and I watched in horror as they began to cut into each other, fighting and dying on the ground below us while magic was thrown between the nymphs perched on our walls and the wizards hiding in the forest beyond.

Gunter rushed out of the castle and straight at a troll, howling with rage, his sword swinging in front of him. Magic exploded around us, cries coming from every direction, and when I looked down at where Gunter had been, he and the troll were both gone and I could no longer see them in the mass of fighting bodies below.

"We have to draw the wizards out," I yelled. Winston roared in what I hoped was approval and not annoyance. "You have to get me down there."

I heard another shriek and turned to see Balmeer beating the head of a giant with his wings, his talons bared, a brilliant crimson in the fading light. Meanwhile, Timbago stood below, waving his hands and dancing about while immobilizing the larger creature from the ground. The goblin finished his spell and the giant's legs cemented together. Balmeer swiped a lethal-looking talon across the giant's face, knocking him off-balance so that he fell over, landing heavily on a group of trolls. Then Timbago scampered away, the large bird close behind.

I looked down at the rolling, heaving mass of fighters, and realized there was no way that Winston could land. My army was on the ground, dying, and I was trapped on the back of a dragon.

Forget that. I wasn't just going to sit up here and hide while the fight went on beneath me. If I was stuck riding dragonback, I was going to use it to my advantage. I was going to be Queen Alicia Wilhemina Munroe the First, my own royal version of the air force.

"Take us higher," I yelled into Winston's ear. "We need to see what's going on from above. I want to see exactly where the wizards are hiding."

Winston flew farther up, and I saw Kitsuna and her mother—along with Ardere and a few other dragons—follow us. I turned from side to side, watching, waiting for a spell to be thrown.

"What are we doing?" Kitsuna screamed.

"We need to take out the wizards. Without them the rest of the army will crumble. But they're hiding in the forest somewhere, and I can't see them. We need to flush them out. "

"What?" Kitsuna asked.

"We need to flush the wizards out of the forest. I just don't know how."

"We're on the backs of dragons." She pointed at her mother's wings.

"Big, fire-breathing dragons," I said under my breath. "Of course. We can set fire to the forest. That should get them out into the open."

"What about the dryads?" she asked.

I looked behind me at the tree sprites fighting at the barricades and then down at the men below, dying under the wizards' attack. There was no choice for me. I had to keep my people safe, even if it meant that the trees had to die in their place.

Kitsuna nodded grimly and tightened her grip on her sword, its blade dripping with a black goo that I thought might be troll's blood. I pulled my sword out of its scabbard and wrapped my fingers around it.

"To war." I lifted the sword over my head and kicked Winston's shoulders with my heels.

His head shot around, and he glared at me for a second before folding his wings in and letting his nose dip forward, dropping us into a deadly dive, straight at the trees where the wizards hid. I gripped the spike at the back of his neck and slammed my eyes shut, desperately hoping we didn't crash-land.

I felt a burst of heat and opened my eyes to see that he'd breathed fire onto the trees, the other dragons behind him carpeting the forest in flames at the same time. He pulled up, and my breath caught at the sight of the blaze below.

Everything was on fire. Dark clouds began to amass over the trees, as rain started pouring down only in the forest, and the dragons wheeled upward before turning back and diving again, breathing fire and feeding the flames so that even the wizards' magical rain couldn't put them out.

Winston flew straight up, circling once, and prepared to dive again. This time, I didn't close my eyes as flames roared out of him in a sickening shriek. There was heat at my back and then a sudden, horrible jerk.

I lost my grip on Winston, sliding off his wing and hurtling toward the ground, my sword slipping from my fingers. Time seemed to slow as I watched the giant who'd grabbed Winston's tail fling him across the field like a piece of dirty laundry.

I hit the ground, and all the air in my body exploded out of my mouth in one giant scream. Everything hurt. Every single thing. Even parts of my body that I didn't know existed howled in pain. I lay there, trying to decide if I was actually still alive, or if this was that one last clear, lucid moment you're supposed to have before you die. Some part of me expected to find myself face-to-face with my parents or Gran Mosely, or some guy wearing a robe and big white wings with a golden light around him.

Instead, I got the hideous, twisted gray face of a muscular, six-foot-tall troll, his dirty hair matted with gunk and a smear of blood across his sharp green teeth. Obviously I wasn't dead, but if I didn't get up I was going to be very soon.

I threw my hand out and felt for my sword. I wrapped my hand around it and rolled onto my side, pulling the blade free from the mess of bodies it had been tangled in. I rolled back over just as the troll rushed toward me, his ax raised over his head.

Without thinking I pushed the sword out in front of me. He lunged, and we both froze, staring at each other as he crumpled to the ground beside me, my new weapon buried in his chest. I grabbed the hilt of the sword and tugged, trying not to panic, but it held fast no matter how hard I pulled, trapped inside the dead creature. I was alone on a battlefield with a wizard who wanted to kill me lurking somewhere nearby, and I was now completely unarmed. My stomach started to lurch, and it was all I could do not to vomit.

There was another explosion of fire above me, and I forced my gaze from the troll's body to search the sky for Winston, hoping he was all right. Instead there was nothing but fire and blood and screaming. A black sphere hurtled toward me and I ducked, covering my head as it exploded behind me. I could feel its heat radiating back at us in waves.

"You ruined everything," the Fate Maker snarled. I stood up, staring at the crazy man who appeared in front of me in ripped robes.

I glanced around, desperately trying to find a weapon while he formed another fireball and hurled it toward me. I dodged it as my eyes darted for a way to protect myself. Nothing. Crap. I was now facing a psychotic wizard in the middle of a battle, completely alone and unarmed. Definitely not good.

"I didn't ruin everything," I snapped, still searching for a weapon. *A stick. Anything that I could use to fight with. Something, anything, that can keep me alive just a few minutes more.* "I'm trying to *save* everyone. These are people, not pieces on a chess board."

"They're nothing!" He threw another fireball at me.

I ducked.

He came forward, anger flickering in his eyes. "This is my world, and I won't let you take it from me. I won't let you destroy everything I've worked so hard for."

"Haven't you heard?" I backed away from him. "The world doesn't revolve around you."

"You know," he said with an evil smile, "your mother said the same thing, and now she's as good as dead, trapped inside the horrors inside her own mind. When I'm finished with you you'll be begging to join her there."

Without thinking, I quit retreating and I threw myself at him, my mind full of rage. I didn't care how powerful he was, I was going to destroy him. I was going to kill him with my bare hands, and then it would all be over. All of it. This war and the pain I'd felt since my mother's accident left me alone. I could end him and then I'd find a way back to her and I'd make the wizards fix her, bring her back to me. I'd force them to at the point of a sword if I had to. All I had to do was end him and then everything could go back to how it was supposed to be.

I tackled him around the waist, and we both tumbled to the ground. I scrambled up and starting punching, trying to find a place to hit him that would hurt the most.

I heard a familiar screech above me. Balmeer. He dove in between me and the Fate Maker, his talons bared, and I was flung backward.

The Fate Maker brought one of his arms up to beat back the enraged roc and threw his other arm out to grab my wrist. In an instant the world fell away, and we were being pulled between one place and another.

Chapter Thirty-One

There was a puff of smoke and the world lurched as we landed, hard, on the floor in the West Tower, next to his worktable.

Instead of waiting for the nausea to pass, I lunged at him, swinging my fists, trying to hit him somewhere, anywhere, before he could recover. "I'm going to kill you," I screamed.

"You'll try." He brought his hand around to smack me in the ear with a force that caused stars to spin in front of my eyes and twist my stomach. "You'll fail like everyone else, but you are welcome to try." He slapped at me again, his aim off this time.

Instead of punching at him, I buried my knee in his ribs and looked for something to use as a weapon. If it was just the two of us I was going to need something to even the odds, if only a little. I wasn't stupid enough to think that I could take on a wizard on my own.

I spied the Orb of Fate. *Just a ball of glass*, Esmeralda had told me—a ball of glass with a silly magic spell on it. Nothing more than a weapon to use against him.

I wrapped my fingers around it and hit him with it. The glass exploded in my hand, cutting deep gashes in my flesh, and my blood splattered across the floor.

The Fate Maker fell back with a shriek of rage, his hands covering his eyes, and I pulled myself to my feet. I kicked him in the ribs as hard as I could before running for the door, desperately trying to get away from him.

"Where do you think you can run to?" he taunted from his spot on the floor. I spun around to see him sit up, blood running down his face as he glared at me. "I can find you anywhere. Ask your mother. She thought the two of you had escaped me, and I found her. If I can find her across all space and time, there's nowhere someone like you can run to get away from me."

"I'm not my mother." I let go of the door handle and turned to face him. "And you don't scare me."

"Liar," he said. He laughed, his voice low and cruel-sounding. "I terrify you."

"No, you make me sick."

"That's fine, Your Majesty. I didn't ask for your approval, just that you sat on your throne and did exactly what I told you."

"Never."

"No? Then you'll die in this room, and I'll leave your carcass hanging from my walls as a reminder to the people of Nerissette just who rules here. They will see your body, and no one will revolt against me ever again."

"You think the army is just going to let you take over again?"

"Do you think they can really stand against me? Against giants? Trolls? Do you think those sniveling weaklings will still fight once you're dead? Or do you think they'll go back to cowering?"

I shook my head. "You can't control them anymore. You've lost them. You'll never rule them again. Not without a fight."

"I will. I'll force Esmeralda to bring through some other pathetic girl as Rose. I'll shower her in love and attention, and she'll never question me because there will always be the whispers of what happens to stupid, silly queens who try to think for themselves."

"Is that really your plan?" I asked, rolling my eyes at him so that he knew just how stupid of an idea I thought that was.

I spotted *The Chronicles of Nerissette* sitting on the table and smiled. This ended here. Today. With me. No one else would ever be pulled into this world, ever again. No one else would be taken without any say. Even if it meant that I could never leave. It was worth it to keep the rest of the people safe.

"You dead, new brat in place. Seems simple enough."

"Nothing is ever that simple," I said.

I grabbed the *Chronicles*. It was time to end the lies, to let the people know that their lives were so much greater than any prophecy could imagine.

I heaved the book into the fire, and the flames burst upward, a bright, violent blue, to consume the book. "So much for another queen."

"It's a book," he said, his voice cold, "nothing more than words on a page. Magic spells for weak-willed wizards in need of guidance."

"How do you intend to bring a new queen through without the book? You can't use the Mirror of the Nerissette without the other relics."

"The cat will tell me where they are. And if she won't, then there are others who can find them. Others who will do the spells, who will break and give me the powers I need."

"And if they refuse?"

He raised his chin and glared at me. "I don't intend to give them a choice."

"There's always a choice."

The Fate Maker stood up and wiped the newest smears of blood off his face. "Do you know the first thing I'll do when I go through the mirror, Allie? Do you want to know where I'll go right away?"

"I couldn't care less," I said, trying to figure out the best way to attack him. I eyed the window—I wasn't sure if I had enough weight to push the two of us through it together. We were at least seven floors up, and the ground beneath was paved with thick, white stones. There was no way anyone could survive that fall, not even a wizard.

"I'm going to go to Jesse's and Heidi's parents and take away the illusions. I'm going to let them feel the loss of those deaths. Then I'm going to tell them how you and your boyfriend killed their children. How you roasted them alive, screaming for blood the entire time and reveling in the battlefield."

"That's not true." I jerked my head toward him and felt my heart sink into my stomach at the cruel smile on his face. Was it? They couldn't have been in the forest, could they? Had we killed them? Oh, God, had we *murdered* them?

Revulsion filled me, and I had to push their faces from my mind.

"It is," he said, a note of triumph in his voice.

"You're lying."

"Am I? Or are you a murderer? Did you kill them like you killed that troll on the battlefield? Did *he* matter? Will you feel guilty that he's dead, or is he someone you'll forget?"

"Shut up," I said, my shame and revulsion growing like weeds in my stomach, as I remembered the look on the troll's face as he died.

"You'll forget him. You know why? Because he didn't matter. He wanted you dead, and you killed him, and it *doesn't matter.*"

"Shut up!"

"Just like all of those people out there. None of them matter, and in the end, all of this will fade away to legend. A story lost in time. The dumb little queen who tried to defeat the wizards and destroyed the world instead."

I looked at him again and then at the window. It was too tiny to fit either of us. Which meant there was only one way to stop him. One way to make sure that he never used the relics to open a portal and steal someone else's life. But I couldn't end this without destroying all of our chances.

"You might kill me, but you'll never step foot in my mother's world. No one else is ever getting trapped here again. And I don't care if I have to destroy every piece of magic that exists to make sure of it. This ends here, today, just you and me."

"What are you going to do?" he asked. "Cry and hope I let you live?"

"No." I shook my head at him. I knew how I had to end this. I knew how to stop him and the first thing I had to do was get rid of Esmeralda. I had to release her from the curse that had trapped her inside the body of a cat and there was only one way to do that. "Esmeralda, wherever you are—I forgive you."

I grabbed the chair standing next to his table and swung as

hard as I could. Shards of burning hot pain ricocheted up my arm as the chair connected to the glass of the mirror.

The room exploded in golden light, and I felt myself flying backward. There was the dull, faraway *thump* from my body hitting the stone wall next to the fireplace. I saw it from the outside. My body was there, sprawled unconscious on the floor, bathed in the radiant light of the mirror, but I wasn't in that body.

I watched from near the ceiling as the Fate Maker collapsed to his knees, his whole body wavering like the last traces of an image on a television screen after you've turned it off. He dropped his head forward and howled in rage while the mirror glowed brighter, filling the room with a searing heat, an intensity that I'd never felt before. Even in my detached state it felt as if the entire world was crashing down on this single point, all the realities of all the worlds suddenly collapsing into this single instant of time and space.

The light grew brighter, making the edges of my physical form tingle and burn. I watched the body below and tried not to think about the fact that it appeared not to be breathing.

There was a high-pitched wail, like the sound of all the air being sucked out of a balloon, and the light receded back through the mirror, the magic of the mirror dragging the Fate Maker along with it. Everything went black. The room, the mirror, the place where I'd been floating. Everything was black, and the pain was unbearable. I wanted to scream, but the sound was eaten by the blackness, and I was left with nothing but silence.

No light. No dark. No pain. No sound. Nothing—and all I could think was that no one had warned me death was going to be so boring.

Chapter Thirty-Two

There was an intense heat, and then the nothingness fell away into jagged spikes of pain.

"She's breathing," someone familiar yelled. I struggled to open my eyes. "Stay back. She's breathing. Give her some air."

Gran Mosely. It had to be Gran. Something had happened. Some sort of accident, and I had been hurt, and we had all been here in Bethel Park the whole time.

There was no Nerissette. No Fate Maker. No war or dead trolls or dragons or any other fairy-tale creatures that lived inside my mind. Heidi and Jesse were alive. We had been in an accident, and everything had been some sort of hallucination brought on while I was unconscious.

"If you don't move back, Iron Lover, I will tie you in vines and leave you in the corner."

Darinda.

I felt my heart crumble. It wasn't a dream. We were still here. Nerissette was real, and I had killed the Fate Maker. I had murdered someone. Two people, if you wanted to count the troll. I tried to open my eyes and winced at the bright light.

"Come now, Your Majesty," Darinda said. "It's nothing more than a bump on the head, and you have an army to congratulate."

"Wha?" I moaned and my eyes fluttered open. Something warm filled my hand, and I found Winston's dark fingers tangled with my pale ones. "What happened?"

"We were hoping you could tell us," Rhys said. I shifted so that I was looking at him.

"Let's get you sitting first," Darinda said.

Instead of waiting for her to help, Rhys scooped me up and set me on the bench beside the worktable.

I glanced around and saw that my friends all looked battered and bruised. Rhys was covered in smoke and grime, the arms of his coat torn, while Mercedes was dirt-streaked with her hair in a messy halo around her face. Kitsuna had a shallow gash above her eyebrow, leaking blood, and I tried not to vomit at the sight of it, remembering the way the Fate Maker had bled when I hit him with the orb.

I turned to look at Winston, and he smiled, his face a mask of exhaustion. He had an ugly bruise forming on his cheek, and his left shoulder and arm were bandaged tightly against his side. I looked down and noticed that he had bandages wrapped around his chest and stomach as well.

They were all here. I gasped for breath as a sob racked my chest. We were all here. We were alive. None of us had been badly hurt.

I stopped and shame filled me again. Not everyone had made it through. We'd still lost Heidi and Jesse and it had been my fault.

"Oh my God." I rested my head against his shoulder and let out another sob. "Are you sure you're not hurt?"

"Just a dislocated shoulder and a couple of cracked ribs," he said before I could ask what happened. "The other guy looks much worse."

"Does he?" I sobbed again and then looked at him.

"I'd let you see." Winston swallowed and looked away from me, lifting his chin to stare at a blank spot on the wall above my head. "But the aurae have already begun burning the bodies."

I nodded, still too numb to really understand what he was saying. "So…did we win?"

"Yes, Your Majesty," Rhys chuckled softly. "We won. When you and the Fate Maker disappeared from the field, his army panicked. It was over within minutes."

"What happened here, though?" Mercedes asked. "We saw the explosion from the window, but by the time we got here the Fate Maker was gone, and you were lying in the corner, not breathing."

"I destroyed the Mirror of Nerissette," I said.

"What?" Mercedes asked as everyone else fell silent.

"He told me that when the war was over he would kill us all and find the relics to go back through the mirror and find another girl to take my place. So I stopped him." I swallowed. "There was this explosion and this light and he was sucked in."

"We should go." Darinda grabbed Mercedes's hand, pulling her from the room and motioning to Rhys and Kitsuna to follow her.

When the door slammed shut I turned to Winston. "How much do you hate me?"

"Why would I hate you?" He stared into the fire, not

meeting my eyes.

"I destroyed our only chance of going home. How can you not hate me?"

He flinched and then glanced over at the empty frame where the mirror had been. His hand trembled as he stared at what remained of what had been our only way back to normalcy.

"You did what you had to so that you could protect your people." He wrapped his non-bandaged arm around me, his eyes still fixed on the mirror's remains. "How could I hate you for that?"

I leaned my head against his shoulder, and we stared at the shattered glass as the last of the fading twilight gave way to the darkness of night.

What could have been moments or hours later, he shook his head and shifted, looking at me for the first time since he'd seen the destruction I caused. He stood up, taking my hand, and helped me to my feet.

"Come on," he said. We walked down the stairs, hand-in-hand, and made our way to the passage that led to the roof. I opened the hatch since he couldn't lift it with only one arm, and he helped me climb up the ladder so that we could stand on the roof, staring out at our kingdom.

He wrapped his arm back around my shoulders, and I turned to the west, watching the smoke rise from near the river. I looked down and saw some of the men of the Leavenwald carrying a board between them, with Gunter resting upon it.

Winston squeezed my shoulders tighter, and I let my head lean against his shoulder. Whatever happened, at least we'd be facing it together.

Epilogue

I was back in Kiirastuli, the Place of Waiting. The floors were cold against my bare feet, and I brought my hands up to rub my arms so that they wouldn't get cold. What was I doing here? The last thing I remembered was being in the library, reading about the Great Goblin Wars.

"Your Majesty," a low voice purred from the shadows, and I froze. "How wonderful it is to see you again."

"Kuolema," I said as the giant dragon slunk into the light. "Why am I here?"

"I thought that would have been easy to see." His face came closer, and I could feel his tongue flicking the air near my ear. "The goddess Fate wants her due."

"She's gotten it," I said, trying not to shiver as his tongue flickered next to my ear again. "I'm here, ruling Nerissette. I'm doing as it was decreed. Besides, Fate isn't real. She's just a made-up thing that Esmeralda created to keep people in line."

"Is that so?" the dragon hissed.

"Yes."

"And now you think you rule by what? The might of a sword? The love of the people?"

"I'm queen because there's no one else. Not because of prophecies or fate or anything else."

"You're queen because that is who you are meant to be."

"Fine. Then as queen I demand to know why I'm here and not back in the library."

"Because you haven't fulfilled your end of the bargain," Kuolema hissed. "You haven't paid back your share. You are a pretender to the throne."

"I am—"

"A murderer."

"No." I shook my head. "No, I'm not. We didn't know they were there. It was a mistake. Heidi and Jesse were a mistake."

"War is coming, Queen Alicia. A war like one that no one on any world has ever seen before. War is coming, and if you are not careful it will swallow every reality whole. The world of nightmares will be made real, and then no one will escape. No one will be free. Not even your mother will be free from the monsters that will be unleashed from inside her head."

"You leave her alone."

"War is coming, Queen Alicia," he said again and began to slither away from me, back into the shadows. "I suggest that you prepare."

Acknowledgments

No one writes a book alone. Especially not someone as scatterbrained as me. So here we go in no particular order.

Thank you to my daughter Ainsley for not only giving me the challenge of writing something that I was willing to let her read but also for reading every version of this story and not telling me that it sucked.

Thank you to Libby Murphy and Liz Pelletier at Entangled Publishing for taking the chance to let me write not one, but three books about this world and cheering me on the entire way.

A huge thanks to Libby and Danielle Rose Poiesz, and everyone else at Entangled who have put so much time into this project and into keeping me sane, as well as my amazing publicity team: Jaime Arnold, Danielle Barclay, Heather Riccio, and Debbie Suzuki. I'd be a lost stammering mess during interviews without you.

And last but certainly not least to my family—Ben, Ainsley,

Max, Mom, and my friends who have read, critiqued, consoled, and occasionally provided a shoulder to cry on as I worked to bring Allie and her adventures to life. And to all the young people who have read this book in its various forms and given me their opinions. Each and every one of you have made my life richer for having known you, and I can't wait to see what sort of adventures your own lives will have in them.

Turn the page
for a sneak peek at the next book in
the Chronicles of Nerissette
trilogy

EVANESCENT

by
Andria Buchanan

Chapter One

I stood in front of the Fort of Neris as the sun came up—alone. The square was never empty. There was always someone around, even if it was just a guard standing watch, waiting for the giants and trolls that could attack our home at any moment. My first sign that this was a dream.

The sun peeked over the horizon, and I watched the red-gold light fill the sky, heralding the dawn. Something slithered against my ankle and I glanced down. The square was flooded, and blood-tinged water lapped at my ankles.

Definitely a dream.

I lifted the heavy, impractical skirts that Dream Me had apparently decided to wear and sighed. Whatever it took to get out of this dream, I wasn't going to find it standing here in a crappy dress, getting waterlogged. I turned toward the main gates, prepared to start the long hike uphill to the Crystal Palace. I really didn't feel like hiking five miles—even if it was a dream—in a floor-length gown, of all things.

"They're coming."

I jumped at the sound of Esmeralda's voice and saw her sitting on top of the water. I stared at the sorceress-turned-black-and-white cat. She had gone missing three months before, during the first days of the war against the Fate Maker for control of my kingdom, and no one had heard from her since. "Es? What are you doing here? Where have you been?"

"I've been forgiven," Esmeralda said. "I have been released, but I still choose to protect you because you are the greatest thing—the only good thing—I have ever done for my people."

"That's not—"

"They are coming," she repeated. "No one is safe. You are not safe."

"Who's coming?" I asked.

She looked over her shoulder, and I followed her gaze. On the horizon a huge black dragon circled in front of the sun. Kuolema. The Soul Eater. One of the four guardians of the Bleak, an eater of the dead, a dragon who called the darkness between worlds his home. The dragon that always haunted my nightmares. But this time there were two figures sitting atop his back. There had never been anyone with him in my dreams before.

A man, raven-haired, hunched his long, thin body over the dragon's shoulders, his black and silver robes flapping around him. The Fate Maker. I tried to stay calm as I moved my attention to the person behind him. All I could tell from this distance was that it was a woman, her crimson skirts draped delicately over the dragon's flank and her red hair gleaming like fresh blood in the sunlight as she clung to the Fate Maker's waist. The hair on the back of my neck stood up and all I wanted to do was run. Run as far and as fast as I could away from her. If she was on the back of a dragon with the Fate Maker, no matter who she was or what she wanted here in Nerissette, it was bad. Very, very bad.

"No." I shook my head and stepped back, lifting my skirts even higher so that I could make a dash for it if need be.

"The world they bring with them is too evil to contemplate."

"But he's dead." I swallowed. "All of you are dead. You. The Fate Maker. Heidi's and Jesse. We have their bodies."

"Are you certain?" Esmeralda asked.

"There were bodies. Skeletons."

"Are you sure they're the right bodies?"

"No, but dragon fire is hot and we did our best to identify them."

"When you looked at them, what did you think?"

"I didn't actually see them myself, but we buried bodies."

"And me? Did you bury me? The Fate Maker—did you bury him?"

"You and the Fate Maker just disappeared into thin air! Like you spontaneously combusted or something. So you're dead—you have to be. Aren't you? What are you if you aren't dead?"

"I am at rest," Esmeralda said. "Or as much at rest as I can allow myself to be now that you're in danger."

"And the Fate Maker?"

"He is coming and bringing an army of monsters with him like this world has never seen. If you are not prepared to stand up in front of the gates of Nerissette and face him, he will drench this world in a river of blood and tears that will wash Nerissette back into the Sea of Nevermore. Then he'll march into The World That Is and burn every world between here and the stars."

"So what do we do?" I begged, my eyes fixed on the dragon, drawing ever closer to us. "What do I do?"

"Don't let him find the rest of the relics that I've hidden. Stop him and stop Fate once and for all. Destroy any monsters that they put in your way, and don't let them find a way to get into The World That Is."

"But how?" I asked.

"That…" Esmeralda bowed her head and I watched in horror as she began to fade away. "I do not know."

"Esmeralda!"

She looked up at me again, her eyes glowing constant even as her body started to shimmer like a heat mirage.

"Don't." I held out a hand to her. "Don't go. Stay and help us defeat him. Then we can all be free. All of us."

"Oh, Your Majesty," she sighed. "I am always with you."

The cat disappeared then, and I heard the beat of the dragon's wings as it flew closer.

"This world, Nerissette, is mine," the Fate Maker's voice taunted from inside my mind. "And I'm coming for it."

Instead of fleeing I stood my ground, waiting, terrified but holding my head high as the dragon swooped lower. He veered toward me as if to tackle me to the ground. No matter what happened, though, I knew I wouldn't move. I was firm, steady, and this—this—was nothing more than a dream.

###

"Your Majesty?" A soft voice sounded next to me, and I felt a touch on my shoulder, jerking me out of my nightmare. The small, smiling maid was leaning over me. "Your Majesty, you were screaming in your sleep. Again."

"Right." I swallowed and then sat up. "Sorry. It was just a

dream. Just a very, very bad dream."

"Of course it was, Your Majesty," the maid said absently. "Now come on, up you get. You've got your Great Hall after breakfast."

The Great Hall. That was today. The one day a month where I sat on my throne and allowed my subjects come to me so that I could pass laws and judge disputes and basically rule them. Otherwise known as the worst day of the month since I'd become the Golden Rose of Nerissette, the rightful queen of the World of Dreams.

"Thank you." I studied her face, trying to remember her name. There had been a lot of new faces around the castle since my coronation three months ago, and I still couldn't keep everyone straight.

"Brigitte," the maid replied. "From Sorcastia. I've only been here a week."

"Oh." I nodded. "So how is it? Working in the palace? Do you like it?"

"Much better than working on a farm, Your Majesty." She smiled. "That was what had been in store for me, but once you came, I knew that I could do better and, well…"

"Here you are." I couldn't help thinking that if war came again Brigitte, and all the others who'd flocked to Neris, would have been better off if she'd stayed put. They still believed the lie that their lives were controlled by the invisible, nonexistent, Goddess Fate.

"Here I am." She laid out a brilliant sapphire-colored dress with silver vines embroidered on it and placed my sword beside it. "Maid to the Golden Rose herself. Dressing her for her Great Hall."

"Right." I rolled my eyes at her. "The Great Hall. Yay.

Bring on the Great Hall."

She giggled lightly. "Master Timbago said that you might say something like that. So he told me tell you that the cook is making eggs in honor of your big day."

"Because that's supposed to make everything better." I rolled out of bed and started tugging off my nightgown.

"Yes, Your Majesty," she said and then smiled at me.

"Come on, let's get me ready to go administer some justice. Deal with some land disputes and maybe argue about a pig or two."

"I heard about your decision on the pig," Brigitte said. "It was particularly inspired. Telling them that they had to split the pig exactly in half or they both had to forfeit their land in repayment? That was brilliant."

"Yeah, who said Shakespeare didn't occasionally come up with a good idea or two?" I shrugged.

"Who?" she asked.

I picked up my dress from the bed and slid it on before turning so that she could do up the laces. "Never mind."

Get tangled in our Entangled Teen titles:

Conjure by **Lea Nolan**

When a mysterious eighteenth-century message in a bottle surfaces, revealing a hidden pirate bounty, Emma, her twin brother, and her secret crush Cooper discover the treasure. But then they unwittingly unleash an ancient Gullah curse that attacks Emma's brother with the wicked flesh-eating Creep and promises to steal Cooper's soul on his approaching sixteenth birthday.

A Tale of Two Centuries by **Rachel Harris**

Alessandra D'Angeli is in need of an adventure. Tired of her sixteenth-century life in Italy and homesick for her time-traveling cousin, Cat, who visited her for a magical week and dazzled her with tales of the future, Alessandra is lost. One mystical spell later, Alessandra appears on Cat's Beverly Hills doorstep five hundred years in the future. How will she return to the drab life of her past when the future is what holds everything she's come to love?

The Summer I Became a Nerd by **Lea Nolan**

On the outside, seventeen-year-old Madelyne Summers looks like your typical blond cheerleader. But inside, Maddie spends more time agonizing over what will happen in the next issue of her favorite comic book than planning pep rallies. When she slips up and the adorable guy behind the local comic shop's counter uncovers her secret, she's busted. The more she denies who she really is, the deeper her lies become…and the more she risks losing Logan forever.

Get tangled in our Entangled Teen titles:

The Reece Malcolm List by Amy Spalding

Devan knows very little about Reece Malcolm, until the day her father dies and she's shipped off to live with the mother she's never met. L.A. offers a whole new world to Devan—a performing arts school allows her to pursue her passion for show choir and musicals, a new circle of friends helps to draw her out of her shell, and an intriguing boy opens up possibilities for her first love. Now that Devan is so close to having it all, can she handle the possibility of losing everything?

Tremble by Jus Accardo

Dez Cross has problems. She's almost eighteen and on the verge of losing her mind thanks to the drug Denazen used to enhance her abilities. People close to her have turned their back on the underground and are now fighting for the wrong side. And then there's Kale... Things couldn't get any worse. Her father is willing to throw everything he has to keep Dez from getting the cure--including the one thing that might tear her apart from the inside out.

Out of Play by Nyrae Dawn and Jolene Perry

Rock star drummer Bishop Riley doesn't have a drug problem. But after downing a few too many pills, Bishop will have to detox while under house arrest in Seldon, Alaska. Hockey player Penny Jones can't imagine a life outside of Seldon. Penny's not interested in dealing with Bishop's crappy attitude, and Bishop's too busy sneaking pills to care. Until he begins to see what he's been missing. If Bishop wants a chance with the fiery girl next door, he'll have to admit he has a problem and kick it.